The Legend Of Blacksky

A.E. BUTTERSCOTCH

The Legend of Blacksky
Copyright 2019 by A.E. Butterscotch.

Publishing assistance provided by TJS
Publishing House
Cover design by TJS Publishing House
www.tjspublishinghouse.com
IG: @tjspublishinghouse
FB: @ tjspublishinghouse

Published in the United States of America
ISBN-13: 978-0-578-60991-1
ISBN-10: 0-578-60991-6

DEDICATION

The time has come for me to throw words of celebration
into the air like confetti. Only a
Divine power could prepare me for such a moment. If you
stay ready, you don't have to
Get ready. Unbeknownst to you, your dialogue is my
recipe. If I make it, you make it.
You've earned a starting spot right next to me.

A.E Butterscotch

CONTENTS

ACKNOWLEDGMENTS

Thank you for letting me introduce myself to the world properly. I own minds when my pen hits the paper like you're my property. I have made this grown man monologue free of monotony. Let's be clear: I'm nice, and before I mention mortals, all praise must be given to my Lord and Savior Jesus Christ: It was you that made my mind soar to new heights. FOOT PRINTS IN THE SAND. From an adolescent to inexperienced man. God's plan. R.I.P Peggy Marie Edwards, Leon Edwards, Linda Edwards, Willie Tarver SR, Annie Mae Blithers, Larry Phillups, Marvin Bush, Cassie Bush, Jhonny Man, Lolly, Showtime, Face, Mookie, Tuna, T-Lover, Tiz, Dooley, BJ, MAE MAE from Auburn, NY, Rodney C from Buffalo, NY. Special thanks to my father, JAMES COSBY BUSH, Shareef LAMAR Edwards, Cassandra Petty Edwards, Tavares Boone, Tamara Scances, Head, Cosby SALTER, and Linda Williams. Love y'all! Peace to Nadiv Tracy. It's repping time for the kid born under the summer moon. This is for those Cancers born in June. Leave your mark on the world while accumulating a fortune. Peace to Miller County, GA and Syracuse, NY and Auburn, NY.

CHAPTER ONE:
FAMILY

As the smell of fried fish, cheese eggs, grits, and hash, wafted underneath the bedroom door, Childish Gambino complained to my parents over and over again about someone in his life not being able to get right. Every day of the week in Syracuse, our local Am radio station made the hit song repetitive. If momma love let her firstborn have some input on the music selection, change would've been taken place like Sam Cooke.

I yawned and stretched my arms out and vaguely heard a conversation between my parents. Tried as hard as I could, but my tiny ears couldn't decipher what they were saying. When I peeled back the covers, my stomach began to growl. Sitting up straight now, my eyes roamed around the room and landed on my little brother Jamel's bed. It was disheveled, and his pajamas in a heap on the floor. I stood up, walking softly on the carpet, then made my way over to the closet door. Before I could pick out my Sunday best, Jamel burst back into our room. There he stood, all of five feet. To me, he looked like a miniature version of Kevin Hart. His breathing was heavy, and he had a suspicious look on his face.

"I think Mom and Dad are inside their room smoking that funny-smelling stuff again," he said. It was nothing out of the ordinary for Jamel to run around the apartment like Sherlock Holmes being nosey.

I looked him up and down then said, "So that's why you busted in the room like twelve?" For those of you that aren't from the hood, twelve means police.

"See for yourself," Jamel said serious-faced.

Anxious to see if his latest accusation had any merit, I turned the metal doorknob slowly and looked around. All clear. The hallway smelled like it had been freshly sprayed with potpourri. There wasn't any concrete evidence of any loud being smoked. I closed the door, then turned and faced my little brother.

"What gave you the impression that they were smoking?" I asked. He didn't say anything for a few seconds. I assumed that he was thinking of a clever reply. Maybe even a lie.

"Every time they come out and spray that potpourri, they go back into their room and start giggling. If you haven't noticed that by now, then you're probably smoking trees too, and if you are, I'm telling Mommy," he warned.

I gave Jamel a serious look, then laughed lat him. I couldn't front on him; every word he spoke contained some partial truth-except the part about me getting high. He was definitely crossing the line with that assumption. That was nothing new; Jamel was a habitual line Grosser. Without a second thought, I stepped forward and put him in a headlock. He moved around and started tussling with me, trying hard to get out of my tight grip. Jamel had heart like the hero Wasil Ahmad, so I knew he would never beg me to let him go. Fact: At any age, bravery can begin to show.

"You ever seen someone get tortured?" I asked, tickling him.
He started laughing, and before I could remind him of the importance of not jumping to conclusions, our bedroom door swung open, making us both look in that direction.

"What's so funny in here?" Dad asked in his heavy southern accent.

My dad was about six-two, two hundred twenty-five pounds. He had an outdated S-Curl and the same skin tone as Viola Davis. He claimed it's from picking cotton as a kid in Georgia.

"Come on, y'all! I like to laugh too," he said, looking from me to Jamel, waiting for a response, with the time ticking away inside my head, I made up something.

"Jamel was telling me about this girl he likes," I said with a smile. I didn't look at my brother's face, but I'm willing to bet it had a dirty look on it.

"Is that true, boy?" Dad asked in a suspicious tone.

A few seconds passed by, and uncertainty hung in the air like a reverse lay-up from MJ. Without warning, Dad broke out into a laugh, but quickly cut it off.

"There ain't nothing wrong with chasing the little girls around. When I was your age, we used to play hide and go get it."

Dad had a huge grin on his face. The kinda grin a father has when he finds out his son has embraced the concept of Adam and Eve and not Adam and Steve.

"There was a slight pause before Jamel asked, "What's hide and go get it?"

I could actually see my father's country mind moving before he answered my brother's question. Which was always a good indication that he was about to say something crazy.

"All the girls hide, and if you find them, you get that prize in between their legs. After I played the game a few times, I didn't even have to chase them gals. Shit! They wanted to be caught by the kid."

"If the object of the game was to catch the girls, why didn't you have to chase them anymore?" Jamel asked in a naive tone.

Dad smiled. "Because boy! After I caught a few of them and showed them the weapon of mass destruction, they started calling me big meat." He grabbed his crotch like Michael Jackson. "And what girl don't like big meat?"

Once me and Jamel established eye contact, we both erupted in laughter. Was this Dad's rendition of the birds and the bees? I thought.

"I'm so sincere," he said, straight-faced. "I was packing way before Green Bay."

Before Dad continued, my eyes darted to the figure standing behind him. Mom was the reason I had a light-skinned complexion. Her tone was the color of a red brick, and she had long jet black hair that traveled down her back. Mom's eyes were grey, bright, and clear. She was full-blooded Blackfoot Indian and the undisputed queen of our household. Her gaze was burning a hole through my father's back. Sensing my mom's presence nearby, Dad stopped talking.

There was a slight pause. Then Mom said, "I can only imagine what you're in here telling these boys."

"Nothing," Dad responded quickly.

Mom stared at Jamel and me real hard, and Jamel blurted out.

"Hide and go get it."

Mom looked upside Dad's head and said, "Don't be telling our sons none of your nasty country stories." Mom laughed a little. "Besides, as slow as you are, I highly doubt you caught anybody."

"I couldn't have been too slow," Dad said. "I caught you."

Mom smiled. "That's because I wanted you to." She leaned in and kissed Dad on the cheek. After they broke their brief embrace, Mom shifted gears and gave us instructions.

"It's time for breakfast," she said. "So go get cleaned up and meet us in the kitchen."

When Mom left our room, Dad smiled. "If I tell you there's cheese on the moon, bring some crackers."

As soon as he left, we raced each other to gather our toiletries and tussled to get into the bathroom first. When we got cleaned up and changed into our Sunday best, Mom called us out to the kitchen.

"You boys better hurry," she said. "You know your Dad doesn't have a problem getting started without you."

"You ain't never lied," Dad confirmed.

After Dad's promise, we put a little more pep

in our step and sat down to join our parents. Sitting at the table on Sunday mornings was a ritual for our family. Mom took her time and fixed four plates.

"Lamar, do the honor and bless this food," Dad ordered.

I took a deep breath. "God is great, God is good, and we thank you for our food. Bow our head. We must be fed, give us lord our daily bread."

It was quiet for a while, except for the sounds of forks hitting plates and chewing.

"This is good, baby," Dad said, breaking the silence. He was telling the truth. Mom always got her mind right in the kitchen. She could write a cookbook if she wanted to.

"The fish is cooked just right," Jamel added.

Mom smiled and said, "If you and Lamar scaled the fish just right, then I wouldn't have to come behind you and do it again."

"I always tell you two boys, when it comes to cleaning fish, take your time, and do it right. Remember, the more time you put into something, the better it turns out."

All this was easy for them to say, they weren't the ones cleaning those slimy fish for hours, I thought.

"Maybe you should get us new knives to clean the fish with instead of those old forks," I explained.

"Those old forks are all you need," Dad

assured me.

"Are you positive?" I asked.

Dad laughed a little. "This reminds me of that time when me and your grandfather went hunting in Upper Missouri, by The River Of Sticks. You were just a tiny boy back then, Lamar. And Jamel, you weren't even thought of yet."

I looked up from my plate and smiled at my little brother. He frowned and gave me a dirty look back. The thought of him swimming around in Dad's scrotum was comical to me. After pausing to take a few bites of his food, Dad started up his story again.

"Now, this wasn't the first time I went hunting in this particular area with Old Bear," he said.

"Old Bear," I repeated.

"Mah-to-he-hah," Mom said softly. "That was my dad's spiritual name."

"Anyways," Dad said. "Being the old Georgia boy that I am, every time we went on those trips, I wanted to prove that I wasn't a slouch when it came to Mother Nature. Now, if that meant hunting food for my family to eat, then so be it."

I looked over at Mom, and even though she didn't show it, I know she had to be beaming with pride on the inside. Here my father was, saying he would basically get on some prehistoric shit to feed his family.

"Your grandfather was one of the toughest men I ever met," Dad admitted. "I mean, here I was equipped with a fifty caliber American rifle, titanium bonded knives, and camo gear. While Old Bear always kept it simple with a handmade Hickory Longbow and a bunch of old as dirt tactical arrows. Every single time we went on those trips, he easily outdid me. Old Bear would say, 'I have made a deal with the deer, mountain goats, sheep, and other small game.'"

"What kinda deal?" I asked him.

"'I will only kill them to feed my family and not for sport," he said. "On this particular trip, he led us over a hundred hills and bluffs. Across beautiful prairies and deep green forests as far as my eyes could see. After a few hours, I began to think your grandfather had gotten us lost, and I said something to him about it. You see, all the hunting trips he had taken me on had me feeling like I knew the area better than him," Dad explained.

When I looked over at Mom, she was smiling like she knew how this story would end.

"When I suggested that I should be the one to lead us back home, Old Bear didn't argue with me. Instead, he shook his head and quickly agreed. After four hours of taking us in circles, I stopped and humbly admitted to him that I was lost. It was at that moment that he turned towards me and said, 'Going there can never tell been there how to get there.'"

My mind was still in the process of digesting the moral when Mom said, "What are your goals for the summer, Lamar, and Jamel?"

As usual, in our house, the conversation could change faster than Clark Kent in a phone booth.

"I'm considering trying out for football at the end of the summer," I announced proudly.

My declaration was met with a smile from my dad and a frown from my mom. Like myself, my daddy was an avid sports fan that still got very enthusiastic when he talked to you about his football career. He would quickly let you know that he played safety for Miller County High School in Georgia before he dropped out of school to help his parents on the farm.

"What about lacrosse?" Mom asked.

Mom absolutely loved that I played lacrosse every year, every chance she got, she would remind me that our Native American ancestors created the game, and by playing, I would be honoring them. Honestly, I wanted to play something a little more physical this year.

"Sounds like my son wants to put people on their ass this year," Dad said. "And you can't do that playing lacrosse." I smiled at how he was able to read my mind.

"Hmmm," Mom responded. "We should talk about the negative side of football."

"What negative side?" Dad asked.

Mom reached over and touched Dad's hand. "I just want to make sure our son isn't trying to fill shoes that aren't his size."

Dad laughed. "I would be lying through my teeth, Marie if I said I didn't want Lamar to give football a shot. After all, baby, he's the one that brung it up." While Dad was talking, Mom was looking into me, and I was looking back at her.

"How many concussions did you have when you played?" Mom asked, putting Dad on the hot seat.

Dad paused in thought. "I had a few collisions. But, I guarantee you that I dished out way more than I received. Besides, concussions are part of the game."

"Cosby," Mom said, calling Dad by his first name. "Let's not forget how you still get severe headaches sometimes from all that punishment you dished out. And you forget things all the time." Her eyes quickly shifted to include me in her talk. "Just remember that this decision is yours to make. We will support you no matter what you choose. Your ancestors walk with you and will always be by your side as well. Honestly, I would like to see you concentrate on your reading and writing skills."

If something was really important to my mom, she would bring up the spirits, our ancestors, and any other paranormal activity if it emphasized her point.

"How do you feel about being a sophomore this year?" Dad asked.

"Excited," I responded.

Nottingham High School was the best school in the world. Academically, athletically, and socially. The cutest girls in the city went there. It was a staple of the Eastside. Go Bulldogs!

Dad smiled and said, "From what I heard, that school is a fashion show. Which would explain to me why you're always trying to get us to buy you all these expensive clothes and shoes."

Out of the blue, Dad always mysteriously heard some shit. It was as if he had the number to some gossiping parents hotline.

Dad was nosey, so I knew if that hotline did bling, his ass was definitely picking up.

"Where did you hear that at?" I asked.

My father looked at me like I was stupid. He picked up a piece of fish with his fork and said, "Lamar, don't ever think in a million years that I don't know what's going on with my kids. Have you forgot that I used to be your age? I'm omnipresent, nigga." He paused. "Do you know what that means, boy?"

I shook my head and said, "No!"

"That means I'm everywhere at all times watching you like a ghost."

I cursed my dad inside my head. His country

ass did the most, sometimes, I thought.

My mother laughed and said, "Just in case you didn't know, I purchased that Webster dictionary for you to study. Clearly it's been collecting dust inside your room because if it wasn't, you would know what that word meant. Besides, I hope you're not getting caught up in that fashion show nonsense?"

"Nope," I said truthfully.

How could I participate in a fashion show with two cheap-ass parents? I thought. Thanks to only a few Ralph Laurens, Calvin Kliens, Lacostes, and Nauticas, I was invisible as a freshman. Just like the same ghost my pops just mentioned. This year I was "Thinking of a Master Plan" like the God Rakim. It included some Hermes, Gucci, Burberry, and hopefully Tom Ford.

"Good," Mom said, snapping me out of my thoughts. "Don't be that fly guy walking around with a GED."

"What's wrong with a GED?" Dad asked. "I got one."

"You know what GED stands for to the white man?"

"Nope," Dad said.

"It's not your diploma, but it's Good Enough Dummy!"

Me and Jamel broke out in laughter. By the look on my father's face, you could tell he didn't think the joke was funny.

"With all these weirdos running around in the streets, being regular is the new style," Mom said.

Mom was right as usual, but I didn't want to be regular. I have to work on my personality this summer, I thought. Before my parents could interrogate me any further, the telephone rang.

"Who the hell could be interrupting our Sunday breakfast?" Dad asked to nobody in particular.

Mom answered. "There's no telling."

The phone rang two more times, and my father looked me in the eyes. "Are you going to get the phone or sit there and pose for animal crackers?"

"Get up," I said, walking towards the phone.

"Good choice," he responded sarcastically.

What the hell is wrong with their legs? I thought.

I picked up the phone. "Hello," I greeted.

"Hi, Lamar. This is Ann. 'Chocolate'. Let me speak to your mom."

I took the phone away from my ear and put the receiver in my hand. "Who is it?" my parents asked in unison.

"Ann," I responded. Mom got up and made her way over to me.

"Here she is, Chocolate," I said, handing my mom the phone.

Ann was actually one of the first people my mom befriended when we moved from Missouri, and after being around her for a little while, I quickly developed a puppy love crush on her. And who wouldn't? She had these big baby doll eyes with a nice body, and she was always dressed in the latest fashion. Her style seemed like it was handcrafted by the gods to be trendsetting and original. Whenever she was in conversation with momma love, I eavesdropped just to hear her wordplay. This woman had a way with words that made me wait for her delivery like she was a female MC; Lil' Kim, Foxy, Remy, and Nikki. When she came around, her swagger could brighten up the gloomiest day. After she started stripping, she stopped coming around.

As soon as Mom hung up the phone, Dad was on her body for information. He was so thirsty, I thought.

"What did she want?"

Mom smiled. "I guess Chocolate is moving into the empty apartment upstairs."

Dad eyed Mom suspiciously. "You guess? How the hell did she find out about that apartment anyway?"

"I told her about it."

Dad shook his head. "Now, why on earth would you do some shit like that, woman?"

"Why wouldn't I? Chocolate is my friend. Besides, I don't remember her never doing anything wrong to you. Give me one reason why you don't like her, Cosby."

"Well, for starters," Dad said. "She probably still shaking her ass at Bottoms Up. I could only imagine the company she keeps."

Mom laughed at Dad's assumptions and shook her head.

"You always seem to jump real, real high when it comes to conclusions. It must be all that basketball you're watching?"

I smiled. It was lit. Sometimes, Sunday mornings took on a life of its own. By the look on Dad's face, I could tell Mom had him in his feelings, and this was supposed to be the Lord's day.

"I like jokes, especially when it makes the truth softer for you. If you think questioning the company Chocolate keeps is jumping to conclusions, then you're tripping with no luggage."

Mom looked Dad in his eyes. "I wouldn't know the company Chocolate keeps, but I'm willing to bet if you ask Simon, he could tell you. He dwells in those places."

"Are you saying Simon is the one who told me that Chocolate is stripping?"

"You're always pretending like you don't know things that you surely know. That's all I'm saying."

While Mom and Dad went back and forth, I got up and excused myself from the table. I almost made a clean getaway, too, but Mom yelled my name out before I made it to my room door.

"Chocolate said she needed help moving her stuff. I volunteered your services to her." I shook my head. "Don't shake your head, because you're not doing anything real around here. The way I see it, you need the money."

I quickly agreed to Mom's terms. When it came to money, I didn't turn down nothing but my collar. I would've helped Chocolate for free, I thought.

"What time is she pulling up?" I asked.

"Six-o'clock," Mom said.

Good, I thought, plenty of time to finesse this situation and get prepared.

CHAPTER TWO:
THE PROPOSITION

By the time six o'clock rolled around, my anticipation of Chocolate's arrival had grown to epic proportions. So before she was due to pull up, I changed out of the clothes I had on and put on some Tommy Hilfiger swim trunks, a grey tank top, white Airforce one low tops and just a splash of Nautica Cologne. I'm on my Jahiem shit! Just in case she got close, I wanted to smell good. If you stay ready, you don't have to get ready. After I was done, I stood in the bathroom mirror and smiled at my reflection. In the summertime, when the sun hit my honey skin tone, it boosted my buzz in the hood high enough to make Winnie the Pooh make an observation. Mom braided my hair into two long cornrows that touched the shoulders on my chiseled frame. Staying active by playing sports keeps me cut up like a hip-hop record.

It wasn't hard to figure out that my dedication to my maturation could only be fed by actual experience. Hopefully, Chocolate would be up to serving me tutelage. She definitely has enough wisdom to baptize me with the Wanya Morris effect.

My strategy was simple, while I helped her move all her belongings upstairs, I would engage her in intelligent conversations that put my charm on display. Unbeknownst to my Mom, who really thinks the Webster's she purchased me is actually collecting dust inside my room, I've spent countless late nights thumbing through all the pages to strop my wordplay. Even though I know it's never going to reach the skilled magnitude of Voletta Wallace's son. I have faith that I can make my vocabulary bigger. One thing is for certain. I keep my line in the water. Let me tell you this again just to annoy you like Mike Jones. I keep my line in the water, and if that shit doesn't work. I put bait on it.

"Chocolate is here!" Mom yelled, snapping me out of my daze.

Several minutes later, when I made my way outside, Chocolate had already backed the U-Haul truck up to the apartment building door. While her and my mom were in conversation, I checked her body out from head to toe. Trust me when I tell you, the whole neighborhood suddenly showed up to do the same thing. I've never heard it so quiet out here, I thought.

She was wearing a polo skirt by some sexy designer who knew what they were doing because it showed off her goddesslike figure. Her hair was longer than a Saturday morning track meet at Manley Field House, and it was styled in French curls. From looks alone, I knew all the bald-headed girls inside our building wouldn't jack her shit and call it fake. Only bad bitches accumulate haters within the first five minutes of their arrival. The cat's paws on her thighs made a trail underskirt to a place that I dreamed of. The gold and diamonds she rocked were dazzling the broke eyes of onlookers. I could picture all the stickup kids' hands itching as they stared in awe. Simple Webster's words couldn't convey how harmonious her appearance is, I thought. Paul, the owner of the building, should've paid her to move in the hood because she was so bad that she just made his property value skyrocket.

I stood there, trying my best to look cool, calm, and collected. Meanwhile, I wanted to jump into their conversation like double-dutch. So you know it took some resolve for me to just sit there and wait for her to acknowledge me. I couldn't help but notice that when she talked, she made these little gestures with her hands that seemed rehearsed. I was so caught up in watching her movements that I didn't hear my name being called.

"Lamar," she said. "Are you going to just stand there or give me a hug?"

Before I could reply, Mom said, "Great Spirits, my son is already going deaf. Get over here and give Chocolate a hug."

I strolled over Cool Hand Luke style, trying in vain not to appear too thirsty for a hug.

"What on earth have you been feeding this boy?" Chocolate asked, hugging me hard. She smelled like fresh flowers and a Dove Beauty Bar. Her skin felt soft like a newborn baby.

"Venison, beans, and rice," Mom bragged.

Chocolate grinned. "Same old Sage."

'Sage'? Was that Mom's Native name? I made a mental note to ask her about it later.

"You have accumulated a lot of shit, girl," Mom noticed. "It's going to take you two all night to get this stuff upstairs."

Chocolate's eyebrows shot up in surprise. "'Us two'? Wait, you're not going to help us, Marie?"

"Nope. My cooking show is coming on. Besides, this is why I had kids, so I don't have to help out."

"That's why you had kids," I mumbled under my breath.

"I heard you, Lamar," Mom said, turning around to walk back into the building.

Once the metal door slammed, there were several seconds of silence between Chocolate and me. 'Her skin is glowing', I thought. She checked me out from head to toe.

"You ready to put this work in?" she asked.

Nasty thoughts flooded my mind. "I love putting work in."

She slowly ran her tongue across her bottom lip, and I could feel my heart rate speeding up. "Are you sure? This is a lot of stuff right here," she said, looking down at my crotch.

"I have a real strong back."

She gave me a hot and sexy look that caused a global warming inside my boxers. "This should be something light for you then," she said.
"We can call this big back Sunday."

Chocolate's subliminal game was mean. Clearly, I had to focus on the task at hand. If I wasn't careful, my dick would be standing straight ahead.

After about two hours of walking up and down the stairs, sweat ran off our bodies. What the fuck does she have in these boxes that could be so heavy? I thought.

"How much do I owe you?" she asked.

"You don't have to come out your pocket like that."

She laughed. "There is no nation like a donation."

I smiled. I had to jack that saying, I thought.

"What are you smiling at?" she asked.

"Your 'no nation like a donation' saying."

"It's true. You just helped me move all my things up here. Now you're talking about I don't have to come out my pocket like that. When you work hard, always get compensated for it."

Chocolate took a seat on one of the burgundy sectional couches, and it gave me the perfect view of her thick thighs. Down boy, I told my dick.

She shook her head and said, "All those stairs. How come this building doesn't have a fucking elevator?"

"Ray Rice would put an elevator in this building before Paul will. You should see how long it takes him to fix something when it breaks."

"Are you kidding me?" she asked.

"I kid you not," I said, staring into her eyes, so she got the message.

"He looked like a tight ass," she claimed. "He had the nerve to ask me to lunch when I paid him the security deposit."

"Stop playing, Chocolate! Paul didn't play himself like that?"

It wasn't like I didn't believe her. I had heard several occasions that involved Paul paying a few stacks for some black pussy.

"And he suggested barbeque," she added.

"What was your answer?"

"I told you, there is no nation like a donation. Seriously! Lucky for him, I smoked a blunt like twenty minutes before he insisted. I fucked that rib sandwich 'All The Way Up' like FAT JOE."

We both laughed.

"Can I ask you something, Chocolate?"

"Ask away."

"How come you stayed away from us for so long?" Her eyes blinked twice like my question caught her off guard.

"The older you get, the more life twists and turns you. And you only live once, so I want to do the things I like to do."

"Like what?" I pressed.

"Growing my brand," she said. "Look at you, all grown up now and asking me tough questions. I'm impressed, Lamar. Your mom and dad have done well with you. What grade are you in now?" she asked, smoothly sidestepping my question like a running back.

"I'm going to be a sophomore this year."

"Where at?"

"HAM!"

She laughed. "Paris in September of Syracuse."

"What is that supposed to mean?" I asked, suddenly feeling a little stupid.

"Fashion show," she said, pointing at my clothes. "I hope your gear is up to par."

"So I take it you went to HAM too?" I asked, purposely dubbing her question like she did mine.

"Did I?" she bragged. "You're talking to one of

the baddest bitches to ever grace the 'T'."

The 'T' at Nottingham High School is the main hallway that leads to most of the classrooms. If you get fly, that shit is like a runway. All the bad chicks post up in the 'T', so I couldn't help but grin at her statement.

"Let me find out, what do you know about the 'T', Chocolate?" I asked.

She smiled and reached in her purse. "Please! Me and Big Sam are like this." She crossed two of her fingers just to demonstrate how close.

Big Sam was a six-four, five hundred pound hall monitor. I liked Sam because he was a gentle giant. He had been the hall monitor at HAM for so long that he most likely knew your momma's momma. His desk was located right in the middle of the 'T', so he could watch everything like a hawk. If you got out of line, he would let your parents know way before the teachers did.

I shook my head. "So, I'm assuming you already knew I went to HAM?" I asked, searching her face for deceit.

"When you assume shit, you make an ass outta yourself."

Chocolate was lying, and I knew it. Gut instincts. Now I knew that I couldn't just be an open book with her. If I was, she would toy with me like a cat does a mouse.

"You smoke loud?" she asked, suddenly

pulling out a blunt and lighting it. Chocolate raised the blunt to her lips and pulled on it lightly. As the blunt made a strange crackling sound, a fruity smell invaded my nose.

"I sure do," I said.

She licked her lips. "Do you wanna hit this?"

"Sure."

Maybe I was imagining shit, but I could swear her eyes moved down to my dick.

"How many times?" she asked in a sexual tone.

I stared at her juicy lips and almost froze up.

"How many times?" I repeated.

Her face erupted in a big ass smile. "How many times have you smoked weed, silly?"

"A few times," I lied.

"Come here," she ordered. "You can't hit this from over there."

I walked over to her like I was that dude and sat down next to her. When she passed me the blunt, I placed it in between my fingers and raised it to my lips. I pulled on it lightly and fought the urge to cough. Puff, puff, puff. Then I blew out the smoke like I knew what I was doing. Now I've heard people periodically describe how high they got the first time they smoked trees. For me, the weed seemed to open up parts of my brain that were dormant before. Diabolical thoughts flooded my mind. Chocolate put her hand on my leg.

"Do you want something to drink?" she asked.

"Hell, yeah! My mouth is dry as hell." She gave me this sexy look that made me fall in love with all her features. And Chocolate didn't have an album out. She came back with two glasses and handed me one. I took a sip, and it tasted good as hell.

"What is this?" I asked, holding the glass up.

"That's moscato." She looked me in the eyes. "I know it tastes good, but you know what else is good?"

"What's that?" I asked, leaning back.

Tasty thoughts came to my mind. Something inside of me wanted her reply to be pussy. Such a powerful five-letter word that could turn standard dialogue superb. You heard? Pussy.

Chocolate smiled and said, "Your conversation."

"You make me better," I said.

"Tell me some of your favorite subjects at school?"

"Gym and lunch," I responded straight-faced and believable.

She screwed up her face. "Are you serious?"

"I'm fucking with you, Chocolate. I take advanced reading and writing classes." I threw it out there just to brag.

She smiled so brightly. "Every time I hear the word advanced, it makes me think about the word talent."

"Don't forget gifted. I try to practice both sides to balance it," I said, talking my shit.

"Once you reach a certain level in this world, talent alone doesn't matter anymore. A lot of people have talent. That means you're going to have to outwork the competition."

"I don't mind putting that work in," I said sexually.

Chocolate smiled, knowing what I was insinuating. "Okay, Mr. 'Put that work in'. So you know everything there is to know about this gift that you are blessed with?"

"Nope," I said. "I'm still learning, but I do know a few th--"

"You can know a billion things, boy. Just know that," she said, interrupting my statement. "All you have to do is master one out of the billion. Then you got something." I could feel her words storing themselves inside my brain. This was black woman wisdom, not plain Jane.

"How do you plan to use your special set of skills to make a living?'"

"One day, I wanna be a journalist and a successful author," I said, unsure of what I really wanted to do.

Chocolate nodded her head. "What genre are you going to target?"

"What do you like reading about?" I asked, flipping the question on her.

Chocolate smiled, and I could see the wheels turning inside her head. "Honestly, I would like to read something that's never been done in my era. Something new. A modern hip-hop adventure filled with twists and turns on every page. I wanna leave the town and go to a place where all my dreams come true. Romance, mystery, murder, sex, and seduction for the streets."

"That's a lot of shit, Chocolate."

She smiled. "You ain't never lied. I know it is, but you're talented and gifted, right?" She paused. "It's been nice playing catch-up with you, but I have to start putting some of this shit up while I feel like it."

Chocolate extended a fist in my direction like I was one of her homies she demoted to the friend zone. Purposely or not, she made me feel like she was suddenly uninterested in my conversation. I looked at her. She did this with the sexiest smile on her face. I sat up on the couch and got serious. It was time to shoot my jump shot with humble talk. Obama.

"Before I leave Chocolate, I would like to run something by your ears."

"I'm listening," she said.

"I was hoping that you would be willing to teach me a few things that you seem very knowledgeable about."

She folded her arms in a defensive posture.

"Do elaborate."

"I need to learn how to charm the pants off all women without it seeming like I'm manipulating them, teach me how to dress with style. Last but not least, I want you turn me into a sexual savage."

The look on Chocolate's face told me that she was taken aback by my bold proposition.

"What do you plan to do with all this information?" she asked.

"Get money."

She looked at me and read my face. "You're serious, aren't you?"

"Very."

"Why me?" she asked.

"You're one of the baddest chicks to ever walk the 'T'," I said, calmly reminding her of the statement she made earlier. "Plus, you're classy Chocolate and beautiful," I added.

I could tell she was trying so hard not to smile.

"You're way too young for me, Lamar. And Marie would kill me for turning out her firstborn."

I smiled. "Mom's not going to find out Chocolate," I responded with conviction. "As far as my age goes, please believe me when I tell you that in this situation, age is nothing but a number."

That saying was so cliché, but true.

She smiled. "If I say yes, what's in it for me?"

Hard dick and bubblegum, I thought. I smiled.

"What are you grinning at?"

"I'm sorry," I said. "Sometimes my mind wanders off on its own."

She raised an eyebrow. "I see. Very interesting. Don't apologize over something you can't control. I still would like an answer to my question, though."

"The only thing that I can offer you of any value is my virginity," I responded, throwing my line in the water. She cocked her head to one side with a sexy expression on her face, revealing she was contemplating swallowing the bait.

"Your virginity," she repeated, amused.

"All yours for the taking."

She paused like she was getting the right words ready for her reply. "Hmm. You're either still high as hell, or you already have some shit with you that's been ingrained since birth because you definitely got the element of surprise thing down to a science."

I flashed her my million dollar smile and turned it off just as quick.

She took several deep breaths. "You're very adamant about all this shit, aren't you?"

"I think we've established that."

"I don't know, Lamar," she said. "You expect me to believe you're a real virgin in this day and age?"

Chocolate looked into my eyes to see any traces of a fib, but I really was on that A.C. Green

31

shit!

"I'm keeping it one hundred with you. Besides, I'm sure there is a way for you to check my authentication?"

She looked at me and smiled. "Stand up."

I did as I was told and stood up without hesitation, then I removed my tank top on my own and noticed a thin layer of sweat had formed on my chest.

"How can you be a virgin with a body like that?" she asked.

"As you would say, these things do happen."

"Allegedly," she responded.

The way she pronounced that nine-letter word made me pay attention to how plump and juicy her lips looked up close. It also made me aware of the close proximity of my dick to her pretty face.

"Are you nervous?" she asked with a smirk.

"Nope," I lied with a straight face. Truthfully, Chocolate had me hotter than the tropics Felony Set rapped about.

"You should be because the truth is about to come to the light."

"Chocol-" She placed one finger to her lips to silence me before I could get her name out. Her gaze moved lower, then she reached up and gently ran her right hand across the crotch of my swim trunks. Her touch made the heart rate monitor on my Fitbit beep twice.

"Take these off," she ordered.

I started shedding my trunks about as slow as a snail, doing my best to heighten the suspense in the room. She watched intently, and from the look on her face, I could tell that she enjoyed the show. When my trunks fell all the way down, my dick sprang out and bobbed in the open air several times, all ten inches of heavy meat, revealing that I had inherited the weapon of mass destruction like a North Korean President.

Chocolate's mouth popped open in awe. "Damn! I can't believe it. Your dick is like Bigfoot! There are always tons of sightings of dicks out there this big, but this is the first time I actually seen one."

She grabbed the weapon with her right hand, and with her left hand, she squeezed my left buttcheek.

"Whoa! Whoa! Hold up!" I yelled.

"What's wrong?" she asked with a smirk.

"I don't know what kind of test you're about to conduct, but I'm not with that Kanye shit."

"I'm sorry. It won't happen again," she promised.

This time she wrapped both of her hands around the base of my shaft, and it took all my self-control to stand still. Without warning, she pulled both of her hands from the base, all the way up to the head of my dick. To my surprise, a thick layer of my pre-cum coated her fingers. She looked me in my eyes and licked my essence off her digits like it was a delicacy.

"Mmmm," she moaned. "You are a virgin."

"So, we have a deal?" I asked, pulling up my trunks.

She paused. "This deal is still something I have to put some thought into. With that being said, I will have an answer for you in a day or two. In the meantime, don't lose your bargaining chip to your little girlfriend across the street."

As I left Chocolate's apartment, I knew there was a good chance she would agree to my proposal. As far as Stacy was concerned, the eyes do hustle, I thought.

CHAPTER THREE:
BONDED BY BLOOD

I hopped out of bed, still drowsy and tired, but very awake. My dick was standing straight up like a miniature bat underneath a pair of slightly wrinkled pajamas by Sleepy Jones. Morning wood in the hood usually meant I had erotic dreams of thirsty thots in short tops and tight leggings, for what's inside those leggings, I've seen so-called players do their fair share of begging. I wanted to be a legend, so I stayed up later than necessary thinking about all the different variations of possibilities if Chocolate were to say yes to my proposal. It equaled more game to my repertoire of sophistication and endless women for my disposal. Not only did I want that local pussy, I wanted to fuck around and become global.

After brushing my teeth for several minutes, hit

those, don't miss those. I used soapy water to wash my face, then used my towel to dry my face. I looked in the mirror. Innovation. I smiled at a reflection that revealed two dimples like MASE. I'm a handsome young man considering I was from deep space, I thought. Class and taste inspires jealousy and hate. Wait! The answering machine beeping non-stop made my thoughts marinate. I came out the bathroom wondering who it could be. My mind flashed back to last night; I couldn't forget about Chocolate seeing Stacy watching us from her porch. The eyes do hustle, especially when I picked furniture up, flexing my muscle. The red numbers flashed five messages, but as soon as I reached over to hit the play button, the phone rang. I picked it up on the second ring.

I knew it was Stacy. "With whom do I have the honor of speaking to so early?"

"Good morning, your majesty," she said, playing right along. It was cute of her.

"Good morning, bae."

"I guess you didn't get my message to call me last night?"

I pulled my face away from the phone and shook my head.

"When I got home, I was tired, so I went to sleep."

My response caused it to get quiet. Crickets chirping and shit. Clearly, she was thinking of a reply.

"You need a cellphone."

"So, you can blow that phone up, too?"

"You never know," she said. "I can't front. It's a realistic possibility. I do have a cocky ass man." At least she kept it a buck, I thought.

"You don't trust me?"

"You be saying that word like trust can just be handed out like candy on Halloween. Trust is like money from a hard labor job. You have to earn that shit."

"So, what's good?" I asked.

"This wetness between my legs if you act right. I haven't seen you in a few days. You act like you're ducking me or something. Can I see you today?"

"After I freshen up, I'll be over there."

"All right, bae," Stacy said. "Don't be making me wait too long."

As soon as I hung up the phone, the door to my parent's room opened, and my dad stepped out. I know he heard part of my conversation with Stacy. The ears hustle too.

"What time did you get in here last night, boy?" he asked.

"I don't know pop, but everyone was sleep, so I ju-"

"It had to be around eleven-o'clock because I was still up at ten-thirty watching the news," he said, interrupting me.

I came to the realization that I would never fully understand why my parents deemed it necessary to ask me questions they knew the answer to already.

His face had a frown. "What took you so long?"

"Chocolate had a lot of stuff in that truck."

"I bet," Dad said. "She probably had stripper poles and all kinda other freaky shit, didn't she?"

I stood there in my b-boy stance while my father attempted to do some exotic fishing. South of France style. Saint-Tropez. French fish and overpriced oysters. I wouldn't take the bait, though. After all, what Chocolate had inside her boxes was none of my business. My pops thought he was Perry Mason, staring at me, waiting for an explanation.

"Well?" Dad said, raising his voice.

"Honestly, she didn't unpack none of her boxes."

He gazed into my eyes. "Are you lying to me?"

"Nope."

"What's done in the dark will always come to the light."

"Anything else?" I asked.

"Actually, I do," he said. He stuck his arm out and pointed to the couch. "Sit down." I walked over to where he gestured and sat down. What now, I thought.

"Out the blue, Simon called me last night." He paused. "He wanted to know what I thought about you working for him this summer."

"At Benz Kitchen?"

"The Greasy Spoon," Dad said,

"Doing what?"

"Now, how would I know some shit like that? Does it matter? You said you wanted to work." He paused. "You do wanna work, don't you?"

"I do, Pop."

"Good boy," he said. "Then do what he tells you. As far as your Native American side, you've been a grown-ass man. It's time for you to start acting like one and help me carry some of the weight around here." Dad placed his hand on his lower back. "My back hurts, son. You're my firstborn, and I love you, but I regret coddling you for so long. Before your grandfather died, he made me promise him that I will never cage your spirit. Old Bear would look into your eyes for hours and hours when you were a baby. He said one day, you would lead this family to unlimited riches without any effort. It's finally time to see if the crazy old man was right, or was he just talking because he had lips. Only time will tell."

"When do I start?"

"At five o'clock," Dad said. "And don't be late."

I thought Dad was done talking, but before he

made it back inside his room, he spun around. "Be careful around Chocolate," he warned. "Everything that looks good, son, ain't good."

Relieved that the convo was over and pressed for time, I hopped in the shower and got out just as fast. Bootcamp style! After changing into my Guess outfit and a pair of black Nike boots, I headed out the door in a hurry. It was an early summer morning outside, and the sunlight illuminated the twelve-twelve baggies and other pieces of litter strewn everywhere. Regular project shit, I thought as I walked across the street.

Before I could even extend my fist to knock on Stacy's door, she opened it, and we both stood there, taking each other in. Stacy is full-blooded Native American, and that was just one of the reasons why my mother liked her so much. She was beautiful without any kind of makeup. Stacy had light grey eyes, jet black curly hair, olive-colored skin, and juicy pink lips that made you just wanna kiss them. She wore a black halter top with tight blue leggings and Calvin Klein briefs. Sexy! Her rose gold necklace with a heart-shaped pendant wasn't flashy; it was stylish just enough to make you notice it.

"Say something, boy," she urged.

"Are you going to make me stand here, or are we gonna take it inside?"

She smiled. "Decisions, decisions."

I stepped forward and ran my fingers through her curly hair, and it felt extra silky and soft. My touch caused her to raise her head to my level, and I kissed those sexy lips that I adored. Stacy's lips tasted like cinnamon, and her skin smelled like rich cocoa butter and a sweet-smelling fragrance.

"Did that sway your answer?" I asked in a sexy tone.

"You're lucky I like you, boy," she said as she moved out the way to let me inside.

When we both got inside her home, she closed the door behind us. Their house was decorated with various Native American trinkets, life-like animal statues, and different dreamcatchers.

"Your mother?" I asked, looking around her crib.

"Not back from the reservation with your mom yet. We're home alone so you can come into my room," she said, leading the way.

I walked close behind her. "Are you sure, Stacy?"

Out of all the times I've been over her house, this was the first time I had been invited into her room, mostly because her mother didn't play that shit. This had all the capabilities of being a symbolic moment for us, I thought.

"If I wasn't, you would know," she explained. "Now, come on."

Stacy grabbed my hand and couldn't help but

notice how plump her ass looked in those blue leggings. Trump should make leggings on millennial girls with nice bodies mandatory, I thought. That would cause his approval rating to go up.

When we got inside her room, she closed the door and locked it.

Stacy pointed and said, "Sit down!" I walked over to her bed and followed directions. I saw with my back to the wall and headboard.

Stacy started rummaging around for something in her dresser. That gave me time to take in the scenery around me; two mahogany bookshelves were in different corners of the room. Knowledge is power. That would explain why Stacy could tell you some information on a bunch of various subjects. She had photos of legendary Native Americans decorating her walls; Crazy Horse, Red Cloud, Tecumseh, and Pocahontas.

Suddenly, Stacy bent over in a way that put her athletic ability on display. Her eyes connected with mine. She wanted to see if I was watching. You know I was–how couldn't I? She did a sexy Kendall Jenner pose of sound body and mind. I sucked my teeth. The mind plays cruel tricks on man, and the media makes us feel filthy. I got enough dick for her and her. Now I'm GUCCI GUILTY. I'm hypersexual without having sex yet. Could you imagine the world's laughter if the aspiring Messiah got transported to Pariahville to grow sugar cane and pick daffodils? When I landed, cloaking devices and laser beams would try and off-set the extraterrestrial black author competitor. That's a real-life trilogy. Alien vs. Predator. This is sexual prose misconduct for highly intelligent women who lust for a great mind fuck. Stay tuned; you're in luck.

Knowing the effect she had on me, Stacy turned around with a smile on her face. Two tiny sticks were in her hand. "What are those?" I asked.

"Sage incense!" She lit both of them with a Bic lighter, and then she placed them inside a wooden holder that collects ashes. She seated herself on the bed, Indian style.

"What do they talk about at these council meetings that we never get invited to?" I asked.

"Well, most of their conversations are about how the white man is still breaking treaties that he agreed to."

"Why would the government sign something just to go back on their word centuries later?"

"So they can take back the land that has high value to them now. They're so good at lying and stealing," Stacy said.

"What can we do to stop this?"

Stacy frowned. "Just in case you didn't know, the U.S. Government is like a poor kid with no toys."

I shook my head. "A kid with no toys?" I repeated. "What's that supposed to mean?"

"They're nothing to play with!"

"That was cute, Stacy,' I said, "But there's got to be something we can do."

"We can exterminate those roaches. I'm talking about punishing them for the decisions they made. Send them to an early grave."

"They'll put you where they put PAC too. Jail. Do you remember Craig Mac's slogan?"

"That Bad Boy rapper from the 90s? He had a whole bunch of slogans that I forgot, and I'm not alone."

"Let me drop some knowledge in your ear," I said. "Just like a crispy piece of swine. You would be Big Bertha's first choice to wine and dine. And that's not the only issue.

"I bet your momma miss you and go through a whole box of tissue. It's real when make her shed a tear because you won't be around next year, and going Upstate is wack. R.I.P. Craig Mac."

Stacy smiled. "I can't front, boo. You lit, but fuck that shit. After what these white people did to both of your ancestors: Native and African. You should want the same get back as I do. Does that sound crazy to you?"

"Executing something without a game plan does sound crazy to me," I said.

"Sometimes Lamar, the best plan, is no plan.

Take them by surprise."

Just like me, Stacy aspired to be bigger than tiny Syracuse. It's the truth. We were both young and determined to be great. 2PAC in Juice.

"Sometimes, no game plan leads to a suicide mission, and I love myself too much to go out like dark skin Jermaine."

Stacy flicked her wrist like she was shooting an imaginary jump shot. "There are situations when you have to sacrifice for the good of the team."

I smiled. "Not if the coach is tripping with no luggage."

"Speaking of teams, we need to strengthen our team. That's why I wanted you to come over so bad. It's time to take our relationship to the next level. Are you ready?" Stacy asked.

"I'm Alicia Keys ready."

Stacy looked deep into my eyes, and it got real quiet inside her room. Suddenly, she jumped up and headed towards her closet. I'm finally about to get some cameltoe, I thought, and I was secretly worried about being a two-pump chump once I got inside that rump.

"Where you going, baby?" I asked in a concerned voice.

"Be patient!" she yelled from the closet.

Seconds later, Stacy was walking in my direction, holding a miniature Indian figurine in her hand. It most definitely wasn't lit.

"Where did you get that from?" I asked.

"From my grandfather, and it's been in my family for a long time."

"Is that an Indian condom?" I asked.

"Don't be silly. Red Jacket is not a condom."

Red Jacket damn sure sounds like a condom to me, I thought.

"Who is Red Jacket?" I asked curiously.

"He was the chief of the Senecas and the head of the Six Nations.

"The Six Nations," I repeated. Stacy gave me a look that made feel like I should know the answer.

"A confederacy formed by six tribes, which consisted of the Senecas, Oneidas, Onondagas, Cayugas, Mohawks, and Tuscaroras. Their combined strength pushed out the white man from Native lands and was strong enough to withstand the assaults from neighboring tribes. Red Jacket was a great leader and a powerful speaker. In rap terminology, this was the original Native G-Unit. They didn't play any games."

"So, what happened?" I asked. "Because even G-Unit broke up several times."

Stacy frowned. "Did you ever see all hell break loose?"

"Nope," I said one word.

"White people, whiskey, and small-pox happened," she said, looking into my eyes. "Three different terrible things that the Native Americans tried to escape from." She laughed out loud. "Even Houdini couldn't get out of that crazy shit! Shortly after that, the pale faces slithered like snakes then took possession of Native lands for their own industry and enterprise."

"So you're saying Red Jacket went down with the ship like the Titanic?" I asked.

"Not exactly," she said. "Like many of our ancestors, he felt so disappointed and painfully hurt that he couldn't put a stop to the white man's continual encroachments onto Native lands. When Caucasians see something they want, they devise a plan to take what doesn't belong to them: people, soil, and oil. Under extreme stress from not being able to spoil their plans, Red Jacket started drinking whiskey to excess. Sadly, the once-great orator became a drunk. This went on for a few years, until one day he just stopped cold turkey."

Knowing that alcoholics don't just stop drinking without something significant happening to make them do so, I asked my next question. "What made him stop?"

"Well, for a very long time, nobody knew what made him suddenly stop getting wasted. Which was odd to other Natives. After all, drinking used to be his favorite. He never talked about it." She paused. "Then, one night under the glowing light of the fire, he told his family and friends this story." Stacy paused again and adjusted her posture. "The day before, he stopped started off like any other day. Red Jacket had venison and whiskey for breakfast. Before the sun was high in the sky, he lay drunk inside his wigwam. He was a broken man. He fell into deep sleep and begin to dream. In his dream, he rode a milk-white horse towards the next village. After a short ride, it started to get dark outside. For the next several miles, the full moon started to cast shadows over the vast prairies. Thirsty for more fire-water, Red Jacket galloped faster and faster to his destination. Suddenly, his horse came to an abrupt stop on its own." The fire on the incense twinkled. "When the animal began to behave in a skittish manner, he knew that could only mean one thing: someone or something was coming. Then, almost out of thin air, a pale face on an all-black stallion appeared. Upon closer observation, the horse's hooves were rotted, and worms wiggled from its nose. Red Jacket woke up from his dream sweating profusely."

"That didn't stop him, though?" I asked. "Did it?"

"Please!" Stacy said. "Red Jacket was a lot of things, but a quitter wasn't one of them. It didn't take long for him to disregard his dream and get started on his daily afternoon binge of drinking firewater."

"He drank and drank until he depleted his supply. Thirsty for more firewater, he threw some of the most prized furs in his collection on the back of his horse," she said with a serious face. "Sadly, he headed back to the fort to do what most Natives did long ago." she paused. "Sell their soul to O-kee-hee-de (the Evil Spirit) for a drink. He sallied forth from the village and over the plains with one thing on his mind: firewater.

"Before long, it began to get frighteningly dark, and Red Jacket started to sober up. Frustrated from his lack of buzz, he traveled faster and faster over the bluffs. Sensing that his horse was tired, he pulled the reins and slowed down. He trotted along in darkness and silence until suddenly, just like in his dream, his horse began to get skittish. Red Jacket gripped hold of his lance tightly, ready for anything."

"His worst fears were confirmed when out of the shadows appeared the same white man on the black stallion moving slowly and methodically in his direction."

"OH SHIT!" I blurted out. "What happened next?"

She smiled and said, "I m trying to tell you if you stop interrupting me."

"My fault. Can I hear the rest of the story, though?"

She made a flat tire sound then continued. "When the white man got close enough to speak, he stopped his horse. He had long curly black hair, long dirty nails, and bloodshot red eyes. The two men sized each other up. The stranger broke the silence and asked Red Jacket the fastest way to get to Seneca Territory. There was a pause while Red Jacket thought for a minute. 'For what reason do you have on Seneca land?' Red Jacket asked. The pale face smiled, exposing his rotted teeth. 'I have something to collect there that has value to me,' the pale face said. Unsatisfied with the white man's motive, Red Jacket smoothly gave him the wrong directions to Seneca Nation. Red Jacket smiled at his cleverness until he heard the pale face scream out. 'Thank you, Red Jacket.'

He spun around on his horse to ask the pale face how did he know his name, but the black stallion and the pale face had disappeared into thin air. From that day forth, Red Jacket never touched firewater again."

"I wonder what the white man had to collect?" I asked, knowing damn well he wasn't there for his health.

"According to Red Jacket, the pale face was the Evil Spirit himself; O-kee-hee-de. He was headed to Seneca land to collect his soul."

The light flickered inside of Stacy's room, and it triggered a supernatural effect inside my mind. Goosebumps formed on my arm.

"Long after Red Jacket's ordeal, he continued to bring people together in hopes of peace and unity." Stacy slowly began to twist Red Jacket's head in a counterclockwise motion until his head came completely off.

"What the fuck is that?" I asked.

"This is a needle, silly."

The African American inside me questioned her on his own.

"What do you plan on doing with that?"

"Do you trust me?" she asked.

"Yes."

"Then close your eyes and stick your thumb out." I had faith that Stacy wouldn't do anything stupid, so I closed my eyes and complied to her request. Seconds later, she broke out in a ritualistic chant. "Me-chwe-ne-hyna-je-bi. Protect me and Lamar from O-kee-hee-de. Give us your strength Great Spirit, our journey in life has just begun, and we will need the shield of your mighty hand."

Stacy gently pricked my thumb, and the feeling caused me to open my eyes slowly. Fresh blood drizzled from the small wound down my thumb.

"It's my turn," she announced, pushing her small thumb forward like Hacksaw Jim Duggan. I pricked her just as softly as she pricked me, then a small trail of blood ensued. She looked into my eyes and smushed our two thumbs together.

Stacy smiled. "May we never forget the day our DNA got mixed, and souls became hitched. We are now bonded by blood."

She placed one hand on my shoulder that caused me to look down at her Calvin Klien briefs. 'Wild thoughts' appeared inside my mind like RiRi. At times like this, all pretty pussy should be placed in hot pink panties. I had to get my paper right in order to be around supermodels that pop Rosé bottles and take shots of whiskey until they felt frisky. Suddenly, Stacy kissed me passionately enough to make my prior thoughts history. Our talented tongues explored each other's mouth. That cinnamon taste came back again, and I started sucking on her neck. She closed her eyes in pleasure. That's a head spin. We were finally about to sin.

Her skin was soft and hot like a Lauryn Hill album, and I could feel her nipples brushing against my chest. The sensation caused my dick to get hard. My hands came up instinctively and cupped her breasts through her halter top. As I pinched and tugged on Stacy's nipples lightly, she let out the sexiest moan. I was ready to do the grown, so I put my hands underneath her shirt and eased it up, right hand on her butt, both of us working as a team to pull it over her head together. She removed her bra in one swift motion and set her bare breasts free. I wrapped my arms around her back tightly, leaning in to suck on them.

When I closed my eyes to savor her taut nipple, she started unfastening my belt, her small hands caressing and feeling on my manhood. As soon as I was about to remove her leggings, a door opened and closed in the house. Caught in the moment, Stacy pulled my body closer like she didn't just hear what I heard.

"Stacy!" Her mom yelled.

"Yes, Mom!" She answered, quickly putting on her top.

"How many times have I told you if you have company in your room, the door has to stay open?" her mom asked.

My eyebrows arched. Who else had she invited into her sanctum? I shook my head. When it came to my virginity, I thought to myself. I got about as much luck as the drummer from Def Leopard getting pulled over by a trigger happy cops and being told to place both of his hands in the air. This wasn't fair. In my mind, I could hear other virgins saying, "I feel your pain," and it would be lame if I didn't appreciate their sympathy. I would get my time to shine soon, though. Willy Wonka would even smile when I made Chocolate sing like a symphony. Suddenly, I could feel Red Jacket's ambition enter me, slowly turning me into the perfect vehicle and symbol of the Great Spirit's handcrafted symmetry.

As I got up to leave, I promised myself to make my abstract writing exciting by weaving Black and Native excellence in my words of psychological warfare.

CHAPTER FOUR:
THE INTERVIEW

I got to Benz Kitchen, the diner that Simon Brown owned, at about four forty-five. The afternoon air was muggy in Syracuse. It was the kinda weather that made young girls walk up and down Salina St. with nothing on. A treat for the eyes, multiple thick thighs, posted up on the block, a plethora of thirsty thots. Girls motivated by dope boys who like to watch. The eyes do hustle.

As I combed the area, I only noticed a handful of cars in the parking lot; the first one was a lunar blue metallic Mercedes Benz C-Class coupe. The second one was a snow-white 350f Lexus Sport with nineteen-inch alloy wheels. Both of them were fly whips, and I could see why parents who couldn't afford them chose to name their seeds after them.

When I approached the entrance, the sign in the

window read, "House special for today is slow-simmered oxtails, sausage, and cajun style gumbo."

When I entered the establishment, a bell hanging from a green ribbon tacked to the top of the door clanged and announced my arrival. A few people looked up from their plates, while other people concentrated on their food. I couldn't blame them. The smell of diced onions, red bell peppers, chopped parsley, and garlic cloves, made my stomach growl.

I took a seat at a table next to the window and looked around. By the way, Benz Kitchen was decorated, 'Even a caveman' could tell Simon's blackness was on full display for everyone to see. Starting with a sign that said, "Proudly Black Owned."

There were three different paintings by Ernie Barnes that covered the walls; A Dream Deferred, Sugarshack, and Walk Of Life. He also had black and white pictures of political and Civil Rights leaders. I'm talking about influential men like Benjamin Chavis, Malcolm X, DR. King, and Obama. Grown men in their suit and tie. It felt empowering to be surrounded by so many icons, and I could hear my ego trying to figure out a way to join these great men.

Suddenly, a female voice approached the dining area from the back hallway. A few ticks later, I connected a face with the lovely voice. She was medium height and thick in all the right places, and she was moving with the athletic swagger of a WNBA player. She wore an all-black jacket and skirt by God knows who. Whoever designed this material, though, deserved some dap on both hands, a hug, and some sorta award.

Her breasts looked edible, and her ass looked healthy. Vegetables. 'The Great Pumpkin'. Nowadays, with all the plastic surgeries, I couldn't tell if her body was real or fake. And I didn't give a fuck. If I had money to burn, I would build a bitch from the ground up like a science project. You know a woman is bad when you can feel that confident elegance about her that radiates outward. Despite not having on any makeup that I could see, her skin complexion was a Nabisco Nutter Butter brown. All the sugar daddies didn't make one sound, but their faces lit up like circus clowns for this beauty that represented the trey one pound. I even wanted to be down. Brandy.

Her eyes, though a light grey, seemed unusually wild like they belonged on the body of an arctic wolf. When this mystery woman sashayed over to the cook and took a blue slip off the tiny hook, cheeked it, then grabbed a plate in each hand, and two more on her arm, it caught me off guard.

"You must be Cosby's son?" A deep voice asked from behind me. It had to be Simon Brown, I thought, and if it was, I must've overlooked him on the way to the seat I chose. He was observing me observe other people. How clever of him. When I turned around and looked into his face, I thought he resembled Morris Chestnut. Out of respect for my future boss, I stood up and made my way over to where he was seated.

"How did you know?" I asked, extending my hand in his direction with class.

"You look just like your father, and I couldn't miss the way you looked at the waitress," he said, shaking my hand. "If you were from the Southside, you would know she works here. Simon had some big ass hands and a firm grip. They most definitely weren't the hands of somebody who lived a soft life. In fact, he looked like he slapped a few people to sleep in his prime.

"Was my facial expression that obvious?"

"Sit down, young man," he said, gesturing to his table with a nod. "When people get distracted by something they want, they unknowingly display all types of emotions."

"My dad said you had some work for me," I said, showing him how anxious I was to work, but at the same time keeping it business.

"How is your dad?"

"Good," I said, one word.

"I'm glad to hear that. Me and Cosby go way back so you can relax with the militant routine. I'm not in the mood to talk turkey right now."

Simon was trying to figure out what kinda personality I was working with. I could dig that. Especially with all the weirdos running around town. He need not worry, I thought. The kid is official.

"That's cool with me. What do you want to talk about?"

"Before you walked in here, I couldn't help but notice you checking out both of those luxury cars in the parking lot."

"The eyes do hustle."

He laughed at the slogan. "Which one of those whips do you think I drive?"

His question wasn't hard to figure out. Hypothetically speaking, If somebody paid me some chicken to kill him, I would dump ratchets inside the Benz. Hood book plot: Bad, Beautiful, Broke, and Busted Bitch. A side piece wants wifey's spot. A thottie bitch and snottie bitch can't duck the karate kick.

"The Benz," I said.

"What makes you think I push that?"

"It really wouldn't make sense for the owner of Benz Kitchen to drive anything but a Benz."

"Right. And nobody told you I drive a Benz?" I could hear the doubt in his voice. The bell rang. Two customers walked in.

"Nope," I said truthfully. As his eyes watched his new guests,

I studied him real good with my eyes.

If I didn't have any fashion sense in the modern world, Simon could be dressed regular to you. He had on a red, white, and blue tee-shirt with a black cat on the front. His matching blue penny loafers were fresh as fuck, so I estimated the Gucci shoes and shirt cost a stack. It was apparent that Simon had adapted to the times and knew how to blend in with the youth. He didn't get left behind like the people who refused to give up baggy pants and 5XL tee shirts. Simon didn't have any jewelry on, just an Oyster Perpetual Day-Date Rolex that read Monday. With something like that on his wrist, his gun must be on him or close by, I thought. After determining his clientele was there to buy food, he turned his attention back to me.

"I gotta give you credit. When it comes to what car I drive, you made the call like Nick Buonicotni."

I was confused. "Who is Nick Buonicotni? And what does he have to do with what we're talking about?"

"Nick was on an HBO football show in the early 90s. They would give the viewers a football scenario where a ref threw a flag, and you had to make the right call. You made the call young blood."

Honestly, I liked how Simon broke down his sports saying to me. It sounded like something I could incorporate in my swagger. There is no nation like a donation, I thought.

"Who did Nick play for?"I asked.

Simon got all excited and shit. "The Dolphins. The best team in the AFC, that's who."

Ain't this a bitch, I thought. "As a loyal Bills fan, I personally hate all dolphins, even Flipper." He laughed this big laugh, but I was dead ass serious.

"The Bills," he said. "Boy, I Love Losing Superbowls. I know you know that's what the 'Bills' stands for?"

"I always thought it stood for Bitch I Like Little Surprises."

He smiled. "I have to give you a job now. All the pain and suffering you've endured, it would be wrong if I didn't."

We talked about sports for about an hour, and he seemed impressed by my overall knowledge on the subject. Little did Simon know; when it came to sports, ESPN raised me.

"You got a girlfriend?" he asked, suddenly switching topics.

"Not yet," I lied. I really was trying to avoid turning this job interview into an episode of Dawson's Creek.

"Good," he said. "You're too young to be worried about girls."

"Why is that?"I asked, cursing myself as soon

as the question left my mouth. I was almost certain that my blunder was about to lead to some sorta story.

"Simon says bitches will fuck your whole life up, especially when you're young and have talent. I know pussy derailed my train to my dreams. When I was your age, I went to high school in Baton Rouge, Louisiana."

"Why come you don't have an accent then?" I asked skeptically.

He damn sure didn't sound like Lil Wayne, Baby, Romeo, or Master P to me. I sat back in my seat, patiently waiting for his explanation.

"That's an easy answer, son. It's the same reason why you don't have a Missouri accent. I've got more years in Syracuse than you have on this Earth. In case your country ass father didn't tell you, most niggas up north have family down south." He paused. "In the late 80s cocaine made a lot of cowards think they were the one. NEO. Niggas died over that weight. Big Pun. So I kept a big gun, shit got real, I let it off a few times, and then went on the run. My folks sent me to go stay with my grandmother in Baton Rouge." Inside, I laughed at his short story, but just like it did you, his wordplay got my attention.

"What do you think about that?" he asked.

"Your short story sounds like the thuggish version of the Fresh Prince of Bel-Air theme song.

Are you sure your name isn't Will?"

Simon grilled me hard. George Foreman. "Will wishes he had the GOD's style. I have the kinda swagger that would make Jada smile, then take off her Jimmy Choo's and stay for a while. I've sold so much product around the way, this generation should call me hashtag dope. You looking at a man that's gotten fly since Hov was drinking 'Cris' on that speedboat. Look at me, youngster. My favorite letters in the alphabet are GQ. Baton Rouge isn't California, and my grams wasn't no Aunt Viv."

"You sound like you didn't like it down there?" I asked.

His face lit up like memories popped inside his head.

"I didn't just like it," he said. "I loved it. What do you know about The Pelican State? Where the food is good, and the Creole and Cajun pussy are great. Them girls hotter than Tabasco sauce, when that Jazz band playing, your soul might get lost. They call that southern hospitality. You can't walk down the road without people blowing their horns and waving at you."

"When they blow the horn at you upstate, you're about to get ran over. Wherever they're going, they ain't trying to be late. All these young dudes my age shooting. It's definitely not safe," I said.

He smiled. "I can relate, and it's funny you

said that. I used to stand in my grandmother's front yard, and every day at the same time, a red 76' Ford Bronco used to come flying by. I guess they were in a hurry too. There was an older light-skinned woman behind the wheel. She had three girls my age in the backseat. They must of figured out the kid was new in town. Each time they passed the house, they became more bold."

"What made them so bold?" I asked.

"They started flashing me their titties. Two of them had big titties, and the other one had itty bitty titties. Her chest was flat like a frisbee. I know her momma seen them flashing me. I went to Gramms and asked her who these women were." He paused long enough for me to visualize all them breasts. "According to Grandma, they were a Creole family named the Dumonts: Berniece, Tracy, Jessica, and Dee Dee. She made&clear that there was hundreds of Dumonts, and then she told me they were notorious in Baton Rouge for putting roots on people."

"Roots?"

He laughed. "You've got the same look I had on my face when my grandmother told me that shit. Root is slang for voodoo and witchcraft. Before she told me that, I used to think that Roots was just a TV Miniseries."

"So what happened next, Simon?"

"My grandmother's blood ran through my

body, so let's just say she knew me well. She said, 'You Yankees always come down here with all your slick talk, not knowing they ain't saying nothing slick to a can of paint. The big city life has spoiled you. That's why you don't have a clue what goes on down here in these Louisiana woods. The deep south is filled with unspeakable evil. I know you don't believe me, but a hard head makes a soft ass. When you go over the Dumonts house do yourself a favor and don't eat or drink anything they offer you, and you better not leave none of your hair behind.'"

"So you took her advice and never went over there?"

"I wish," he said. "That shit my grandmother was kicking went inside one ear and came out the other one. Benz block don't raise scary niggas. Plus, I was a young, thirsty boy back then. That's a real bad combination." He paused. "And it didn't help that Tracy Dumont looked like Jasmine Guy."

"Jasmine from the Quad?" I asked.

"Hell no," he said, confusing the shit out of me.

"Jasmine Guy has a twin?"

He smiled. "I'm talking about the Jasmine Guy from It's A Different World. The young one. You with me now?"

"I think so," I responded sarcastically.

"Good. I hope you're not one those people who take two hours to watch 60 Minutes?

Anyways, after laying my game down flat for two weeks, I finally got her to understand."

"Understand what?" I asked.

"I told her pretty ass we're taking our masks off by doing all this talking shit over the phone, so when I came over there, the only thing left for us to do would be futuristic fucking."

I smiled real wide. "Just like that, player?"

"Look here, Lamar. Simon says that 'Jodeci Cry For You' shit don't work with some of these women. Don't be that man named Dan who be spoiling these girls and getting them all hot and bothered. Just so a veteran like me can come through on that thug shit and lay the pipe."

"Who is Dan?" I asked, confused again.

"Dan stands for dumb ass nigga. Nowadays, every woman gives a man a little burn, but it's what you do when you get in the game that counts. You gotta own that pussy when you're inside it." He paused to let his words sink in. "The day I finally went over to the Dumonts', I was shocked at how big their land was. You should've seen this shit. The property looked like an old-school plantation. There was more Dumonts than my eyes could count, and they all stared at me like I was prey. When I got to the back door of Tracy's house, she was waiting for me and didn't waste any time inviting the God in. Their house was decorated with all types of African drums, masks, and pottery.

Tracy grabbed my hand and led me straight to her room. Once that door closed, I beat that pussy up on the bed, floor, and dresser. Bob the back blower was in the building."

"You went meat to meat without a condom?" I asked in a surprised tone.

"Back in those days, you didn't have to strap up like you do now. There wasn't all these sexually transmitted diseases around. Don't get me wrong," he said. "We had crabs and gonorrhea, but you can get rid of that shit. I'm telling you that I was putting in that work, and suddenly her sister Jessica busts in the room.

"I was butt-ass naked when she said, 'My momma wants to meet you.' I definitely thought a nigga was about to get kicked out the house because all the noise Tracy was making. While Jessica was looking at my dick, I got dressed as quick as possible, then Jessica showed me where her momma's room was. The crazy shit is before I could even knock on her door, Berniece yelled for me to come in.

"I stepped inside her room and closed the door behind me." He paused. "When I looked at this woman, I was shocked as fuck. From the waist up, Berniece was naked, and her breasts stood up like apples on her chest. I couldn't stop staring."

"Yeah, right," I said. "You're making this shit up as you go along, Simon."

He looked at me and shook his head. "I'm not that kinda fella who has to lie to kick it. I never made shit up, besides my bed in the morning. Now I even got a few women who do that for me. Berniece was light-skinned with a keen nose. She had a cute face, sexy lips, and curly hair. This fine bitch looked the same age as her daughters. It was as if she was drinking some secret elixir that stopped the aging process. I stood there, gawking at her as she asked me a whole bunch of questions about New York State. When she was done, she told me to go enjoy myself."

I thought about what he was saying and shook my head.

"Where they do that at?" I asked.

"Baton Rouge," he said. "When I left Berniece's room, I stopped at the bathroom to go wash up. After I locked the door, I grabbed some soap and placed my dick in the sink. Her pussy didn't stank, but it had a scent to it that I had to get off. Suddenly, Jessica jumped from behind the shower curtain and reached inside the sink and grabbed my dick. She said, 'I know you don't think you're leaving without letting me sample this New York dick?'"

"That's crazy," I said. "Did you hit that, too?"

"Nope. I got the fuck outta that bathroom and made up a quick excuse to Tracy explaining why I had to bounce. It was too much weird shit happening all at once."

"That story was official," I said.

"I wish like hell that was the end of the story, but for the next three weeks, I went over to Tracy's house 'For old times sake' like Freddie Jackson. Every time I went through that door, Berniece made me these delicacies that I couldn't get enough of. When I got home some nights, their house was all I thought about. One day while I was getting dressed, my grandmother said, 'I see those Dumonts got their hooks deep inside your soul boy. Now I warned you not to eat anything over there, but you did. For the past three weeks, I've watched you walk four miles in a hundred-degree heat to visit those Dumonts.'"

"I told my grandmother she was overreacting. The Dumonts didn't have any roots on me. I could stop going over there anytime I wanted to. She said, 'Prove it then, badass'. I was anxious to prove my grandmother's superstitions wrong, so even though my dick begged me to keep going, I stopped going over there. The first day was a piece of cake. I kept myself busy around the house, and nothing happened. The second day, Tracy blew up the phone like Dave Walker, the late-night stalker. My grandmother had to threaten her in order for her to stop calling. The third day, I got sick ass hell; throwing up, headache, sweating, and diarrhea. I thought I was going to the upper room high in the sky. It took my grandmother a week to nurse me back to good health." He paused. "I never stepped foot on the Dumonts soil again. A few years later, after I'd made my way back to Syracuse, I received a phone call from Tracy. To this day, I'm still trying to figure out how this bitch got my number."

"Two years is a long time to try and reconnect with someone. I guess you did put it on her," I said. "What did she have to say?"

Simon stared at me, but he didn't say nothing. Then a frown crossed his face. He was acting weird as fuck.

"What did she want?" I asked again.

He rubbed his chin. "She told me that she had a two-year-old daughter named Sharon, so I said congratulations, but what the fuck does that have to do with me? That's when she told me that the little girl was mines."

I shook my head. "And you just jacked what she said?"

He glanced at me like my question was crazy.

"Please," he said. "Momma raised me to be a lot of things, and a fool wasn't one of them. I hopped on that midnight train to go take that DNA test. When I got there and looked in the little girl's face, I knew she was mines before I got the results back."

While I was enjoying the rest of Simon's story, the Nutter Butter brown waitress calmly walked right up to our table. She was fine as hell as she cocked her head to one side.

"How many times are you going tell that story, Dad?" she asked. "We both know Mom just had your nose open."

Oh shit, I thought, hoping my facial expression didn't show how perplexed I was. It was a struggle to hold my composure, but I did it. Sharon never broke eye contact with me. She seemed to be studying my reaction. I stood up and extended my hand in her direction. "Pleased to meet you. I'm Lamar."

She smiled the most beautiful smile, holding my hand. Her hands were soft and supple, which made me question what she really did at Benz Kitchen.

"Well, I guess you know my name already, I'm Simon's ambitious daughter."

Simon looked at me and smiled. "I just hired Lamar so he can help you out around here, so don't run him off like the other people you've trained."

"You know I wouldn't do anything like that, Dad," she said, walking away just as quickly as she came.

"I'm sorry for staring at your daughter like that," I said.

"The eyes do hustle," he said, using my line on me. "You got the job, and I want you to start Friday. I have faith in you that you won't disappoint me. If you're anything like Cosby, you won't. Benz Kitchen is a great place for you to stack that money. I pay well. Are you ready to get this chicken?"

"Born ready," I said.

CHAPTER FIVE:
A TASTE OF CHOCOLATE

That night, while I sat on my bed dreaming of Leer Jets and coupes, Mom popped up inside my doorway without making no noises whatsoever. It didn't surprise me, because she could be a ninja when she wanted to be. If sneaking up on you was her plan, there was no stunt she couldn't pull. Jackie Chan. Her gray eyes twinkled in the darkness.

"Today was a big day for you," she said in a sweet tone that all loving mothers use.

"You could say that again."

"That's why I'm standing here, so you can tell me about it?"

Before I answered my mom's question, I assumed she knew exactly how my day went already, and she just wanted to see if I would keep it a buck.

"I spent some quality time with Stacy today."

"Good," Mom said with a smile. "You know how much I like that girl."

"How come you like her so much?"

"Stacy is a beautiful Native girl, and she comes from an honorable family. She isn't like the rest of these fast ass girls around here." Mom paused. "I'm not trying to be a grandmother already. Besides those important things, she reminds me of me when I was her age; young and not afraid to fight for what we love, or who we love."

"I haven't seen that side of Stacy yet." I admitted.

"If you keep flirting with every girl you see, there is doubt in my mind that you will. Remember how young you are and don't be in a rush to get old. It's a whole bunch of stuff that you didn't see yet. That doesn't mean it's non-existent. I know Stacy is a quiet, but sometimes the quiet ones have the best personalities."

"I like that, Mom," I said. "That was fly."

Mom smiled. "You've always had a thing for the truth."

"I took a blood bond with Stacy today," I shared.

"O-kee-pah Ka-se-kah," Mom said, speaking the Native language.

I shook my head. "What does that mean?"

"It means the conductor of ceremonies," she

explained. I don't know why, but the hip-hop head inside me thought of Styles P. "The blood bond is your first step in finding out your purpose here on Mother-Earth. Tomorrow, I have decided it's time for you to go see the Shaman." She paused. "Stacy volunteered herself to be your chaperone to the Onondaga Reservation."

"How come you're not taking me?"

"As a young man, you must walk this journey to 'Form your medicine' alone. Be alert. Most likely, the Shaman will predict deception in the darkest hour, rewards of risk that uncloak unfamiliar faces and cowards, but you're my son, that means you're connected to a higher power." She paused. "I heard you start work at Benz Kitchen on Friday," she said, switching topics on a dime. "I would assume you know to be careful because Benz Kitchen is in the heart of the hood. You've always seemed to like new challenges Lamar, so look at this job as one, but keep your eyes open."

"I know, Mom," I agreed.

"Good, my child," she said. "Knowing is half the battle. Before it slips my mind, Chocolate called here earlier and said she needed your help hooking up a hose for her water bed."

"Okay."

Mom left quietly, then I got ready to go upstairs. 'It's going down', I thought. Young Joc.

When Chocolate opened the door, she looked

so sexy that the Hershey Company should have seriously considered naming a candy bar after her pretty face. I couldn't front. She was milk chocolate personified. She was wearing a burgundy sheer dress with gold accessories. The two colors collaged with her skin complexion perfectly and made me think of African American royalty.

She looked into my eyes and grinned. "For a minute, I started to think that Marie forgot to give you my message."

"All I know is, as soon as I got your message, I came up here. Those colors look real fly on you," I said, changing topics.

"Thank you. Remember that it's important to find out the color that brings out your skin complexion the best." She moved out of the way to let me in. Once I was inside, she closed her door and locked it. Chocolate smelled like weed and expensive perfume. I imagined the fragrance was called 'Salute' by Melissa Day.

"Do you have an answer for me yet?" I asked.

"Actually, I do. Sit down," she ordered, gesturing to her couch with a nod. I took a seat on her sectional couch, and Chocolate sat down beside me, then she crossed her legs like Sharon Stone in Basic Instinct. "I've given your proposal some thought, and I decided to accept your offer."

"What made you say yes?" I asked curiously.

She smiled. "I have a few reasons why I'm

saying yes to you and not no. Would you like to hear them?"

I smiled back. "Of course I do."

"First of all, as a black woman, I couldn't pass up my chance to nurture black male brilliance, so while you're in my presence, absorbing my knowledge should be a priority. If you listen closely, you have a chance to reach the stars, because everything I say should make you want to shoot down lyrics in your notepad. Bokeem Woodbine. And when I'm done with you, your bullets should change gun laws. Columbine. Real special people in this universe do things with a unique design."

This was one of the reasons why I wanted Chocolate to be my instructor. Her words were so inspirational that they caused bombs to go off inside my head like Funk Flex was inside my cerebral. It took some resolve to resist my urge to act like a groupie.

"As a young man, you already have the potential to have the U.S. Open Solane Stephens down the road seasoned with savvy and focus. Only a great mind can create, and leading by example makes ordinary people wanna be great. If you're looking for knowledge and wisdom, I'm offering you a full plate. You're packing, and what can I say? I love the pipe. The things that we share in this apartment are between me and you. If you start pillow talking, you're on your own like Patti

Labelle. I won't confirm it," she warned.

"What makes you think that I'm just going to start pillow talking?"

"These things do happen," she said. "Real good pussy makes men do the craziest things."

"And yours is that good?" I asked.

"Grade A," she promised, looking deep into my eyes.

Chocolate looked so sexy that she froze me as if she were Subzero. Intimidated, I looked away for a split second. She had that kinda effect on me, and she knew it. Suddenly, Chocolate reached out and gently placed her hand under my chin, turning my head to face her again.

"You're not gonna do that are you, Lamar?" she demanded.

"No!"

"Good," she said. "I don't want this to jeopardize the relationship I have with your mother." She paused. "The first and most important thing that I want to teach you is knowledge of self."

"Are you trying to say that I don't know myself?"

"Calm down. Don't get defensive, because I'm not trying to insult you. You have so much to learn about life."

"Like what?" I asked.

"Just know that before I even considered such an arrangement, I did my homework on you. It was a small precaution to make sure my time isn't wasted on you. Styles P believes 'Time Is Money', and so do I." She held one hand up and rubbed her fingers together, flashing me the silent cash symbol.

"What kinda homework?" I inquired.

She sighed and said, "If I remember correctly, your birthday is June twenty-fourth. A Cancer with a twist of Gemini. I'm a Pisces. A water sign just like you. I know this is hard for you to understand, but together we are so powerful. I have carefully picked out distinctive lessons that will boost your writing ability to unheard-of levels."

I didn't know enough about that astrology shit to match wits with Chocolate. True story.

"What does astrology have to do with writing?" I asked.

She smiled. "I want you to listen carefully to what I'm about to say because I'm about to break everything down for you like Chris Brown did at the end of his 'Loyal' video."

Chocolate's simile triggered thoughts to go off inside my head like guns in the hood on the fourth of July. The fact that Chris did all those moves Chocolate was alluding to with a pair of construction Timberlands on was a testament to his skill and bravado. After those B.E.T Awards, the one that he performed 'Man In The Mirror'. I had wasted countless hours debating with my father after the show - about who was better, MJ or Chris?

I pictured people in their late forties like my father saying. 'Fuck, no! Ain't nobody better than Mike.' That thought caused me to smile real wide.

"There you go with that smiling to yourself shit. Dream state," she whispered. "What's on your mind when you zone out like that?"

"Nothing real," I admitted. "Break it down, though."

"There is so many great men and women that have walked this Earth at one point. I'm talking all time. My next question is, where do you think you rank all time?"

Chocolate's question was deep but simple for me.

"I don't," I said honestly.

"Not now, but one day you will. I honestly believe that. The question is, do you believe that? Do you want to be lost in the pages of history or make history? Most people walk around content with not accomplishing anything significant in their lifetime." She paused. "I want you to know that your brain is capable of remembering every situation with dialogue, every song lyric, and every movie quote. I envy you for that. In fact, you will even break down these words thousands of times inside your mind. Imagine a writer who can recall anything at any time. Crazy! What are you going to do with this talent? Make people think when they read your material or describe some fucking bushes for two pages? Do you know the average author is well into their forties when they pen their first novel?"

"I didn't know that," I admitted.

"Why do you think it takes them so long?"

"They were probably out doing more important things, like having children, falling in love, and traveling the world," I guessed.

She smiled. "Your answer, which is right, actually coincides with your first lesson. All the things you just named are life-altering experiences that help shape who you are as a person. The deeper the experiences we have, the deeper your content will be for your books."

"Is this considered a life-altering conversation?" I joked.

"For someone else, maybe not. But for you, fuck yeah! Which is why any money that you earn from my teachings entitles me to a percentage of your proceeds."

"I don't have a problem with that."

"Good. There is no nation like a donation!" She paused. "What do you think about nineties rap music?"

"Dope," I said one word.

Chocolate reached under her coffee table and pulled out a huge stack of material that included magazines, books, and albums from hip-hop legends.

"I remember the artists had catchy lyrics that made you want to rewind their tapes over and over again like that Nelly song. They didn't dumb their lyrics down for you to understand. You had to get on their level or get left behind. That's how your writing should be, like a classic rap album by PAC, BIG, HOVA, and NAS. Tell a story that transcends color, but at the same time, move the crowd like Rakim."

"You really think that I can be that good?"

"These things do happen," she promised. "If you think it, so you are."

"Why do you repeat the same sayings?"

"Because that's my style. Plus, repetition is the mother of all skills. It's like this new generation forgot that one of your greatest goals should be to handcraft your own personality. If you had one chance to meet with someone important, would they leave there impressed with your conversation? When I'm done with you, they will be. Just know that! Your style will be original and fly, just like mines." She paused. "We have done enough talking. Are you ready for your next lesson?"

"Born ready," I declared.

"Get on your knees," she ordered. "Since you like proposals."

Her mood seemed to shift right in front of my eyes.

"Are you serious, Chocolate?"

She frowned at me and said, "Does it look like I'm playing?"

I got up, and she helped me kneel on the carpeted floor, then she positioned her body directly in front of me.

"Today, I'm going to teach you how to use your tongue for more than just chit-chat." She laid back against the pillows and got into a comfortable position. "Don't do anything unless I tell you to," she said.

It seemed like Chocolate was deciding exactly how she wanted to teach me this lesson. Meanwhile, I felt like I was being punished, but for some reason, I was extremely aroused by her theatrics.

"Are you nervous?" she asked with a smirk.

"Yes."

"Take my panties off."

Damn! This woman had me harder than penitentiary steel, thinking with my other head. I quickly went to snatch her panties off.

"Stop!" she commanded. "Your technique is all wrong."

"Yes, Chocolate," I replied, chastened.

"When you're trying to turn a woman out, think like EPMD and LL Cool J."

"What?" I asked, confused.

"Slow Down Baby," she said. "And look me in my eyes when you take my panties off. It turns me on and shows me you have confidence in yourself.

You wanna let these young girls know that when they fuck with you, it's real. Eye contact does that."

"Anything else?"

She paused. "For now, no. You may begin."

This time my gaze was way more primal and direct. I slowly slid my hands up her legs, and her skin was nice and smooth. I'd been waiting so long to touch Chocolate that my mouth started to water. Little did she know, I was hungry for her pussy.

"I've been waiting to suck on your pussy since I was an adolescent," I declared, keeping it a buck.

"Nasty talk is always nice, but your actions will prove if you're telling the truth."

When my hands made it to her knees, she spread her legs slightly. I took off my Guess shirt and threw it on the floor with an attitude that could pass as believable. She jacked it too. Silly of her to think she was the only actor in the room, I thought.

"Are you okay?" she asked. I didn't answer her back. She swept her hands across my muscular chest and gave me this look. Sexy ass, I thought. I placed my arms on her hips and slowly begin pulling off her Red Laperla panties. I wasn't surprised by the brand name. Her pussy was so pretty. Clearly, it deserved to be in the most expensive lace. Without warning, I gazed deep into her eyes and pushed both of her legs up to her chest. The look in her eyes revealed an intensity at my boldness. I was on auto-pilot despite her orders.

"Take your time," she reminded me.

My pleasure, I thought. As I slowly started licking between her thighs with the long laps of my wet tongue, she let out a very low moan.

"Oh yeah," Chocolate said, softly running her fingers through my long hair.

The sensation of her massaging my scalp calmed me down and made me relax. I had to steal that technique, I thought. When I started licking the valley that separated her thighs and pussy, she began a sexy pant that echoed throughout her apartment. Her spine arched in response to my hard work and dedication to learn.

"It's time for you to make me cum," she announced, placing both of her hands over my ears and maneuvering my face in her place. I thrust my wet tongue in and out of her pretty folds with the intensity of a starved kitten drinking fresh milk, so when she slapped the shit outta me, it caught me completely off guard.

"Spell your name in this pussy," she demanded.

Her boldness and audacity lit a fire within me that made me want to suck the soul out of her pussy. I licked her so passionately in the shape of an L and slathered my tongue across that thin strip between her ass and pussy for letter A. When I got to letter M, I sucked and slurped on her clit, then swirled my tongue around inside of her wetness. She tasted like cucumber melon body wash and exotic soap from France. I could feel her natural juices running down my chin and licked my lips to savor her flavor. A small amount of pre-cum came out of my dick on its own.

When I got to A again, a sound came forth from Chocolate that she couldn't control. It had to come from deep within her soul, I thought. I sucked on her clit harder, taking charge. Sensing my takeover, she opened her mouth to give me another order. I ignored her and slipped two fingers inside her wet pussy. Her insides felt hot like Phoenix, and my whole hand quickly became coated with her juices. She trembled under pressure, and when I pushed my fingers in and out, while simultaneously licking her clit, her legs started shaking uncontrollably.

"Stop it!" she yelled.

"No!" I disobeyed. "Repetition is the mother of all skills."

The fact that I was smart enough to rebuttal her line made her stare deep into my eyes. This time, I didn't look away. It wasn't until I tasted her delicious cream on my tongue that I realized how hard she came. Her sounds of pleasure caused my dick to swell up like a bee sting. Without warning, she sat up and freed the weapon of mass destruction from my shorts. All my pent up frustration burst, and I filled the palm of her hand with torrents of sperm.

"How did you make me cum while pleasing you?" I asked.

"Don't be shocked," she said with a sexy smile. "These things do happen."

CHAPTER SIX:
DREAM VISIONS OF A LEGEND

We stood there staring at the wooded area around us on the outskirts of the Onondaga Reservation, where Stacy's mom dropped us off and immediately turned back around. The morning air was nippy, considering it was the summertime. Stacy came up with the bright idea of walking to the main village instead of riding there. It was so much green everywhere that I wished it was money and weed rather than trees, shrubs, and grass. Besides the birds chirping and the squirrels roaming around, it was relatively quiet. No loudmouth hood buffoonery or early morning hustlers getting to the bag. There were no cars, trucks, and the contaminated air that came along with them. Just me, my girl, and nature. The silence was only broken by the sound of our voices.

"How come you wanted to use Pat and Sam instead of riding to the main village?"

She gave me a confused look. "Who the hell are Pat and Sam?"

My sarcastic parents introduced me to Pat and Sam at an early age. I used to ask them how I would get to basketball and football practice. It was my way of hinting to them that their firstborn needed a ride.

Dad said, "Ask Pat and Sam to take you." After walking around the city of Syracuse a few times, Pat and Sam had had enough.

"Our two feet," I explained. She laughed.

"Walking is good for your heart," Stacy said as she zigzagged and worked her way through the wooded underbrush.

"My heart is fine," I promised. "My feet are a whole nother story, though."

"For an athlete, you do a lot of complaining. If you keep crying, what is the baby gonna do?"

"The baby would've got a ride to the main village in a car seat, but clearly you're on Dora The Explorer time," I responded.

"Please, I'm way more sexy than her." She stopped and posed like I was about to take a picture of her.

She was wearing a fly dress by Victoria Secret with a flannel shirt tied around her waist. On her feet, she was rocking a pair of construction

Timberlands. The ones that every hood in America loves. Stacy had her long hair wrapped in a blue bandanna 2PAC style. It made her look thuggish, but at the same time, she looked feminine. I had on some regular degular shit. Levi 501 jeans, a blue Buffalo Bills hoodie, and a pair of black New Balance. We both had on matching Eddie Bauer backpacks. I had a Flying Squirrel sleeping bag in mines, a flashlight, snacks, water, and my dad's Estwing Sportsman's Axe. At the last minute, I stuffed it inside my bag just in case I had to make a split decision.

"Why did you have to wear that omen out here?"Stacy asked.

"Don't be mad I'm representing my mob," I said, tapping the Buffalo logo on my hoodie. "We're going to the Superbowl this year," I declared with a straight face.

"A square peg could never fit into a round hole," Stacy said, pointing at my beloved Bills hoodie. She laughed, but I didn't.

"And who is going to lead you to the big game?"

"Tyrod," I responded.

"Sure he is, I can see it now. The Bills vs Browns in the AFC championship game. Then they would advance to play the Bears," she said, sarcastically. "Bills fans always have these high hopes until about week six, and then you don't hear them anymore."

For the real men who watch sports, It's their dream to have a cute girlfriend who can carry on a factual conversation with them on several different sports topics. I'm one of those young men, so I actually thought it would be fly of me to put Stacy up on game, but I had no idea how much of a monster I created until she started quoting Jemele Hill and Cari Champion. To add insult to injury, her Bills analysis was accurate. Buffalo hasn't been to the playoffs since DMX was hot, I thought. And they fired Rex Ryan, gave Tyrod an extension, but got rid of the receivers he had chemistry with. You know I did what every Bills fan does when people take shots at our team.

"Are you sure you didn't get us lost Eagles fan that's never been to Philly?" People from New York with football teams from a different state they never been to were counterfeit to me. At least I liked a New York team that actually played in the state. When The Bills finally do win, I will be right there, conducting the ultimate celebration.

Stacy smiled. "Now you're contesting my tour guide skills?"

"I'm just saying," I said. "My Fitbit is saying that I took ten racks worth of steps."

"We're almost there, lazy."

"I remember Papa Smurf used to rock the Smurfs to sleep like this," I responded.

Suddenly, a weird feeling passed through my body that words couldn't explain. I scanned the area on instinct, and out the corner of my eye, I spotted a large shadow in the thick shrubs watching us. My Fitbit stopped counting steps because I stopped taking steps. Real talk.

"What's wrong, baby?" Stacy asked, noticing she was suddenly walking alone.

I pointed as I spoke. "Something is inside those bushes." Stacy trained her eyes in the direction I alluded to, but she had a look on her face like she didn't see it. I was on point like Chris Paul, though. Maybe it's because, in all scary movies I saw, black people are always going out like dark skin Jermaine, I thought. I wasn't trying to be another unsolved mystery to go down in history.

"Where is it?"

"Right there," I said, pointing again to the same spot.

When the shadow finally emerged from the bushes, it was a big ass deer. Strangely, the animal locked eyes with me and didn't immediately run away.

"A deer," Stacy said in a sarcastic tone. "There's a lot worse things inside these woods than that."

I smiled. "Like what?"

She twirled around. "Like me!"

After maneuvering through the heavily

wooded area for another twenty minutes, we arrived just outside the main village.

I looked down at my watch. It was almost nine in the morning, and the roads were still relatively quiet. I checked my surroundings. No new cars, one diner to eat at, no big city buildings, and the people who occupied them. So this was the reservation?
I didn't fully understand why I couldn't tag along with momma love to these council meetings. By the looks of things, the old heads could use some input from a modern mind.

We took the trail that led right to the Shaman. It was Stacy's idea. She said we should avoid all the main roads to get there. The trail began to veer off into a backroad, and we came across a few hidden houses in the wilderness.

"Look," Stacy said. "You already have a fan club."

What could I say? I'm a handsome young man, I thought. I saw three people walking around casually on their property without a care in the world. Sometimes, Stacy acted like she was the only person allowed to look at me. I ignored her smart ass comment and kept it pushing, though. We passed a few more houses, and I noticed several girls noticing me. The eyes do hustle!

Stacy suddenly pointed. "That's the medicine lodge right there."

My eyes followed her finger. There was a

young lady standing by the bushes that concealed the front entrance of the sacred building. She was a pretty, tall, reddish orange-skinned girl with a nice body. Her hair was dyed blood red, and it was cut short with the left side shaved completely off. It was different, but at the same time, fly. She was wearing a black dress that hugged her curves, red shoes, and gold jewelry. From her outfit to her look, I could tell she wanted to distinguish herself from all the other Native girls on the reservation. Her plan worked because she definitely had my attention. This mystery girl was accompanied by two big bowling pin-shaped red men with thick muscular arms and menacing expressions. This girl was either somebody important on the reservation, or she thought she was. Only people with money to pay goons have a security team.

When she looked up and saw us, her face lit up with mixed emotions. She stopped the conversation she was having with her team and quickly closed the gap between us. For the second time on this trip, I felt something inside me stir. Up close, she was even more striking; her skin was creamy, and I liked her dark brown eyes. There were tiny freckles placed perfectly on her face. It was like the Great Spirit himself took time out to sprinkle them on her face like a topping. As Stacy stood by my side like a Jadakiss song, a small crowd began to form up.

"Here comes this stupid bitch," Stacy

whispered.

From the tone of Stacy's voice, I assumed she had some beef with this girl that wasn't fully cooked or done meat. How else could you explain her project girl response? After a few seconds of silence by everybody, Stacy spoke up. "As we walked past a few of these cabins, I almost thought you wouldn't show your face today, Layla."

Layla rolled her eyes at Stacy's response, and for some strange reason, she looked right at me.

"I've been waiting on you," Layla said like Gladys Knight at the Apollo.

"I know you're not talking about me," Stacy asked in a challenging tone.

"For just this once," Layla said sarcastically. "You're absolutely right. I'm talking to him."

Layla established eye contact with me, and she had a flattering, flirty, and fun look on her face. Cuties, beauties, and dimes. I loved the summertime, I thought.

"Me?" I asked. "I don't think we ever met before, so you can't be talking to me."

She placed her hand on her hip and smiled. Naturally beautiful results for my soul. A natural glow could never get old.

"Your name is Lamar, right?"

"How do you know my government name?" I asked.

"Be easy," she said. "If you were a lame, I

wouldn't know your name. You're Marie's son, though."

"My mom told you my name?" I asked.

"I have my sources, but please believe me when I say those sources don't include Marie."

Her voice made love to my ears, and I looked directly into her eyes. I quickly studied them. I'd seen those eyes somewhere before, I thought. Weird. Stacy wasn't happy with our conversation that excluded her participation.

"Did this mystery person tell you that I'm his girlfriend?"

Layla shifted her weight to one side and folded her arms. A good indication that she was about to say something spicy.

"Talk to me nice, Stacy. My source would never mention you, because they know I don't worry about insignificant details."

"Insignificant?" Stacy repeated. "I can see homeschooling has finally put some big words in your vocabulary, but you don't scare me."

With all the mass shootings in America, homeschooling didn't sound like a bad idea. When mentally unstable white kids get mad, you might have to rock a bulletproof book bag. Sad. R.I.P. to all those kids, I thought.

Suddenly, I could see the anger in Stacy's eyes. "Watch your step, Layla. I'm TTG."

For people who don't know modern lingo,

TTG means trained to go. It was bottle popping talk. Fighting words. Before Layla could respond, I strategically cut her off. A smart move from a calculating boss.

"Can somebody tell me what that means?" I asked.

As I pointed to the top of the medicine lodge, blue streams of smoke rose into the cloudless sky. Layla moved closer to me and looked in the direction of this smoke. She said, "Usually, people don't want no smoke." She gave Stacy a dirty look. "That smoke means it's time for you to see the Shaman." Her closeness made me feel something. Something deep inside my body. If our paths ever crossed again, I definitely wanted to ask her if she felt the same thing.

Suddenly, a man appeared at the front door of the medicine lodge wearing blue jeans, cowboy boots, and a great number of quills of the raven that formed his stylish headdress. His presence was commanding, and the small crowd that gathered became quiet. These people respected this man enough to be silent without him giving the order to do so. That's power at an early hour.

"That's my dad," Layla bragged. "The Chief."

Seconds later, this powerful man called out my full government name. Several people standing close by stared at me, and the crowd parted like Moses parted the Red Sea. It was as if I suddenly became contagious. I inhaled deeply and braced myself for whatever might come next, and the next thing to come was a tight hug from Stacy. She did it in a calculating fashion, but I could still feel her passion. Her hands roamed the small of my back. I can't say I was surprised by the show of affection. This is what women do when another wooer is looking in your direction.

"Remember, baby, in the face of danger, you must always show how much heart you have," Stacy said.

Did she know who the fuck I think I am? Over Stacy's shoulder, Layla shot me a quick mischievous grin that captured my attention and moved my emotions. Her eyes had this carnal quality that made it hard for me to look away. It was a turn on.

As I started walking slowly towards the lodge, I heard a few whispers from the crowd. When I got closer to the chief, I couldn't help but notice his reddish-skin was blotched with age and spotted with the same freckles his daughter had. He looked into my eyes, then down at my feet. Creepy shit! He placed both of my hands inside his, examining them, looking for something. Then he sniffed the air around us. His face became more lively and expressive.

"You may enter the lodge now," he said. "The Shaman waits for you inside."

When I got six feet from the lodge, my brain told my mouth to momentarily halt so he could broadcast what's inside my heart. Your odyssey is about to start too, so it's till death do us part, but don't be a retard. Cherish this Good Book that's guaranteed to get the world hooked; I told you, I keep my line in the water with bait. If this sounds evil to you, turn back now. It's not too late.

I opened the door and walked inside the lodge. My heart started beating like a bass drum, billows of smoke from a fireplace made it hard for me to breathe. FAB. I could see the lodge was decorated with antique smoking pipes, kettles, and weapons. The heat from the fire caused sweat to drip down my face, and I used the back of my hand to wipe it off.

"You may be seated now!" a booming voice said from the thick smoke.

When I took a seat, I didn't remember when I first noticed the man seated across from me, staring at me. He wore the skin of a black bear, the head of which he used as a mask. There were groups of buffalo, and human skulls placed all around us to form the perfect circle. At my feet was a small teacup with ancient Native markings on it. About thirty seconds passed without a word being exchanged. Suddenly, the voice spoke again.

"I am not the chief, but what I'm about to say are words from his mouth. He has told me that you are here to 'Form your Medicine'. You also want to talk to the Great Spirit."

"What the chief says is true," I said.

"You will now drink the tea that I have prepared for you."

I picked up the cup and drank half. It tasted like shit, and after I finished all of it, there was a moment of silence, which the Shaman quickly broke.

"Is there anything else you seek?"

"I would like to know my Native name?" I asked.

Right after I asked my question, I began to feel things; my ears started to hum, my chest tightened up, and my fingers tingled. Suddenly, the room began to fade and get real fuzzy. I thought, did this Shaman just poison me? I tried to get a grip, but I couldn't. I vaguely heard his voice like it was slowly coming towards me down a long tunnel.

"I know that you seek a Native name, young man, but soon you will have a Chinese name, my friend." He paused. "Long Gone." His promise was followed by pounding laughter in my ear.

I've never hallucinated before, at least not knowingly, but when the entire lodge begin to shake like a stripper, and the bottom of the floor fell from beneath my feet, I knew there was a first time for everything. As I descended into a free fall, I yelled for Stacy. It didn't do me any good, because I couldn't even hear my own voice. Everything became Kodak Black and quiet. All the stars in the sky seemed within my grasp. This was that Kanye testimony "Touch the Sky" that tested my faith. Good thing I wasn't phony. R.I.P. to all my homies.

Out the blue, wolves howled in the distance, and birds began to chirp loudly as my feet sunk into what looked like red clay. The surface of this clay was polished and clean. Somehow, I'd been transported to a primitive world beyond my wildest dreams. When my eyes set directly in front of me, they zoomed in on a sight that I'll remember for the rest of my days.

A tall, muscular, and extremely imposing Native American was sitting Indian style directly across from me. He was wearing a shirt made of two brown deer skins, expertly dressed and stitched with porcupine quills. More information came to me. Suspended from his shirt, from his shoulders to his hands, was a fringe of a bunch of scalp locks. There was no doubt in my mind that he snatched those shits off his victims' heads in battle. I looked around some more. We were both seated under the skylight in the middle of his wigwam. Over the fireplace and hanging from a pole was a pot with something smelling good as hell coming out of it.

The interior of his wigwam was decorated with his bow and quiver, battle-axes, different lances, and a raven headdress. I rubbed my eyes because I still couldn't believe what I was seeing. The old man finally looked up and gave me the once over, then he smiled.

"You have decided to wake up and join us again, Blacksky." His voice was filled with certainty and bravado. This Native knew me that's for sure, but how? I thought.

"Who are you?" I asked. "And who is this 'Blacksky'?"

He laughed the laugh of a villain on the last stage of a video game.

"Do not tell me that the peyote has melted your brain. I am your grandfather and the chief of the Blackfoot Nation." He gazed at me like I was crazy. "You have been on a spirit quest to 'form your medicine'."

"How long have I been sitting in this same position, grandfather?"

"For about two days," he declared.

Multiple thoughts began to form inside my brain. Where the hell was I? Could one person exist in two different realms?

I let my eyes drift around the wigwam. Did my grandfather know that I was trapped inside Blacksky's body? Suddenly, a sharp pain shocked my brain, and tons of useful information flooded my cerebral. I realized it was information that was embedded in Blacksky. No wonder why I could explain everything around me in vivid detail.

Somehow, I had managed to quantum leap back a few centuries but was allowed to keep a modern mind. This had to be the Great Spirit's design because it damn sure wasn't mine. While my grandfather stared at me suspiciously, my brain downloaded more information.

"What now, grandfather?" I asked, thirsty to learn more about the body I had inhabited. "Please tell me, grandfather," I said. "What happens now?"

"I am proud that you have completed the first process in forming your medicine, Blacksky. Now it is time for you to take your first squaw." He laughed a little. "When ho'gà:hgwë't (the sun goes down), you will become a man."

Was I really a virgin in both worlds? I had a girl but was still on a drought. This was some pitiful shit to talk about. If I couldn't get any pussy from one of these squaw thots, I would be an embarrassment to the people that died on my block. Which meant it was time to put this abstinence to a stop. Watch! I'm about to draft a Native girl before my time even runs out on the clock.

"Who is this squaw you speak of?" I asked.

"She is the beautiful daughter of my friend One Horn. A tried and tested warrior with whom I have fought many battles alongside. How! How! I have agreed to give him four horses, three guns, and several pounds of tobacco."

My brain quickly decoded the Blackfoot lingo.

How! How! was like saying that's a fact in my generation.

"Do you think that this squaw is worth that?" I asked.

Grandfather gave me a piercing look like I should know these things I ask. "Fire That Burns is the finest young dresser of skins in our whole nation. Her services could be of great value to any warrior in this village, but I have heard that Fire is a hard young squaw to deal with."

I smiled at my grandfather's confession. A quick lesson. The dream world kept me guessing. "What makes her so hard to handle?"

"This is not something that I have made up, Blacksky. I have heard these words from One Horn's mouth, and this is his only daughter. He has told me many times that Fire wishes to live a warrior's life; fight with honor until you die. It is One Horn's belief that you are the only young warrior that could tame her. I have gifted you ten horses and a new wigwam to make this feat easier for you."

I nodded my head as I registered the information he gave me in my brain and said, "Thank you, grandfather."

"The way that you will thank me is by making me proud tomorrow during the hunt for the animal that fills your medicine-bag. May the Great Spirit be with you, Blacksky. I have no more to say," he said in a dismissing tone.

When I exited my grandfather's wigwam, my brain told me exactly where to go, and I was taken aback by the scenery. The entire village was in full motion, and my eyes were treated with a panoramic view of history. Every person around me had a distinctive red skin complexion, wild horses ran around freely, and every dog looked like a wolf. Stern warriors stood in their separate groups wrapped in painted robes. Their heads were decked and plumed with War-Eagle quills. I shook my head and smiled because my world suddenly wasn't the same anymore. How, how!

CHAPTER SEVEN:
LAYLA FIRE'S PERSPECTIVE

Who is Layla Fire you might be asking yourself? I can guarantee you that you're not the only one asking the question. You could ask the handful of people that know me that same question, and you would probably would get different answers from each one of them. I'm the baddest, smartest, and toughest girl on this reservation that nobody truly knows.

I'm the extraordinary combination of brains and beauty that real men have wet dreams about, but don't be fooled by my pretty face, slim waist, and nice ass. You are in the presence of an assassin; A sexy assassin, who loves money, power, and respect. I'm new school Native American, and the reason why I say new school is because the young people in Syracuse are silly enough to think that all

Natives still look like the Indians on 'Dances with Wolves'. I'm royalty on this reservation because my father is Chief Red River, head distributor of marijuana in Onondaga county.

Listen carefully. This is a PSA. I hate the white man, the state, and the crooked government that they work for; their treachery has gone on for hundreds of years against my people. How could I not hate a race who introduced whiskey and small-pox to my people? The fatal disease ravaged entire Native tribes and made so many of my ancestors perish. Fast-forward to present-day America, and the white man's deceit is right there on the surface for everyone to see. The same land that my ancestors have fought so many bloody battles for was eventually all snatched back by the pale-faces. How could I not hate a government that has broken so many promises and treaties? They've given us small patches of dirt when the entire country was ours to begin with. Natives were allowed to build casinos on this dirt, and because it generates billions of dollars, all the white man's trickery seems to have been forgotten by my people.

Native and African American blood is soaked into the soil of this country, and it has been used as fertilizer to grow the white man's businesses. In honor of every single one of my ancestors who are in the 'Fields of Elysian', I made a vow to myself to never stop fighting until I've taken back all the land that was wrongfully taken from us. Beware of a woman with fire inside her belly and courage inside her heart. The Great Spirit has consumed my soul and mixed me with Harriet Tubman, Geronimo, and Crazy Horse. Believe me when I say I have and will use by whatever means necessary to shift the balance of power back to the Natives. If you do not feel what I am saying, then this isn't for your sensitive ears. This is that revolutionist talk from a revolutionary bitch who won't stop until a giant image of me is carved into several American mountains. Because of my goals, the majority of my time is spent scheming on ways to make all my enemies disappear.

Recently, an intriguing situation was brought to my attention by my dad and another reliable source. According to them, Sage, a high ranking member of the Onoda'ge:ono' council, would be bringing her son to go see the Shaman. Normally, outdated council affairs are of no concern to me, especially when I observed that when it comes to the palefaces, they like to talk their problems out. I say, fuck that! I don't negotiate with non-negotiable people. Anyways, the fact that Sage was bringing her son would be normal under any other circumstances if she wasn't a shifter like me. Most people outside of the Native American culture have never heard of shifters, and laugh at the thought of something like this being possible. I promise you that if someone put money on your head, you would be the dead testament to make people start believing a little faster. You don't think this is a fact?

If they were alive, you could ask the numerous Syracuse wanna be drug dealers who aspired to make history by being the first to run off with pounds of my father's weed on consignment. They are history now. So silly of them to forget a classic Christoper Wallace commandment. We definitely wanted our money even if it rained, sleeted, hailed, or snowed. Agahgwaga' has too much to turn my head while people pull stunts. The facial expressions on each one of their faces when I shifted could help out the Scared Straight program if they showed the kids.

Not every Native can shift; it has to be passed down through your bloodline. Even if it is, it still takes practice. Unless you're a natural. I'm a millennial shifter, and that means because of evolution, I can shift into three animals: one air and two land animals, to be exact. The old school shifters can only change into two animals. As you would imagine, the old school shifters are more dangerous than us because, over the years, they have mastered getting in and out of their shifts faster. Practice makes perfect.

The first time I shifted, I was ten years old at Green Lakes National Park. That day, my mother didn't take me swimming in the designated area were everyone else swam. Instead, we walked deep into the woods to a secluded spot that signs posted saying 'No Swimming.' Even though I wanted to, I didn't question my mom's judgment. Like most young Natives, by age ten, I was a skilled swimmer anyway, and it wasn't like I couldn't handle deep water.

I remember her grabbing my small hands and leading me out to deepest part of the lake. Then Mom suggested that we should have a contest to see who could hold their breath the longest underwater. She knew I would say yes, and played on my need to always compete. We took turns diving down as long as we could, and then resurfacing. Like any other time, we were having so much fun at Green Lakes. Suddenly, after about four minutes on one of Mom's dives, she didn't resurface.

Anyone who has ever been on the brink of a major catastrophe where a possible death is involved will tell you the worst thing you can do is panic. I can't front. I panicked. Just before I was about to dive back down, she resurfaced, but she wasn't breathing. My eyes became moist with tears as I stared at her lifeless body. Most people view death as a natural, inevitable event. I thought about all the precious time we spent, and I couldn't let my mother die right in front of me. Suddenly, my heart rate started to pick up, and I felt this weird sensation coming over me. I could feel my small body going into metamorphosis. In an instant, blood rushed to my head. The structure of my body became stronger, and I reached out and latched on to my mom's arm tightly. I was amazed at how quickly I was able to pull her heavy body to shore.

It wasn't until I looked down at my shaggy fur and sharp claws that I realized I shifted into a grizzly bear. Out of the blue, Mom opened her eyes and reached out and touched me. That nurturing feeling made me calm down. "Take deep breaths. Inhale and exhale. That's how you control it,'" she advised. That was many moons ago. Ever since that day, I've worked real hard at mastering my craft.

A crack in the branches snapped me out of my memories, and I stopped dead in my tracks. That's when I saw him. He was about six-foot-one, a buck ninety, long hair, and honey-brown skin. He looked unique and different from anyone else I'd seen. African American mixed with Native American. What a combo, I thought. As I moved closer, I noticed he was standing next to this 'blacktop' bitch named Stacy. Where was Marie? I remained still and blended into the bushes like the chameleon. If you didn't have a keen eye for does, then I could sneak right up on you and wouldn't even know. As I stood on my toes and moved my large eyes around, his eyes locked onto me, and I froze like Onondaga Lake in the wintertime. My body was warning me of danger. He pointed in my direction, but Stacy couldn't see me. I blinked. He blinked back. It was like he could sense that someone had shifted around him. Did he know that I was so much more than a mammal in the bushes? Maybe I'm jumping the gun, I thought. Knowing full well they were going to see the Shaman, I took off through the bushes going about 30 miles per hour.

Okay, when it comes to clutch preparedness, I've been known to move with a purpose. I decided to wear my black Lacoste dress with red H&M shoes. The material on this dress is soft, feminine, and very pretty, just like me. Except for the soft part. When it comes to fashion, if I like it, I buy it. I don't window shop. I'll always get to that bag I pray. Dallin's The Appeal to the Great Spirit. I sprayed on some Jimmy Choo L'Eau perfume. It smelled so good on me that some of the Native girls on the reservation wanted to taste this honey pot, but I like dick. Seconds later, I left my cabin to go welcome our guests.

About forty minutes later, Lamar and Stacy came walking towards me like I had expected. When he came closer, 90s4s female rap came to mind. Even though I'm not a rapper, the way I see it, life is so real that all young millennial women should have a hot sixteen bars somewhere inside them. I wanted to give Lamar this pussy before we spoke one word to each other. I didn't wanna fuck him for his money like the reverse of white porcelain. That's Blac Chyna. All my bra and panties are designer. Christian Dior. Daddy's little girl likes to ride the dick until you snore. I've always regarded my special place as exclusive, but with this hot pink & wet pussy, he could be abusive. Beat it up. I knew I couldn't do the Erykah Badu See you "Next Lifetime" when we turn into butterflies". Whole families were about to cry if I didn't get my way. Tears would not fall from my eyes on any day.

I quickly decided to ask some questions I knew the answer to already. Some slick shit from one calculating bitch.

"I've been waiting on you," I said, looking down at his crotch.

"I know you're not talking about me?" Stacy asked, knowing good and got damn well I wasn't.

"For just this once," I said. "You're absolutely right. I'm talking to him."

Stacy cut her eyes at me, and I could tell she wanted to exchange a few barbs. We were on sacred reservation land. Any place else I would've got at her. That includes Mars. Usually, I gave out free trips to the Beautiful Hunting Grounds. She had a four-leaf clover. This is a place where I send so many clowns.

Suddenly, Lamar pointed. "Can somebody tell me what that means?" He slickly interrupted our war of words. He made me feel corny words were my only threat. I'm known to pop bottles like rappers. You get fly I'll slap ya! I took a deep breath and explained to Lamar what that blue smoke meant for him, and after my father went through the routine that is customary when anyone comes to see the Shaman, a light went off inside my head. It became clear that the blue smoke meant something entirely different for me.

There is an old Native American prophecy that says one day a powerful man will come along and reunite 'The Six Nations'. It's been several years since the elder council members talked about this, but after meeting Lamar, I could see why their hopes were renewed. Call me a little skeptical, but you know the next step was to go have a look at the Native American Book of Prophesy for myself. This just happened to be the perfect time to sneak into the place where the book was being held. Detective shit. Twelve.

Some minutes later, I found myself at the backdoor of the council's private library. After skillfully picking the lock, I closed the door behind me. It eliminated all the light from the sun. Good thing I wasn't afraid of the dark. Shit, some of my best work is done in the dark! I put whips in park if you're phony. I'm the Native American big homie.

I moved around until I found the light switch. When I did, I pulled the string. Now I could see a small room about the same size as a walk-in closet.

There was a mahogany table with two matching chairs and two bookshelves. I quickly went through every single book until I came across one that was unlabeled. Could this be the fable? I blew the dust off the cover and took a seat at the table.

The book started with a detailed description of some of the most powerful Indian Tribes ever assembled by the Great Spirit: Blackfeet, Sioux, Comanches, Seminole, Crows, Apaches, and the list went on and on. After reading several pages, the book confirmed what I already knew, that these tribes are enemies with deep-rooted hatred for each other. It made me think about the shifters code for this generation; all Reservations are sacred ground for shifters, and you cannot attack another shifter on sacred ground. The 'blacktop' is the equivalent of the old world plains, so on the blacktop, anybody can get clipped off. I kept turning the dusty pages, and the book started to mention some Indian legends like the Sioux Chief Crazy Horse, the Apache leader Geronimo, Hiawatha, Pontiac, Red Cloud, and Red Jacket. Strangely, each of their sections had blank pages in them.

As I kept reading, something captured my attention. It was a picture of a Native American war chief dressed in a rare all-white buffalo skin robe, and his face was entirely covered with a grizzly bear mask, by his side stood a small warrior no more than about seven years old. Unexpectedly, the light flickered, and I squinted my eyes, trying to get a better look at his photo. He was standing there like he was ready to put some work in if need be, and he had the nerve to have his little bow and quiver slung with a small robe of beaver skin draped over his body. Very cute, I thought. I turned to the next page, and it was blank, and the next one, and the next one. The light flickered again, making a bunch of goosebumps break out on my arm. WTF, I thought, this is some X-Files shit. I took a deep breath and quickly looked around the room to make sure I was still solo.

Out of the blue, I had an epiphany. All the great chiefs and warriors I read about are shifters and dreamwalkers. Of course, this was just my hypothesis because I'm a dreamwalker. The Elders say the Great Spirit has only blessed a small percentage of Native Americans with this gift. The gift that I speak of allows me to go back a few centries in my dreams. You have no choice where the Great Spirit places you. I've been dreamwalking for two years to a Blackfoot village in Upper Missouri. This sounds crazy, right? It's all facts, though. Lying is for bozoes and fake jewelry bitches who swear their neck is froze. I haven't run into any dreamwalkers like myself thus far, but I'm definitely not stupid enough to think that I'm the only Native blessed with this gift. Believe me. I've watched intently for any little quirks or mannerisms that seem too modern for the dreamworld. The keyword is intently, unbeknownst to Stacy, who thinks I'm slow because of homeschooling, my wordplay is smooth like a Bentley, which means it doesn't take long for complicated things to make sense to me. Does that sound crazy to you? If it does, then you're a mess. Put this shit down, honey, and take a rest.

Before I left the tiny library, I concluded that the reason all those pages were blank was because all the great warriors that I spoke of had their chance to rewrite history by using their dreamwalking ability, but failed. I headed back to my cabin with renewed hope that I could be the one who alters the fate of my ancestors.

CHAPTER EIGHT:
LAYLA FIRE'S DREAMWALK

My cabin has a deyétä':hgwa' (telephone), a gayá'daha' (television), and a bunch of other electronics. A lot of the elders on this reservation don't like modern devices. They say the white man's gadgets stunt your creativity and make you stupid. Of course, I know plenty of stupid Natives on the reservation without one gizmo. You could say that I'm new age Native American with a twist of old-school. Which means I watch Reality Tv and can't picture a life with no phone. Do you wanna be one of my new followers on the Gram? Type in Layla Fire and look how fat my ass is in my posts, and that's a fact, not a boast. As a millennial, I can show you how to do the most, throw the Syracuse Blends CD in my foreign and coast.

I gave my arms a long stretch and got up off

my bed, walking softly on my pretty polished wood floors until I made my way over to the closet, where I put all my weapons and concoctions in.

After looking around for a second, I found just what I was looking for, and I walked back over to my bed and took a seat. I opened the tiny box inside my hand and pulled out one dose of peyote: a strong hallucinogenic drug from the cactus. No dreamwalk could be successful without it. Our Shaman loves high-grade marijuana, and I needed the peyote that only he could get his hands on. Fair exchange isn't a robbery.

A couple of minutes after I ate the tiny capsule, my stomach started to feel nauseous, and I know what that feeling meant, so I laid back and relaxed my head on my pillow. My head was spinning, and as I looked around my cabin, the bright yellow sun peeked through my window blinds like a pedophile on Dateline. Suddenly, the peyote began to take its usual effect on me. The wooden walls inside my room started melting away like marshmallows over a fire. In no time at all, I could hear the familiar sounds of my Blackfoot village in full swing; birds chirping, wolf dogs barking, and redmen and women gossiping.

When I finally opened my eyes, my vision was still cloudy and unfocused. I'm still sleeping, I thought. I put my head under the elk-skin sheets and looked down. The hair on my pussy, once clean-shaven, was now thick and bushy, a good indication that I wasn't in Kansas anymore. I peeled back the sheet and sat up straight. My eyes roamed around the room until they landed on my clothes.

I got up off my buffalo-skin bed and walked barefoot on the red soil to grab the dress I designed. Once it was inside my hand, I held it out in front of me. It was made of two goatskins, trimmed with ermine, and ornamented with porcupine quills and white beads.

After two years of heavy practice, and I do mean heavy, I groomed myself into the best young squaw to dress skins in our village, maybe the nation. That depends on who you ask. I'm good at combining their primitive style with a modern touch. I don't care where you are on Mother Earth. Talent hates the missionary position, which means she always finds her way to the top.

Without a doubt, things are a lot different in this century for women- I'm talking Flintstones. All the Native men in our village believed that squaws should do the manual labor. I took a breath to calm myself, because you know I didn't agree with this shit, and I wanted to Wildout like Nick and turn one of these primitive men into my bitch, but that would put me at risk. I still let my father know every chance I got how fucked up a situation this is. I'm cautious how I do it, though, because I don't wanna set off any red flags by rebelling against the times.

As I slipped my dress over my head, I was stopped dead in my tracks by my father's voice. It's crazy how you speak about somebody, and they pull right up on you. "Chin-cha-bee!" he yelled, calling me in the Native language.

"Did you call me father?" I asked. He had the skin complexion of an unripened Red Delicious apple, and his long black hair flowed down his back. His eyes were as dark as night but sparkled like coals.

"You sleep like you are a white odö'ni'à:h (baby)," he said.

I smiled. "I do not."

"I have come to tell you that I have talked to Chief Crowfoot, and we have agreed in principle that his grandson Blacksky will take you as his first wife." Dad paused before continuing. "It is our belief that his heart is strong enough to tame your wild ways." How! How!

"Blacksky?" I asked. Truthfully, I know who he was. He was the spoiled grandson of the first chief of our whole nation, and I'd seen him around the village a few times. He barely said anything to anyone. I personally didn't know him yet, but like always, there was a lot of tribal gossip assuming why his demeanor was so aloof.

"Crowfoot has given Blacksky a new wigwam for you two to live in, and he has promised to give me four horses, three guns, and two pounds of tobacco."

My father's lack of compassion in this situation made me stare down at the hard-packed earthen floor of bur wigwam and shake my head. You can't make this shit up, I thought. Our village is a modern-day Yemen, where father's roll the dice for you, and all you can do is pray you don't get a lemon. If squaws could run from this transaction like their last name was Simmons, they would turn into Sanya Richards-Ross until they got lost. I'm so heated, I thought.

"It is not fair that I am being sold to someone that I do not even know. How come I cannot find a warrior on my own?" I asked.

"I do not wish to anger you, Chin-cha-bee," he said. "But do not mistake my order as a choice. You cannot do any better than the grandson of a chief anyways."

"What happens to my place inside this wigwam?" I asked.

"Listen to me, Fire," Dad said. "As my daughter, you will always be welcome in this wigwam, because it is my blood that runs through your veins, but you will take your place by Black-sky's side."

"No'yeh (my mother) needs me here," I complained.

Dad nodded. "I believe what you say is true, so you can still help her when you have completed your quota for Blacksky. He will need you to dress his buffalo robes and other skins for the white man's market."

This also meant that I had to tend to the horses at night, J. dress skins by day, cook and serve his meals, then fuck on command. I would barely have time to decorate the robes with my special touch, I thought.

"What day is this taking place, father?" I asked.

"Today," he said. "After the sun has fallen from the highest point in the sky."

I shook my head. "You have given me away today?"

"There is no use of us talking about this. I have decided that this is good for you. Chief Crowfoot's blood runs through Black- sky's veins, and that means he will have just as much fire in his heart as you. One day you will thank me for my choice," he said, walking away from me.

And I had to stand there and take it. I wasn't in a position to pull a Joan of Arc stunt, doing something that you don't wanna do for the greater good. That doesn't make you a punk. What I didn't understand was our family wasn't poor, and we didn't need the free handout. I guess my father really liked this Blacksky kid, and that was saying a lot because One Horn never spoke highly of any of the other young warriors. Which was understandable, they weren't Steph and Clay. They were more like lethargic vajay-jay from sha-nae-nae. That was for you bitches in the dark like Ray, let 'Presidents represent you like Jay'. Lyrically speaking fellas, I'm tight and wet pussy on a hot day. Mysterious thoughts for you to ponder, you never know what I might say.

As the sun began to casually dip in the all blue sky, I knew it wouldn't be long until the agreed-upon hour approached, and despite the speck of uncertainty in my mind about how things would play out with my new husband, I couldn't just wear my emotions on my sleeve. "This shit was bigger than me," like Nino Brown said in New Jack, and I refused to sacrifice my entire two-year dreamwalk for a small gripe. That's wack. I had to stick to the script and execute my plan, so I decided to rock a dress I made of swan's down that is ornamented with the quill of ducks, I secured them from a secrete pond, but that's a whole nother story. DuckTales. My all-white moccasins are .made of mountain-sheep that like to skip from ledge to ledge. As I put the finishing touches on my gown, I gave myself a quick look of approval.

When you're pretty, you don't have to pretend to look good, not every woman knows how to use their beauty to get her way, I'm not them though, soon I would have Blacksky eating shés'a:h (wild strawberries) out of my asshole. Suddenly, my father appeared by the ornamented curtains in my living space. "The time has come for us to keep our agreement."

I nodded. "Yes, father."

"This is for you," he said, extending his arm. He handed me a satchel made of deerskin, and I reached for it. "The Great Spirit has advised me to give you these weapons. Maybe you can persuade Blacksky to let you hunt like you have persuaded me."

"Thank you," I said, taking the satchel from his hand and embracing him tightly. The bag felt heavy with new instruments of destruction; no doubt prayed over by the village Shaman. It took me one year of dreamwalking just to game my father into letting me go on small hunting trips with him. In most cases, a warrior's path is forbidden by squaws. During those trips, we bonded, and I soaked up everything he taught me; tracking and killing buffalo, throwing thirty arrows in one minute, the use of my shield to protect my body parts, how to be deadly with my tomahawk like Nightwolf from. Mortal Kombat, and how to be a nightmare with a scalping-knife.

The union between myself and Blacksky was held in the center of the village in an open circular area, this small piece of land was always kept clear as public ground, just for situations such as this one. Groups of warriors, squaws, dogs, and children were gathered on the tops of their Earth covered wigwams, and nearly all of them were screaming as if Chief Crowfoot himself was eloping. As I patiently waited by my father's side for Blacksky to arrive, to my left, my ears picked up on some Native gossip from Mourning Star. According to her, I had leapfrogged some other squaws who were interested in the chief's grandson, and she didn't see how Blacksky could accept a tomboy as his wife.

If this primitive bitch only knew that my shifting ability allowed me to hear every word she said, she would pipe down, and she would be even more frightened if I paid her a little visit when I did shift.

After several minutes, I thought she was done talking, but what I heard next made me smile. Let her tell it, every squaw inside Chief Crowfoot's wigwam walked funny and had huge smiles on their faces no matter how much work they were given. She said the word around the village is that Crowfoot has a horse cock, and the thought of him sticking it inside her sent shivers down her spine. I wonder what Two Bears would think of this? I thought. I was glad I didn't just ignore her. In fact, know I knew I had to watch this bitch around my husband. I didn't need to hear any more words from her. I could see the cock hungry look in her eyes, and I didn't blame her. All of the warriors I'd seen at the river cleaning their body had tiny dicks, and that included Two Bears.

When Blacksky and Eagle Eyes bent the corner, even the wolf dogs started howling. This was striking imagery you had to see to believe. Blacksky was wearing a robe made of three gray wolf skins and a headdress made of two ravens' quills. As he approached, he had a smooth swagger to his step that reminded me of a Big Daddy Kane record I heard on 'Digging in the Crates', and it seemed out of place for this era. Eagle Eyes had two horses by their halters, and Blacksky had the other two, plus the gifts agreed upon by both parties. With one flap of Blacksky's arms, the crowd quieted down. The light show of power made my pussy wet.

"One Horn, you have agreed with the chief and promised me the hand of your daughter, which I see you are here to keep your end of the bargain. As you can see, I am here to keep my end of this agreement also," Blacksky said.

Eagle Eyes led all four gëödanëhgwishö'ö (horses) by their halters and gave them to haka:wak (my father). I assumed that the other agreed upon gifts were inside the pack-saddle on one of the stallions. Haka:wak (my father) bowed his head and said a long prayer to the Great Spirit. He asked him to bless us with a strong union for the rest of our lives. And just like that, the ceremony was done and over with. I've always dreamed of a glorious wedding in the dreamworld, but this is all I would get. Hagówähgo:wa:h and yegówähgo:wa:h. That means king and queen in the Native language.

After Blacksky and Eagle Eyes helped me move my belongings into my new living quarters, I took some time to get myself situated. I decorated the places I might spend the most time in, and I wasn't concerned about who would hate it. When I was finished, I sashayed over to the center of the wigwam. Blacksky and Eagle Eyes were seated by the fire on gorgeous robes, handcrafted, garnished, and stylishly painted with hieroglyphics. As I took out a pot and placed it over the sunken curb of stone to boil, their conversation got real quiet. It made me feel out of place in my new wigwam. De'knö'e's (I don't like it). Regardless of how I felt, though, I was anxious to prove my worth to Blacksky as his new wife, so I figured, why not start by preparing a feast that showed him I live that life.

In no time at all, I flicked my wrist and had the entire wigwam smelling like a Native American bistro. Aknó'ëh (my mother) groomed me for important moments such as this, and unbeknownst to these two red men, my four-course meal would eventually loosen their tongues in my presence. Suddenly, Blacksky broke from his talk and looked me directly in the eyes. I stared right back in hopes of a mutual seduction.

He smiled. "Those dishes that you are preparing smell so good that I cannot concentrate on

Eagle Eyes' words."

I started smiling because those were the first words that he ever spoke to me.

"Blacksky," I said. "I have prepared a big dinner in your honor. I hope you like roasted buffalo ribs with pemmican, fresh turnips from the prairie, lightly flavored with berries, and well-cooked antelope in marrow fat?"

Blacksky nodded his head. "I guess what they say about you is true."

"And what is that?" I asked, taking his bait.

"They say you are the best young squaw in our tribe."

I grinned. "They said that about me?"

"Haga:de' (my grandfather) also said that no squaw can dress skins like you in our nation." His pronunciation of grandfather sounded funny to me, so I smiled.

"Thank you," I said. "I am honored to have that label."

Eagle Eyes looked over at me skeptically. "Squaws have always been good at two things." He paused and looked at Blacksky. "Work and play."

Ganyo:' I thought, which means pheasant. Most of the young Natives named after birds seemed to act like them too.

Blacksky frowned at him and said, "You have a strange way of complimenting someone, my friend."

"So, do you believe that they are good for other things besides work and play?" Eagle Eyes asked.

Eagle Eyes reminded me of an insecure girl who needed someone else to validate his point.

Blacksky paused before he spoke. "I am glad that someone in this wigwam can cook because I cannot. Can you cook, Eagle Eyes?"

Eagle Eyes hesitated before he responded. He said, "I see your point, my friend."

I looked at Blacksky thinking to myself, this is why my father liked him so much. His words were like gajíhsö'dö:je', a flying star.

Blacksky smiled at me and said, "You may finish cooking for us, Fire."

As I separated all the food into different serving dishes, Eagle Eyes pulled out a beautiful pipe and a tobacco-pouch made of beaver skin and filled with the Native tobacco, k'nick k'neck. Eagle Eyes picked up the pipe and passed it to Blacksky, who then drew his flint and steel, raising a small spark which he lit it with. He drew a few strong pulls and said, "I think there is no need to hunt so far away from the village tomorrow."

"Look around your wigwam," Eagle Eyes suggested.

Blacksky quickly looked around and said, "What is wrong with my wigwam, my friend?"

"The Chief has given you this wigwam, but you do not have any trophies killed by your own hands. Tomorrow we cannot come back with simple elks, antelopes, and mountain goats," Eagle Eyes paused. "We must kill something big." How! How!

"Something big like what?" Blacksky questioned.

There was a moment of silence before Eagle Eyes responded.

"We must kill an (o)nyagwai' (bear) or the dzó:nyödah (eagle). Our hands will be dipped in blood, and all the older warriors will show us more respect."

Blacksky gave Eagle Eyes a long look, then said,

'I do not like the idea of chasing a grizzly bear or the War-Eagle, my friend. This could be a very dangerous thing." How! How!

"What you say does have truth," Eagle Eyes admitted. "But we must be unafraid of the warrior's path while we are on Mother Earth, for the Great Spirit will walk with us." How! How!

I smiled at Eagle Eyes' words because it sounded like some shit D-Block would say. Little did he know, the Great Spirit could walk with you and talk with you, but if you are unprepared for the plains, you will perish.

"I agree with you," Blacksky said with noticeable reluctance. "Tomorrow, we will be brave, but not stupid and careless."

Damn! My new husband sounded very confident in himself. His words were calm and deliberate, and his voice induced goosebumps on my arm. He was already stimulating my mind, so I knew my juicy pussy would be next. I fall hard for men who are just as ambitious as me. I wanted everything out of life, and so should he.

After finishing the meal I prepared, and a brief discussion about the weapons they would take tomorrow, the two friends agreed to meet early in the morning. Once Eagle Eyes was gone, Blacksky walked to our bedroom, and I followed close behind him. When he removed his tunic, revealing his bare chest, it grabbed my attention. I peered at his hands and smiled. Then my eyes slowly trailed up his arms, over his biceps, shoulder, neck, and eyes. Those eyes have a familiarity to them, I thought.

"No, Blacksky," I said.

"No," he repeated. I walked toward him. runway style without even trying. I'm a bad bitch in any realm. Dollicia Bryan.

I reached him. I placed my hands where his were, at the collar of his tunic.

"Let me do this for you," I said. His abs are so sexy, I thought.

Interrupting my thoughts, he asked, "Are you okay, Fire?"

"No," I replied. "There are some things about your trip tomorrow that I do not like, Blacksky." He had one of the sexiest. Native names to come off my lips, so I put some emphasis on it.

"Oh," he responded, rubbing his chin. "What is it about my trip that bothers you?"

I exhaled first. "Listen to me! What I am about to say will be the truth. There are not any grizzly bears or the War-Eagle on Blackfoot lands."

One of his eyebrows cocked. "Perhaps you can tell me where to find them?" He chuckled. "I have heard you know things like this."

"The River Of Sticks," I blurted out.

He smiled mischievously. "Then, we will head in that direction."

My heartbeat quickened. "The River Of Sticks is on the Crees land, one of our most hated enemies. I do not wish for you to get harmed, Blacksky."

"Thank you for your worry, but have you been to this river that you speak of?"

"No," I responded sarcastically, and turned his question back on him. "Have you?"

He smiled at my agitation. "This will be my first time."

"Then please let me join you tomorrow," I sincerely begged.

A hint of a playful smile appeared on his face. "You have the right plan, Fire, just the wrong man."

This was the second fly remark he made to me, and I was in my feelings now. "It is your first hunt, Blacksky. Which means that I have more experience than you."

His sexy eyes took me in slowly, and I could see a trace of anger on his face. He tried to hide it, but o'gadë:gë' (I saw it for myself).

He took a step back and replied, "Show me?"

I raised my hands slowly, in a fake surrender, a little trickery just to get the upper hand.

"Is this what you want, Blacksky?" I asked seductively. A quick glance down at my chest made me notice how hard my nipples looked poking through my dress. His eyebrows lifted and blinked in distraction. He started grinning like it was a game and eased his way closer to me. My first attack caught him completely by surprise, limiting his chance of blocking my one-two punch combination. The blows landed as slaps, and he lost his balance and fell behind some blankets. I smiled at my small victory. When he slowly got up off his ass, he nodded in acknowledgment of being duped by yours truly.

"That was nice and unexpected Fire," he admitted.

"Please, do not be fooled by this pretty face. My past is decorated with the souls of people who have slept on my skills."

"I promise you that I'm wide awake now," he said calmly. "Let me see if you can accomplish that again while I'm paying attention."

"There are no rules, and there is no mercy out on those plains, Blacksky. Only death for the unprepared," I warned. How! How!

"Are you finished teaching me your lesson yet?" he asked.

There was an aggravated pitch to my husband's tone. It was as if I had lit a fire deep within him. Without warning, he removed his leggings and unsheathed the biggest dick I've ever seen. How could I concentrate with a huge red o:nyö'sgwä:e' (cucumber) calling me? My pussy instantly got wet, and I bit my bottom lip. Juices seeped from my wet sex and ran down my thighs. My demeanor, once cocky, had been adjusted, giving away my heightened state of excitement. He looked deep into my eyes, and the look he gave me neutralized my legs.

"You cheated," I declared loudly.

He smiled, knowing I was silly putty in his hands. Suddenly, he burst forward and wrapped his muscular arms around my waist. His eyes stared deep into my soul and said, "There is no mercy inside our wigwam. There are no rules, Fire!" He ripped my dress off so passionately that my duck quill ornaments fell to the red earth and scattered. I stood there, butt ass naked, still gawking at how the Great Spirit had blessed him below the waist. He backed me into a corner like the police did innocent African Americans and shot me a deadly look of

135

passion. When he leaned forward and kissed me slow and deeply, his lips were as soft as one thousand raven feathers. As if he had practiced this moment, he took his opposite hand and started a slow massage on my scalp. The feeling was nurturing, and my eyes rolled to the back of my head.

He picked me up off my feet with ease and finesse, then walked our bodies over to our bed. I could feel my pussy quiver with anticipation. After gently laying me on my back, he knelt between my thighs and whispered.

"You are so beautiful."

His compliment caused an instant orgasm to wash over my body. I dipped two of my fingers into my wetness, and when I pulled them out, he grabbed my hand and licked my tiny fingers clean. He closed his eyes like he was savoring my juices.

"Agega'has (I like to eat)," he said. "You taste like shés'a:h (wild strawberries)."

Having my new husband tell me in the Native language that my pussy tasted like wild strawberries made me even wetter. This is what made me different from most of the other squaws. I kept a clean honey pot, just in case a busy bee wanted to suck on it. I also ate plenty of fruits, so even my secretions tasted sweet. Horny as fuck now, I grabbed his massive horse cock, and the bulging head on it swelled up. Hot. I loved cock. The sight of it made me want to get more filthy. When I slid his dick up and down my dripping wet sex, it became coated in my juices. Volcanic. I was ready for that dick. He aimed his longpole at my opening and guided deep inside my hairy wet prairie bush.

"Sa:wëh! (it belongs to you)," I screamed in the Native language.

For the first time in my life, the impact of a dick caused my pussy to mumble things on its own. She was possessed. Mourning Star actually told the truth about something for once. I didn't mind walking funny because of a big dick. In fact, I would do it with a smile. When I attempted to wrap my wet walls around his foot-long cock, he was ready for it oddly and fucked me even harder. Dick, like this, could make a certified rug muncher go straight. With each one of his deep strokes, my pussy snapped and popped like she was in the Armed Forces. I felt bad for questioning my father's good choices, especially when I bit my bottom lip from an intense orgasm. Father knows best, I thought. Not to be outdone by this primitive boy, I started rocking back and forth and meeting him stroke for stroke. This was my old-fashioned throw that pussy back move that guaranteed a man busted a nut faster. Our cohesion, along with the mixture of pleasure and pain, drove me delirious. I dug my nails into the small of his back because I wanted him to feel what I felt. Suddenly, I decided to lock my snapper around his dick once more. It was my second time using the ball draining move. His facial expressions shifted to pleasure, and his eyes rolled back into his head. My pussy was so wet that lust juices ran down my leg. This time Blacksky lost control and shot his warm seed deep inside me.

To my shock, he kept going with the stamina of a virile savage His magical stroke busted my hairy pussy wide open as powerful orgasms washed over my body. I would kill over him, I thought. It was that good. He fucked me all night, and when he was done, my pussy was sore in a good way, one of those ways a woman can look for her whole life and not find. My Erotic Rating: Extremely pussy pleasing big dick. If any squaw fucked my husband, I promised to kill that bitch. How! How!

CHAPTER NINE:
BLACKSKY

Sometimes, you wake up, and your whole life has changed like a Ginuwine song. Divine. My soul was calm because my dreams suddenly became real. And since real inspires real, free Meek Mill and all the other talented felons that took a plea deal. When you get home, chill like Guy, birds chirped in unison in the sky, sun rays poured through the skylight, and warmed my body. I gazed at my new wife. Damn, she was a hottie. This woman reminded me of Cinderella, wearing that black and yellow. The wild spirit inside me turned mellow. She broke my virginity in a dream world. Now I had feelings for this girl. Diamonds and Pearls. R.I.P. to Prince. It's crazy how life doesn't make sense. I removed Fire's leg from my hip as gently as possible, and quietly slid from underneath her tight embrace, then I kissed her softly on the forehead and got up to get dressed. Her legs were cracked open like eggs. Pussy is the best, skin to skin with no vest, wet, but warm like a nest. Tell me why I felt blessed? Was that because I'm a mess? I was thirsty for more it to test.

Moments later, I stepped out of my wigwam, wearing a buckskin shirt with matching leggings and moccasins. The sunrise was just rising above the hills and bluffs, creating a classic view for my eyes. As I went to go check the traps Eagle Eyes set for small game, I spotted a herd of antelope frolicking in the distance. It boosted my morale, and in that moment, all my stress seemed to magically leave my body. Mother nature had her own way of bringing bliss to people who wanted it. Out the blue, a voice whispered inside my ear.

It said, "Thy shall come my way, Blacksky...Commit yourself to me, and I shall bring all you want to pass." I shook my head and exhaled deeply. The dream world gave out eureka moments without me even condoning it. That's supernatural components. After discovering the traps didn't have anything for me to kill inside them, I headed to the river to bathe.

My brain reminded me that it was customary for our tribe to get clean at the river in the summertime. While I strolled through the woods, my mind, like any man, became flooded with sexual thoughts. I wondered why I felt so connected to Fire already. Why the hell did her eyes look so familiar to me? After one night of lusty sex, our bond seemed to instantly strengthen itself. I mentally pictured her throwing it back like a Sunday on WBLK in Buffalo. It seemed odd that a primitive squaw would know when to contract her pussy around my longpole.

I arrived at the place where most of our Natives learned to swim. In the distance, I could see several Blackfoot sentinels protecting the sacred ground where women and little girls bathe. They were heavily armed. When I removed my tunic, the morning sun glistened off my body. I was cut up like cocaine during a drought because when it came to physical fitness, I wasn't a slouch. I jumped into the river and swam back and forth, cutting through the current like a sharp knife. Suddenly, I slowed down and took thirty quick breaths. Getting air inside my lungs made the exercise easier for me.

"Look, One Wolf. It is the future chief of Blackfoot Nation," a voice chided me. My brain quickly told me that this voice belonged to Two Bears: He was the leader of a group of village troublemakers, a muscular red-skinned man in his early twenties. Dreamworld or not, I hated bullies. The expressions on Two Bears and One Wolf's faces made it clear that they had disdain in their hearts for me, and it was obvious that they were here to push my buttons. Honestly, I didn't know how Blacksky would react to this situation if I wasn't commandeering his body. As a millennial with an old soul, I was quick to unleash my spirit within. In my generation, we groomed ourselves to win. Fuck, if there was two OP's, let the games begin.

"When I do become chief," I said. "You will get the same treatment as the village dogs."

"Is that so, Blacksky?" Two Bears replied. "This is real big talk coming from a young warrior without any medicine yet."

"Do not worry, my friends. After today, I will have my medicine," I promised. How! How!

"Yes! Eagle Eyes has told everyone in the village that will listen to him that today is the day that you will hunt for your protector throughout your short life. Your medicine-bag will be filled with swans' down and sweet-scented grass," Two Bears said.

"And do not forget the quill of ducks," One Wolf added. They both laughed.

Their sarcastic remarks were loaded with Native innuendos that were meant to violate my manhood. Especially since the Natives that rocked swan down and duck quills were squaws. I smiled. I had a way with words too that couldn't be taught. Watch my generation. Philippe Patek. Long dick his squaw from the back and tell her look back at it.

"My friends! I hear your two squaws love sweet-scented grass and duck quills. Should I bring them some after my hunt is over?"

Two Bears frowned. "You need a good beating, Blacksky, and it is me that will give it to you."

Suddenly, he started walking towards the water in a manner that was supposed to frighten me. I remained calm, but don't get it twisted, I was ready to go like the last day of a prison bid. One Wolf grabbed Two Bears by his arm and pointed towards the sentinels.

"Now is not the time," he warned his friend.

"You are right, One Wolf," Two Bears agreed. "We will deal with this fool when so many eyes are not watching."

They both turned around without another word and walked back towards the village like I knew they would: Most people who do a lot of talking won't throw rice at a wedding. Just know that. I stood at the water's edge, watching their two red-skinned bodies dwindle in the distance. When they were both out of my sight, I was only left with my thoughts for about ten seconds. That's when my eyes spotted Mourning Star and Sunrise headed in my direction. From where I stood, I could see that they were both dressed in short shirts made of sheepskin. Their hair was parted at the top and styled with vermillion, petite sexy frames, swagger

143

on a million. The morning sun hit their bodies just right, and it gave their skin that up-north glow.

Since Mourning Star was Two Bears' main squaw, I quickly looked around to see if he was actually smart enough to use a stratagem on me. After combing the entire area with my eyes, I concluded this wasn't the case. I still didn't feel safe. When I placed my sights back on the two squaws in front of me, I noticed their pace wasn't hurried anymore: When two women pull up like Huggies without a credible threat around, I'm like most men. I started thinking with the head that's closest to the ground. Mourning Star looked straight out into the waist-deep water I stood in and spoke.

"It is such a nice sedéhjiah (morning) to take a swim," she said.

"The water is perfect, and the current has slowed down. Ga:jih, sadé'sgoh," I said, telling her to come and join me in the water.

She looked around and smiled. "You know the sentinels are watching us, Blacksky, and we did not walk here to go swimming."

I was a little surprised by her statement.

"What is it that you have come for then?"

She smiled. "We have come to wish you luck on your hunt to form your medicine, and we want a favor from you."

"Of course, that depends on the favor you seek," I said, making my way out of the river slowly and methodically. I could feel my big dick swinging back and forth like an expensive timepiece used by a hypnotist. They couldn't resist the gift, and both women gasped and looked like they didn't believe their eyes. I smirked. No woman could look away from the American cucumber that just put my wife in a slumber. That's saucy BBC talk, skills on display, a custom dick down on a nice day. Mourning Star slowly looked up.

"Did you drop something?"

She bent over to pick up my tunic and leggings. Right away, I noticed that she wasn't wearing anything underneath her skirt. Her clit and labia swelled up right in front of my face. The splendid sight caused a large vein to pop-up on one side of my shaft. I laughed and quickly decided to put my leggings back on; I had already shown them I was ten men strong.

"What is this favor you speak of?" I asked, breaking the silence between us.

Mourning Star slightly raised an eyebrow. "Blacksky, we would be in your debt if you could bring us some swans' down and duck quills to dress our skins with."

Like Fire, Mourning Star and Sunrise dressed skins in our village, but theirs didn't sell like my wife's. I wasn't taken aback by that. Two monkeys can't sell bananas. I smiled at the irony of this whole situation. Amazing. These things do happen.

"I hope that the nice smile on your face means that you will honor our request?" Sunrise asked.

"You will be rewarded nicely for this favor," Mourning Star, added. She licked her lips sexually.

I quickly contemplated some primitive thot action in my mind.

"Yes! We will meet tonight after my hunt is over at the wigwam of my friend Eagle Eyes," I confirmed.

"We will be waiting on you, Blacksky," Mourning Star promised.

As the two squaws walked away, I yelled, "Jigwas ësgö:gë' ae'!." Which means I'll see you again soon. This was a calculating yell because later on I promised myself to "Put it in Her Mouth" like Akinyele. I looked down at my dick and smiled. The world we know lacks radiance, warmth, and companionship. That's why I'm happy one of Mother Earth's ugliest bitches would be on my arm when they pulled up: karma! Mourning Star would get introduced to my premeditated flower cycle: lovely duck quills, sweet-scented grass, then, I'll "Just Beat It" like Michael. My longpipe and long tongue will make them go psycho, follow me loyal disciples, and you'll be able to visualize this nasty Native American plot: pretty Blackfoot squaws in flocks, all primed to grab black superhero dick. Hancock.

Chocolate's teachings are on deck. You don't

like it? Say less, I'm doing this for the culture and to get her respect. I've provoked deep thought and the universal attraction for women who love ambition, big dick, money, and power. You've been granted permission to read this naked at a late hour. I let out my signature War-Whoop. My hocus pocus pussy worship and conjurations lead to orgasmic rain showers. Please, ladies! Refrain from putting up that mental tent. Deep inside your mind, it is I that pays the rent. Mind fuck. This is such a cinch that my deep-pocketed supporters will make a contribution while you sit the bench. Do remember, there is no nation like a donation. I have prepared a talented speech for my congregation that will cause some speculation.

"My sexy lady friends, glorious Negros of this free world. This is that head honcho flow for the cheese and hearts that are nachos. I arose to the sounds of the gourd rattles and rawhide drums with delicious dialect from the deity of a deep dimension for you to decipher. For this sharp-witted chicanery shit, you may need a diaper. I pledge to always put you first, kneel down in your times of trouble, and offer my back to hold up the Earth. Rocking army fatigues and Timberlands. I've arrived inside your hearts without having a pow-wow first." I had better stop, I thought.

"Don't stop, Blacksky," my conscious said. "Talk that shit, and you'll make us rich. Your full body of work will stand the test of time. This hip-hop inspired masterpiece is one of a kind."

Welcome to the lyrically acclaimed journey about getting wiser from a hybrid three one fiver. Do not forget the name Blacksky, for I'm one extraordinary young man and a living testament of the Great Spirit's hands.

CHAPTER TEN:
STRONG MEDICINE

When I returned to my wigwam, strangely, Fire was nowhere in sight to wish me luck in the next step in forming my medicine. I figured she went to her parents' wigwam to help her mother, or she was now at the river bathing. I looked around and noticed a satchel made of deerskin. When I picked it up and opened it, I smiled: It was packed with fresh buffalo meat, two rabbits, one tin cup, a frying pan, one plate, a tin kettle, and some knives. Haga:de' (my grandfather) ain't never lied when he said Fire could be of great use to this guy. So far, she was perfect. Last night, we exchanged pleasure and lust. By doing this small gesture, she was earning my trust.

A few minutes later, I started doing my weapons check on my inventory. Not being prepared for whatever, that would never be a part of my story. I decided to go with my bow that was made out of bone sinew. It was deadly enough to kill a whole crew. There were a hundred arrows in my quiver: fifty bone and fifty steel. While I sharpened my lance, I heard horse hooves pull up, and I knew it was my good friend.

"Are you sure you have enough weapons for our trip?" Eagle Eyes asked sarcastically, from the entrance of my wigwam.

"As far as I am concerned, my friend, we could never have too many. There is no telling what we will run into."

Eagle Eyes smiled. "It sounds like you are ready to be a warrior."

"Your heart is strong, and my heart is strong. We are already good warriors." I noticed he was without a valuable weapon.

"Where are your lance and shield?" I asked.

"I have been told that too many weapons will make my gëödanëhgwih (horse) go slower," he said.

"How! How! The same person that told you that should have told you it is better to have it with you than get caught without it," I explained.

"Not to worry, my friend. I will be fine," he responded.

Ten minutes later, we took off from the village at a rapid rate, under the sounds of the lute and cheers of our family, who stood out in front of their wigwams as we gradually lost sight of them. We went over picturesque grass-covered bluffs and knolls. Even though it was highly unlikely, I never wanted to wake up from this scenery that my mind made so real. For hours we rode through wild fronts and rugged cliffs. The mountain sheep walked around in great numbers in this area and skipped from ledge to ledge while clinging to the sides of the wall. It was as if they were a circus act and didn't even know it. I wondered if they could do it with a few arrows coming at them.

"Pay close attention," Eagle Eyes said. "The War-Eagle is known to be in this area, my friend."

The spotted War-Eagle in our nation had high value. Mostly for the beautiful bird's tail feathers that are used to decorate the heads and dresses of warriors. If this kid born in June could secure several plumes, it would immediately change my position in my tribe's eyes. I snapped my head around and only saw a few regular birds flying overhead.

"Tell me why we cannot just bring back some elks, antelopes, and buffaloes?" I asked, gracefully maneuvering my horse down another sloping hill.

"Do you see your ahšö´nyashä (clothes)?" Eagle Eyes asked with a trace of humor.

I quickly glanced down at myself. "What is wrong with my ajà'dawi'sha' (dress), my friend?" If you asked me, as far as primitive linen goes, I was fly.

Eagle Eyes stared at me like I was clueless, then he spoke.

"We have no medicine or trophies on our tunics."

Trophies in the Blackfoot Nation was just another name for scalps, which are snatched off the head of the enemy during battle as proof of their demise. It's also evidence of a Blackfoot's claim as a warrior.

"I hope you know that we are hunting grizzly bears and the War-Eagle, not other redmen," I reminded him.

The look on Eagle Eyes' face gave away his thirst for a glory road path. That path leads you directly to the battlefield. And that battlefield is the reason why there is a six squaws to every red-man ratio in our nation. That's a lot of Native Americans living and dying at the edge of civilization.

"Sometimes I cannot believe you, my friend," Eagle Eyes said as he rode alongside me, shaking his head. "Yahso:t (your grandfather) is the head principal chief of our nation." He looked at me and pointed to his heart. "Where is your fire, Blacksky?"

I had to laugh. "My Fire is somewhere dressing skins."

"I am sure it is," Eagle Eyes said with some sarcasm. "I have seen so many warriors get soft when they spend too much time inside their wigwams with squaws."

I contorted my lips and shook my head. "Are you trying to say that I am getting soft, my friend?"

"No! But you do not need to spend all of your time with the squaws," he suggested. "They will play games with your mind, my friend."

Never that, I thought. I mentally pictured them playing games with my red cock. That was my plot.

"Speaking of squaws," I said, switching topics. "After our hunt, Mourning

Star will be meeting me at your wigwam."

Eagle Eyes eyed me suspiciously and said, "Why would Two Bears main squaw be meeting you at my wigwam?"

"It appears that she and Sunrise seek the big duck quill for their skins," I said in a sexual manner. "I plan on giving it to them tonight." We both laughed.

"That is funny, but this can easily turn into a serious matter, Blacksky," Eagle eyes warned.

"Good. I want him to take it personal. Two Bears thinks he can teach me a lesson, but tonight class will be in session for him. "

"Be careful, Blacksky. I have seen Two Bears snatch many scalps from off the heads of seasoned warriors. He and One Wolf have formed strong medicine."

Growing up on the East side of Syracuse popped out of me, and I mimicked. "He and One Wolf have strong medicine!" I stared at Eagle Eyes skeptically. "You speak as if you are scared of Two Bears and One Wolf. How can you question the fire inside my heart when you don't want any smoke?"

As our horses entered the edge of a deep green forest, our conversation was interrupted by screams that belonged in a low budget horror flick. I dismounted off my horse quietly and motioned for Eagle Eyes to do the same. Somewhere to our right, there was a clear-cut sound of a Whiteman's voice. For the moment, the brush where we stood concealed our location, but we couldn't see anything. I silently signaled Eagle Eyes to follow my lead while I changed positions. While we were inching closer in the cover of some bushes, the white man cried out in pain again. We still couldn't see the body these screams were attached to, so we both moved forward cautiously.

When we stopped and peered out from our new hiding spot, I was shocked at what I saw. Unbeknownst to Eagle Eyes, it seemed the universe was attempting to quench his thirst for the glory road. I thought, Mother Earth sure has a way of granting requests at an inopportune time. From my quick assessment, there were six men in total right in front of us. Five Knisteneaux warriors, one of Blackfoot Nation's most hated enemies. Their unmistakable red and black war paint made it easy for me to identify them.

They had captured themselves a white trapper, and they had him tied up to a tree. He was dressed as if he were a member of a special cavalry with a stylish hat made of raccoon fur. I thought, why would this paleface be stupid enough to travel this deep unto red-man lands? Seconds later, the silence was broken again, this time by conversation.

"Your people have been told not to trap anymore nöganyá'göh (beaver) on red-man lands, and yet, here you are," the Crees warrior said.

His voice sounded authoritative, and I concluded that he had to be one in charge of the rest of the Crees.

"My friends, you have mistaken me. I was not trapping beavers on your land. I am but a poor beggar just passing through these woods on my way back to the fort, the trapper said in a sincere tone that was believable.

I thought to myself, how did this trapper know the Native lingo? And were the Crees smart enough to pick up on that like I just did?

"Blue Fox! Check his things to see if the paleface tongue tells us lies," the Crees warrior commanded.

As Blue Fox approached the trapper's horse and took off two satchels from the white man's saddle, I noticed something.

There were two more Cree sentries in the trees that I didn't initially spot. I silently alerted Eagle Eyes to their presence with my hands. Seconds later, Blue Fox dumped the contents of the two satchels all over the grass. Like everybody else in attendance, I quickly scanned the ground. A coffee pot, ammunition, a frying pan, some fresh antelope meat, and, most importantly, no beaver skins.

"There are no nöganyá'göh (beaver) skins here, Red Hawk," Blue Fox said, confirming what everybody else had seen already.

Red Hawk gave the trapper a half-smile that died faster than an unarmed black man pulled over by twelve in .a white neighborhood. Then shit got real quiet.

"It does not make any sense," Red Hawk said. "But I am not easily fooled by paleface trickery." Nobody spoke. Then Red Hawk backed out a huge two-edged knife with its scabbard made of the skin off a grizzly bear's head.

Out the corner of my eye, I saw that Eagle Eyes' facial expression was one of a worried man. Rightfully so. I glanced left and right. The sentries hadn't moved one bit. When I turned my head forward, Red Hawk was making a tiny circle incision on the trapper's stomach.

"My friends! You're making a big mistake, and my people will come looking for me," the trapper cried.

The white man started gasping for air out of fear and let out a melodramatic scream that echoed throughout the forest. It sounded as if someone had backed out a gun on Keith Sweat. Red Hawk ignored his plea for mercy and pulled some rope off his horse. The trapper refused to die with dignity.

"Please! Don't kill me, Red Hawk! I have something for you if you let me go," he begged.

"You are in no position to trade, but that is just like a paleface to try and bargain his way out of his grave. Tell me, my friend, what could you possibly have for me?" Red Hawk asked with a cynical chuckle." Your soul is in my hands."

Red Hawk walked over to the trapper and tied the rope to his intestines. It was at that moment that I noticed Red Hawk had the other end of the rope tied to his horse. With every breath the trapper took, blood oozed slowly from his stomach wound and covered his pants with a dark-colored red stain.

"Treasure," the trapper whispered weakly. "I have a map."

There was an excited murmur from the Crees that stood around Red Hawk. Their leader waved them to silence.

"What treasure do you speak of, white man?"

"I have a map in my pocket," he mumbled. "If you help me find it, we can split it."

Red Hawk laughed from deep within. "If it is a split that you want, my friend, it is a split that you will get."

Right after those words, he let out a loud whistle, and his horse leaped forward, yanking the trapper's guts out of his stomach. Blood and intestines sprayed everywhere. Eagle Eyes gasped loudly and gave away our position, then froze in terror. Instinctively, I drew an arrow from my quiver as quick as lightning. The first twenty arrows that left my bow sounded like miniature missiles in the open air and easily found their targets. Two Cree warriors fell from the trees they stood in with a thud. Five more to go, I counted. I glanced across from me at Eagle Eyes and saw him looking back at me. He was slow to react, and it was clear that he wasn't ready for combat. I pointed and directed his attention to the two Cree sentries that were headed in our direction.

Their movement was followed by the twangs of their bows and the whizzing sound of arrows in the air. They attempted to hide their bodies behind the trees, but I could clearly see arms and legs sticking out in plain view. When one of them exposed himself by peeking out from his hiding spot, my bow was already stretched taut and locked in on his body with an arrow. The string on the bow had a sweet country twang as I unleashed the arrow. Direct hit! Four more to go. Several more arrows were sent in my direction, and this time, two of them grazed my leg and right shoulder. If I didn't bring my shield, I would've paid for my stupidity with my life.

I gasped in pain as blood spotted through my tunic, and I quickly switched my attention back to the battlefield. Somewhere to my right, a warrior cried out in pain, and I changed directions and headed there. Suddenly, I heard another cry sounding like Eagle Eyes. I silently cursed myself for leaving his side and took out another arrow from my quiver.

When I got to Eagle Eyes, he was

laying at the edge of a wild and ragged cliff. A Cree warrior lay slew next to him with two arrows embedded deep inside his chest cavity. The hair on the crown of his head had also been removed, and a thin trail of blood ran down his face. I checked his pulse, and he was no longer breathing. Three more Crees left.

Eagle Eyes was bleeding from a lance wound to his stomach. Blood oozed out with every intake of breath he took and covered his tunic and leggings with its dark red stain. In his hand, he had the scalp of the Cree warrior gripped tightly. I knelt down and gently lifted up his head.

Eagle eyes slowly opened his eyes. "I am sorry I gave away our position, Blacksky."

"Do not worry about that now. It is not your fault," I whispered into his ear. "We walked right into this."

Eagle Eyes coughed up some blood and then spoke. "One of the Crees is coming with me, and his scalp is mine," he bragged, holding up the bloody lock for me to see. Fresh DNA ran down his wrist.

"I am proud of you, my friend. You fought bravely."

He smiled. "It seems like I will not be

returning to the village with you this time. Instead, I am headed to 'The Village of the Dead'."

"That is not true, Eagle Eyes. Your spirit is headed to the Fields of Elysian, where all the great warriors will greet you."

Eagle Eyes gasped and let out a small breath. "Take this from me," he said, handing me the bloody scalp lock. "Place this on your tunic to honor our friendship." He paused. "It is time for you to leave, Blacksky. I do not wish for you to join me just yet."

As I watched, my friend took his last breath, a tremendous amount of sorrow begin to numb my body. This hunting trip cost me a good friend. Inside, I became enraged, and as soon as I reached a standing position, a Crees warrior headed full speed in my direction with his lance in his hand. My right shoulder had a slight pain in it, so I .swiftly switched hands like Bo Kimble, a tribute to my fallen comrade. I aimed carefully. The shot upon its release was an emotional one for me, and the impact of my arrow knocked the Cree off his feet, causing a crimson mist to hang in the air like early morning fog. I unsheathed my scalping knife and walked right up on the fallen warrior.

This whole ordeal had quickly turned real personal for me. How! How!

All of a sudden, a solid force smashed into my body from behind. The collision sent me sprawling over the cliff head first. I craned my neck, desperately looking for something to break my fall, but there was nothing. Just the horrible sound of the wind blowing harder and harder as I descended into what seemed like a bottomless pit. I fought for air, and I was falling so fast that it made me forget about all my minor injuries. I closed my eyes, and my brain, spirit, and soul started to form thoughts that were new to my body.

Everything went completely silent, and I could feel some sort of foreign energy coursing through me. It felt pleasantly weird. It was as if my cells were going through a change in physical form from the inside out. As I looked left and right, my arms metamorphosed into beautiful brown feathers, and my feet suddenly changed into big powerful talons. With one flap of my wings, I broke my fall and hovered overhead. Out of desperation to live, I had somehow magically shifted into huge bird.

CHAPTER ELEVEN:
THE TREASURE

If the Great Spirit had wanted red men to fly, he would've given them wings. Well, he gave me wings, and I involuntarily let out a small hoot. Ptilopsis leucotis. I turned into a sneak diss; the irony of going from a bird-watcher to an actual bird tickled my feathers. In urban neighborhoods in America a bird is slang for a brick of coke, or an unmotivated man and woman; any woman over thirty with several kids, never had their own man, no car, no job, an expert on their friends' relationships, and no plan for the future. That's a bird bitch. Any man in his late twenties still walking, smoking weed all day, he idolizes reality TV stars instead of making his own mark, pillow talker, and hater. That's a bird ass nigga.

With one flap, I pushed off with the skill of a

renowned aerialist. As the hot sun warmed my special primary feathers, I took some deep breaths and turned my gaze upon the beauty of the view. I was definitely elated to be alive because if I checked out, I wouldn't have been able to see these mighty forests of stately cottonwood trees, the thousand hills, bluffs, and dales. I'm talking tall green. Kevin McHale. My hearing, eye-sight, and sense of smell had suddenly increased ten-fold. New information flooded my brain with things I couldn't possibly know, like the two squirrels hidden in the brush ten feet ahead. The congregation of prairie dogs barking in the distance.

Cracking branches and the sound of conversation made me grit my teeth in anger. It was the pressure wave of danger. I glided high into the sky and landed on a set of branches right over the top of Red Hawk and Blue Fox's head. A flight path. Stealth was of maximum importance because I wanted them dead. The smell of fatality already hung thick in the air like a backflip by Jessica Dime. I shook my beak. At times such as these, how could ass be on my mind? What is a man to do?

Patience will forever be a virtue, so I relaxed myself to concentrate on the two warrior's conversation. They walked around our two stallions we left behind, checking the packsaddles and satchels. As they stuck their hands in the bags, Red Hawk started speaking.

"This satchel is made of a fine deerskin. My young squaw will like this." He paused. "Blue Fox! Who do you think these two warriors were?"

Blue Fox rubbed his chin. "From the direction they were retreating to, it is my guess that they are Blackfoot-our most hated enemy."

"What do you think they were doing so far from their village at this age?" He walked over to Eagle Eyes' dead body and grabbed him by his hair. As he unsheathed his scalping knife and violated my friend, I closed my talons tightly. When I got my claws on Red Hawk, he was going to die a painful death.

"I do not know for sure yet," Blue Fox admitted. "I believe that they were hunting. They have fresh buffalo meat packed with two rabbits and many hunting weapons."

"They have fresh buffalo meat," Red Hawk repeated with a slight smile. "That does not make any sense, my friend. These two Blackfoot must have passed many animals before they reached this point."

Blue Fox paused and said, "You are right, my friend. Which means the only other thing that makes any sense is the forming of their medicine."

I thought about Simon Brown's slogan at Benz Kitchen because Blue Fox made the call like Nick Buonicotni. How! How!

"Let us see if he can form his medicine from

the bottom of a pit," Red Hawk said jokingly. "His family will not even find his body to bury it in 'The Village of the Dead'."

I'm just going to be a man about it like Toni Braxton requested. Their conversation was hard for me to listen to. Inside, I was infuriated. They killed Eagle Eyes and bragged about killing me, but I wasn't dead. Soon they will be, I thought.

There was a brief moment of silence before Blue Fox spoke.

"Look at the two stallions the warriors left behind. The one that I pushed over the cliff has fine weaponry for just a lowly brave."

Red Hawk looked at our horses and weapons. "If they were not braves, who do you think these young warriors were?"

Blue Fox paused before he spoke like he was thinking really hard about something. "The young warrior that I pushed over the cliff easily killed many trained Crees before I ambushed him. The skillset he possessed makes me believe that he is a relative of Chief Crowfoot." He paused. "If this is true, Red Hawk, trouble could be headed our way."

Red Hawk sucked his teeth and shook his head disgustedly.

"What are you saying, Blue Fox?" I could hear the aggravation in Red Hawk's tone. "I have never known you to be scared of any man."

"Like most of the Crees, I am sure that the

stories the elders tell of Chief Crowfoot have also reached your ears. The Great war chief is not to be taken lightly. His medicine is so strong that he has made many Crees disappear?"

"What do you mean, 'disappear'?"

"Many of the elder Crees in our nation that have gone against Crowfoot have gone on hunting trips and never returned to their wigwams to eat what they killed. They say Crowfoot was possessed by the Evil Spirit himself after the elders in our village killed his only son. When he is hunting you, he is said to be like a ghost."

"Sounds like a red-man's fairy tale," Red Hawk said. "When it comes to the elders, my friend, believe none of what you hear and only half of what you actually see. Besides, the only thing that worries me is how long it will take us to find the white man's treasure." Red Hawk pulled out a tiny map and continued. "I do not know how to figure out this silly map the paleface has drawn.

Red Hawk pointed to a spot on the paper. "Call me crazy, my friend, but I think we have been to this place before."

Blue Fox looked at the map and said, "This is the old Beaver Hunting grounds."

"Exactly, my friend," Red Hawk confirmed. "If we leave now, we will be rich by nightfall." How! How!

"Let us pray to the Great Spirit you are right."

As I sat perched on a branch watching the two Crees pack up our weapons and food, I knew if I waited and watched long enough, they would make a mistake. Red Hawk's nervousness was easy for me to spot. Treachery and betrayal oozed from his pores, creating a strong odor for me to smell.

When they mounted our stallions, the two horses shied as if they could sense foreign riders were aboard. A shout came from Red Hawk, and he took off into the woods with Blue Fox not too far behind him. Moments later, I darted out after them through swirling clouds of various insects rising from the brush and wildflowers. Rodents of all shapes and sizes began scattering in different directions to escape my wrath, but they need not worry. They were of no concern to me.

Red Hawk rode with my stolen bow across his back and an air of invincibility that suggested he wasn't worried about anything. If he knew I was stalking him with the determination of a serial killer, his disposition would instantly change. Scalping knives dangled from their waists, and they each carried big round shields of hide and razor-sharp lances, weapons that they would never get to use on me, not if I could help it. There was a new level of enthusiasm in playing in the game of death that sent chills under my brown feathers. For the first time in my young life, I felt like I was moving with a sense of purpose. Some people joined the armed forces, gangs, and an assortment of other groups just to feel what the Great Spirit was blessing me with naturally. I felt fortunate.

The trail to the treasure took us all through herds of buffalo on countless clay and grass-covered hills. We passed through prairie dog villages, and my incoming arrival overhead was met with loud chatter as they attempted to give up my location. Little snitches, I thought. I cut through the air sideways and doubled back over burrows just to give them something to really talk about. When I let out a few shrieking hoots, they scrambled back to their little piles of excavation and hid.

With four powerful flaps of my wings, I easily caught up to my target. Flying with the late afternoon summer wind blowing onto my feathers calmed my soul and made me notice that it would soon be dark out. I wondered if the two Crees had gotten lost as we traveled away the rest of daylight. Immediately, my eyes clicked into a night vision that was so mesmerizing that I was taken aback. There were so many stars glowing in high definition, and I'd never seen stars like this before. I was up close and personal.

It made me feel like I was closer to the Great Spirit than I have ever been. It gave me the kinda high that would make Willie Nelson and Snoop smile. The moon was full of bright gray and white, lighting up the forest like a personal nightlight.

Something else was happening to me right underneath the moon and stars. It was as if the moon strengthened my body.

When the galloping of their horses stopped, my thoughts and attention instantly focused on the task at hand. As Red Hawk and Blue Fox dismounted from our horses, oblivious to them, I landed on a branch not too far away from them. Blue Fox retrieved a small shovel from one of the packsaddles and looked around like he was unsure where to start digging. Red Hawk had the same exact look, a puzzled frown, but his eyes were on Blue Fox too.

"Perhaps we should take another look at the map," Red Hawk suggested. "It could not do us any harm,"

Blue Fox strode over to where he was standing.

"Yes! Let us give the map a look." The muggy night air caused him to wipe the sweat from his forehead. "I believe that is the tree that is on the map right there," he said, pointing to a huge cottonwood tree.

Not too far from the tree, a river flowed freely. Its waters were filled with floating rafts and driftwood. Then it dawned on me that maybe this was a tiny shore. I figured there had to be a lot more of these shores all over the river. My mind started moving and going over the stored information in my brain. It definitely didn't seem normal that a trapper couldn't find this location on his map, and the two Crees could. That's weird to me, I thought. Then out of the blue, it came to me. The trapper couldn't read the treasure map because a red-man drew it, which meant the trapper had to be headed to some village to get help translating it. Poor fellow got picked off at a crucial moment like Russell Wilson, I thought. I still couldn't believe he didn't audible and give the ball to Marshawn Lynch. I shook my head.

Blue Fox had been digging for about fifteen minutes without so much as a word. He was focused. Eager to be doing something himself, Red Hawk walked over to my deerskin satchel he booked from me and commenced to bringing out my damn fresh buffalo meat, two rabbits, and the pot. When he withdrew his flint and steel and raised a spark with which he got a fire started, it became clear that he intended to make a delicacy for the whole forest to smell.

A few minutes after Red Hawk put all the meat in the pot with some sage and yellow butter, the sound of metal on metal vibrated in my eardrums.

"I have hit something with my shovel," Blue Fox confirmed.

I quietly switched tree branches to get a better look inside the hole he dug. Red Hawk ignored the food he was cooking and assisted Blue Fox in attempting to push away the rest of the mud from around the box. They both pulled the handle together until it moved some. Then they wiggled it free and pulled it out. It was a small black treasure trove with a skull and crossbones symbol on the front.

"Open it," Red Hawk urged passionately.

Blue Fox flipped back the lid and revealed that the box was filled with a fortune in gold coins, jewelry, diamonds, rubies, trinkets, and a solid gold crown seemly fit for a king. The prospect of unlimited wealth and glory contaminated the air and immediately changed the feelings and emotions by the river.

Red Hawk's face split into a huge grin. "The treasure is real, my friend." There was a brief pause before he bent down and picked up the crown and said, "When I enter our village with this crown upon my head, the elders will give me the title of the strongest medicine man in our nation. They will have no choice but to make me a chief. Do not worry, my friend. You will stand next to me."

My eyes probed some new shadows moving around the surrounding forest while simultaneously waiting for my opportunity to intervene. The eyes do hustle! I turned my head all the way around in a counter-clockwise motion and saw five white wolves no less than fifteen feet away. It seems Red Hawk's delicacy was attracting some unanticipated.

Blue Fox let his arms fall, and his eyes rose to

stare intently at Red Hawk at an angle in the darkness, a crooked grin twisted up his mouth. He laughed loudly as if whatever he saw was amusingly counterfeit. "Without me," he said dryly. "You would have never found this treasure on your own. It is me who deserves the crown that you wear. You have lived a soft life of giving out orders and not engaging in combat like a real warrior should."

I let out two hoots into the open air, my way of instigating Blue Fox's words even more. Red Hawk stared at Blue Fox in shock, unaware of the Rap God Christopher Wallace's mantra from my generation. 'Mo money, mo problems'. How! How!

"Why does Blue Fox think I am not a real warrior?"

Blue Fox sneered and pointed at Red Hawk. "I have never seen you meet another Blackfoot in one on one combat, but I have seen you murder an honorable when his back is turned like a coward."

There was a long silence until Red Hawk replied. "Let Blue Fox prove that I am the coward you say I am."

Both men backed up then squared up, knowing full well of the consequences of their words to each other. I thought, it's lit!

The two Crees circled one another like prizefighters. Blue Fox swung first, throwing three quick punches in rapid succession. The first two punches merely grazed Red Hawk, but the third one landed solidly and knocked off the crown.

Blue Fox laughed out loud and said, "Yes! This will be easy."

He was confident in himself. Noticeably aggravated, Red Hawk started forward, swinging wildly, hoping to land something meaningful to change the course of the fight. Instead, he was rewarded with a right cross that caused a small trickle of blood to run down his face. Unable to contain his success in the fight, Blue Fox rushed forward with his own attack. He never saw that Red Hawk had backed his scalping knife out until the last moment, just before it sliced through his jugular vein. The impact of sharp steel on flesh made a distinctive sound, and Blue Fox fell down to the red earth. Red Hawk walked slowly and stood over his friend.

"Now I have murdered you." A huge smile was plastered on his face. "There are no rules in a fight."

It wasn't until Red Hawk turned around that he became alarmed. The whole ordeal was unfolding so fast that he barely had time to raise his arm to defend himself from the grizzly bear's attack. Unfortunately for him, he lost his balance and never seen (O)nyagwai's right claw headed in his direction. The collision knocked Red Hawk down and sent blood with tiny bits of flesh floating through the air. He laid on the ground, trying to catch his breath and made a moaning sound. He barely had time to regain his balance before he was attacked a second time. Red Hawk was stunned by the power of the blow, his legs gave out, and he collapsed to one knee. He touched the side of his face gingerly, shook off what he might actually feel there. He spat a wad of blood in the dirt and stood back up, finally coming to the realization that this fight was to the death.

Red Hawk backed up a few feet and bent over to pick up his lance. Once they squared up, (O)nyagwai' stood up on both of his hind legs and let out an ear pounding growl that rattled the entire area. His growl was a warning, a warning that we were on his turf, a warning that he could kill without a conscience. I thought, too bad Red Hawk didn't know (O)nyagwai' just wanted the food to eat. Red Hawk pushed forward, gripping his lance tightly and stabbed at his target from every direction. Each stab was out of desperation to live long enough to wear the crown. Red Hawk was just getting into rhythm when the grizzly charged him to the ground. This time the animal moaned loudly and began mauling Red Hawk.

Dead silence ensued for a few seconds, and nothing could be heard except for the heavy breathing of (O)nyagwai', who was slowly crawling off the body of Red Hawk. I took a small breath and realized the situation was back under control. I flew down to Red Hawk's body and landed on his chest. He slowly opened his eyes.

"You are Hihí:ih (a great horned owl) the O-kee-hee-de," he whispered weakly. Which basically meant he thought I was an evil owl.

"It is Blacksky," I corrected. "Grandson of Crowfoot." There was a look of terror on his face that could stay in a person's mind forever. His blood squirted, pumped, and his guts leaked unto the red earth. When his legs spasmed twice then stopped, I smiled. I didn't have one iota of sorrow for him.

I shifted back into human form with surprising efficiency and walked over to (O)nyagwai'. His guttural moans set off some unexpected feelings and emotions within my body. As I petted his fur coat and comforted him, I said, "Maho-peneta (the Great Spirit) will welcome you to the fields Elysian, my friend. As you cross over to the other side, may my words soothe your soul."

I stayed by the river and worked deep into the night, taking my two-edged knife and stripping (O)nyagwai' of his fur coat and sharp claws. It took me many hours to scrape the fleshy side of his skin without the proper tools. The real graining and dressing will be done by Fire, I thought. When she was done with it, the whole nation would pay homage. After I reburied most of the treasure, I prayed to the Great Spirit for giving me the patience to see the situation clearly, then I prayed for my friend Eagle Eyes, who would not be joining me as I mounted the stallion and headed back to Blackfoot Nation.

CHAPTER TWELVE:
THE GLORY ROAD

The next morning at sunrise, I climbed the bluffs and finally made my way back outside the village. In the distance, our sentinels let off some black smoke signifying my return. When I approached the front entrance, I purposely tapped my feet against my horse to reduce his stride to a light trot. I entered the village at the right time because everyone was in attendance to welcome me. They all formed what looked like a huge Soul Train line. Why lie? I didn't mind. Now they could catch me in all my splendor. As my horse slowly made its way down the line, the morning sun hit the gold crown on my head, and it cast a blinding reflection that made my onlookers put one hand up over their eyes like they were saluting me. (O)nyagwai's claws hung from my neck, and his fur coat was draped over my muscular body. This is how you upgrade your life & look: starring Blacksky, The Big Dick Bandit.

Everybody seemed shocked into silence for a few seconds. They couldn't understand it. Then I started to hear small side conversations from the crowd. "Do'ogwe:nyo:h (it's impossible) ëhse:go'(you will take it), knoe's (I like it)" they whispered. When I passed Two Bears and One Wolf, their eyes were filled with jealousy, rage, and sorrow. They looked mad I didn't disappear while I formed my medicine and envious that I created a lane that would be unwise of them to swerve into. Please believe it. The young killer was still in the cockpit. Run-tell-that. Go gossip. There's one thing about the circus, the clowns never change. I flashed my smile, and they looked more upset. On the flip side, my appearance caused all the squaw's heads to spin in my direction. I looked into some of their eyes; no connection. Mourning Star and Sunrise gawked in disbelief. "We want to play with your longpole" They whispered. Pretty girls with filthy mouths. A turn-on without a doubt.

I shifted my eyes away from the crowd to the back of the line where Fire stood with my beloved grandfather. His face was serious, but at the same time, proud. It felt so good to see two people that I cared about waiting on me. To my surprise, when I dismounted off my horse, I could feel a strong flash of jealousy from Fire, and when our eyes met, she tried in vain to hide her facial features. Her love of battlefield glory was starting to seep outta her pores. I greeted my grandfather and presented him with the gold crown off my head. The village broke out in deafening shouts of applause. He smiled, seemingly impressed by my gallant conduct. Truthfully speaking, when I secured it from Red Hawk's grip, thoughts of it decorating my grandfather's head was already on my mind. There is no nation like a donation. Especially when it's family. That's dedication. Grandfather waved everybody to silence.

"Let every Blackfoot in this village be silent, and do not speak till I am done. Look up at the sun. Blacksky has formed powerful medicine for all to see. Soon he will be a great chief," he declared, raising my hand as if I just won a prizefight.

The crowd erupted for a second time, causing me to quickly look around at all the different emotions on people's faces. There was an even combination of smiles and frowns at my newfound respect. Grandfather smiled and placed his arm around my shoulder.

"Come on, Blacksky," he said. "We have a lot to discuss." As we made our way towards his wigwam, Fire looked at me and asked, "Do you want me to bring your packsaddle and satchel inside for you?"

Fire was looking sexy as hell. I thought many-beast-sessy-bon. Which translates into absolutely nothing. It was just the first thing that popped into my mind to describe Fire. She was wearing a dress made of a plethora of white wolf skins and embroidered with porcupine's quills. Her craft was on full display. Her long hair glistened in the sun and was well-groomed like no other squaw in our village. Her skin was glowing like she had been on top of our wigwam butt ass naked eating tropical fruits the whole time I was gone.

I nodded to her and said, "Yes! But, do not take too long; it has already been too long without seeing your pretty face."

"I hope that is not the only thing you want to see?" she said in a sexual tone.

I smiled and walked up closer to her. "Sawë'nöih (you're crazy), Fire?"

"I am only crazy for you Blacksky."she said.

"When I am done we--"

"You can play with your squaw later, Blacksky," Grandfather interrupted.

When I entered my grandfather's wigwam, I heard Fire sucking her teeth at his comment. Good thing he didn't hear it. I was led near the edge of a curb of stone where I took a seat on a handsome robe that had been laid out for me. Grandfather seated himself directly across from me on another robe a short distance away from me. Before any words had a chance to be spoken, Fire walked in carrying my packsaddle and satchel. I gave her a quick approving look as she set them down and turned around to leave.

I watched her ass cheeks bouncing from left to right as she made her way back to the entrance. Suddenly, she stopped mid-stride like she had seen a ghost. O'ke:ge (I saw her). An untrained eye would've missed her strange reaction, but ever since my shift, my vision and senses were more focused and alert.

As she stood there like her feet were in quicksand, I put my neck on a swivel to see the reason why. She was staring at a painting of a Native American war chief dressed in a rare all-white buffalo skin robe. You couldn't see the chief's face because it was covered with an (o)nyagwai' (bear) skin mask. By his side stood a small boy who had my facial features. Fire turned away from the painting and walked rapidly out of the wigwam. I made a mental note to ask her why the painting caused her to have that kinda reaction.

When I returned my attention back to my grandfather, he gave me the once-over then smiled. Before he spoke, he took up his pipe and took out a tobacco pouch made of snakeskin. I sat there in observation mode as he pulled out some k'nick k'neck (tobacco) from the bark of the red willow and a piece of castor. He mixed the tobacco with the bark and pulled out a fine powder, which was made of dried buffalo shit, a little of which he sprinkled over the top. For half an hour we passed that shit, literally, and neither one of us said a word. We just enjoyed good feelings amid billows of smoke and pantomimic signs.

I was higher than a gagö:swe:s (elephant's) ass when he asked, "Tell me Blacksky, how did you manage to form the strongest medicine this village has seen in a long time?"

The direct question caught me off guard. "It was my plan to hunt buffaloes, elks, wolves, and antelopes to form my medicine. At the last minute, me and Eagle Eyes decided to take the glory road by hunting an (o)nyagwai' (bear) and War-Dzo:nyodah (war-eagle)."

He laughed. "I have taken this road you speak of, and it is bumpy, challenging, unpredictable, and painful."

"The road cost my friend Eagle Eyes his life."

My confession caused him to pause and stare at me in confusion.

"When you and Eagle Eyes decided to hunt for a grizzly bear and War-Eagle, you knew full well that they wouldn't be found on Blackfoot territory."

"You are right," I agreed. "We both knew that there was a chance that a lot of red-earth would be covered before we found this medicine."

I could see my grandfather's mind coming to

its own conclusions while I told him my version of the truth.

"Hmm," he said, taking another pull from his pipe and blowing out the smoke slowly in my direction. "I wish to hear how you ran into the Crees?"

"How did you know we ran into the Crees?" I asked curiously.

He smiled. "Unless you have fought in two battles against us, visited Red Pipe Stone Quarry, and your name is Blue Fox." Grandfather pointed at my tunic. "Which the pictures on that tunic have indicated."

I looked down at the tunic I had on and remembered that after I shifted back into human form, I was ass naked and had to throw on Blue Fox's tunic. My grandfather had noticed what the entire village didn't. The eyes do hustle!

When I looked up, he was peering at me and waiting on my response.

"We entered a deep green forest in search of strong medicine that seemed close by, but we were distracted by the screams of a paleface."

Grandfather looked at me contemplatively. "For what purpose would the white man have on red-men land besides the trapping of nöganyá'göh' (beaver)?"

"Like you, Grandfather, we believed that the paleface was trapping beavers until we drew closer and discovered that seven Crees had the paleface tied to a tree. We sat in the cover of the bushes while the Crees dumped out the paleface's satchel. There was not one beaver tail on the red-earth. I was sure that the Crees would let him go since he was honest about not trapping beavers."

"You can always count on a Cree to be a hano:go:t (weasel). What happened next?"

"The paleface was scared, and he yelled out that he had a treasure map of some sort, in hopes that this would save his life. He even yelled out that he was willing to split the treasure with the Crees. Of course, the Crees killed the trapper sadistically and took the map anyways." How! How! I paused. "The sight of blood and guts all over the ground was too much for Eagle Eyes, and he gave away our position to the Crees. We had to engage in a life and death battle after that. Eagle Eyes and five Crees were killed in this exchange. I followed the last two Crees to the treasure, and they paid for Eagle Eyes' death with their life."

I took out some hidden jewels I stashed from the treasure trove and placed them on the red-earth.

"I have never spoken to you about how much I hate those same Cree warriors that you fought yesterday, but now is a good time I have decided."

Out of respect for my grandfather and myself, I took off Blue Fox's tunic and threw that shit right on the ground until burning it became an option.

Grandfather had the most serious look on his face. "When your father was on the glory road, he forgot about the most important things in a red-man's life: like loving a red-woman, being there to raise his son, family safety, and peace of mind. These are the things that you can lose chasing glory. Do you think glory is worth peace of mind?" he asked, waiting patiently for my reply.

"No," I said, and meant that shit.

"Sometimes anger pushes you to do things that are hard to explain," he said. "For countless days and nights, I cried piteously to the Great Spirit over the death of your father, the murder of your mother, and the kidnapping of you." A single tear fell from the corner of his eye. "On one dark night during a full moon, O-kee-hee-de the Evil Spirit consumed my soul with a murderous rage that I could not control." How! How!

He picked up the small handful of diamonds and rubies then examined them carefully. The early morning sun hit the jewels through the skylight and lit up the entire wigwam with their authenticity.

He paused slightly. "I have heard your story, and now it is time for you to hear mine. Listen to me, because what I am to say will be the truth. How! How! Like you, I will drop jewels on the red-earth that will be wise of you to pick up." He paused. "Your father, Gwë'di:s (Nighthawk), was in love with the glory road since the day he formed his medicine. In his plight to become one of the greatest Blackfoot warriors that ever walked the earth, he continuously carried war into our enemies' country. His heart was strong, and his hands were always dipped in his victim's blood. Despite his love of war, your father was a good red-man. When you were born, Blacksky, I asked him to slow down and enjoy the life the Great Spirit was creating for him." He paused and placed both of his hands together in prayer. "Instead of slowing down, Gwë'di:s (Nighthawk) accomplished some of the most brazen war-excursions this Nation has ever seen. Nobody could figure out how this young warrior could slay so many of his enemies alone when he was outnumbered most of the time."

Grandfather laughed as if he knew something I didn't. "Your father was the youngest Blackfoot warrior in this nation with a headdress of eagle quills and beautifully polished buffalo horns. The honor of wearing buffalo horns is only given to those with the highest authority in our Nation, and your father had proved that he had the leadership to lead all warriors on the battlefield. At a young age, he was involved in some extraordinary battles."

I shook my head and wondered where my grandfather's story was going next. There was no question something bad happened. While my grandfather paused the story, I thought, how bad?

Suddenly, sadness appeared in my

grandfather's eyes again. "One morning, your father took you and your mother to the river to bathe, and he was ambushed by the Crees."

"Where were the sentinels?" I asked in an angry tone.

"The Crees tricked our sentinels by hiding under the skins of dead buffalo. They were able to imitate the movements of these animals while grazing. Red-man trickery. By the time our sentinels noticed the deception, the Crees came out of the surrounding forest from all directions. Your mother and father were unarmed, and The Crees slew them easily and stole you by using this stratagem. That night, o'gáyë'gyö:nyö:' (lightning strike repeatedly) and I burst forth from this village. Over and across the plains I went, towards the Crees Nation, which was not a short distance away."

"How far was it, Grandfather?"

"I do not know, but my bloodthirsty rage made me move faster than an antelope. As I crossed distant grassy bluffs, I came face to face with (O)nyagwai', and it shocked me when he did not attack me. Instead, he gave some unexpected respect and let me pass. His behavior was not normal, because anyone who has ever hunted an (O)nyagwai' knows that he will attack anything with two feet. It was not until I stopped by the river to get a drink and saw my reflection in the water, that I figured out why he did not kill me. It seems I had shifted into a huge wild dago:ji' (cat) with tufted ears and a short tail." My grandfather's confession made me sit up straight like I had been suddenly and unnecessarily tased by twenty-first-century police. "That seems to have gotten your attention," my grandfather said knowingly. "When I finally reached the Crees village, I laid secretly in the grassy bluffs studying what wigwam you could be in. Certain that I had seen your shadow in one of my enemy's wigwam as he hopped into bed with his squaw, I pranced softly on my paws and entered this wigwam I speak of without being noticed. While you slept peacefully in a separate room, I savagely murdered anyone who moved their bodies or lips to speak of my presence.

"When I was done, I snatched you up as quick as o'gáyë'gyö:' (lightning struck) and made my way back to Blackfoot Nation. When you woke up and walked out of my wigwam the next morning, the entire village looked at you like they were seeing a ghost. They took turns asking me how I managed to pull off the feat of getting you back by myself. As only you can imagine, Blacksky, I made up a believable story for their ears only. The same story your father made up for the elder's ears, and the same story you have tried to fill my ears with today."

"Grandfather," I said, trying to explain myself, but got waved to silence.

"It did not take me long to figure out that after I shifted for the first time, it was not an accident. Your father must have figured out his gift at an early age and kept it a secret which would explain all his success on the battlefield at such a young age. You see, Blacksky, it is my belief that even though I have trained you to be a skilled warrior, you could not have killed Dzardak Crees as well as snatch the skin off an (o)nyagwai' (bear). Does that sound crazy to you, Blacksky?" he asked calmly.

"No," I responded just as calmly as him.

The look on his face told me that he wasn't mad that I lied to him. Instead, he showed me why he was the head of our family and the chief of Blackfoot Nation.

"I do not know what it is, but something about you has changed since I gave you peyote to form your medicine. I wish to hear the truth this time on why that is, Blacksky."

"How did you know?" I asked.

"When I look at you now," he said, staring at me. "I see that your eyes have changed, and I have held you for hours as a baby, so I know these things to be true. The eyes never lie." How! How!

He kept All Eyes On Me like the PAC album Chocolate made me listen to, waiting for me to speak. I said, "Grandfather, it is hard for me to explain, but I will try." I paused. "I have traveled here from the future and somehow merged souls with Blacksky. In my world, I was also forming my medicine, and that journey brought me here to you. It is as if I exist in two different realms now."

My grandfather's mind seemed to be moving a mile a minute, probably trying to digest what I just fed him. I wasn't tripping with no luggage, though! I understood that this was some heavy shit to spring on him.

"I have heard the elders speak about this when I was a tiny warrior," he said, looking up through the skylight as if he were reminiscing." They had a name for what you are describing, and it is called dreamwalking. As I remember, you were born under a full moon on Wë'ö'dahgwa'(June) dewáshë:h ge:ih (24). The elders say that the people born on this day have magical imaginations and powerful dreams."

There was a silence between us, and my mind was moving now. What my grandfather said had me speechless. How could I be born on the same day in two separate realms?

My grandfather interrupted my personal thoughts. "The people of the willows used to say that there are only but so many souls on Mother-Earth to be recycled when someone's soul is headed to Fields Elysian. It is my belief that your father's soul has found you in the future and blessed you with the power to shift as well as dreamwalk. It is like your father wants you to change the red-man's destiny."

"Do you believe that I am the only one with this gift? And have you seen anyone else acting suspicious in our nation?" I asked a double question.

He paused. "It would be foolish of you to think that you are the only one from the future that knows how to use this gift. Besides, we should be more concerned with what you plan to do with your gift. I have heard that the white man rises like a great cloud in the east and is taking many red-men lands. They must not reach Blackfoot Nation."

CHAPTER THIRTEEN:
DUCKQUILLS

As much as I wanted to interrogate Fire about her reaction to my grandfather's painting, eat the delicious food she cooked, then get that dessert between her legs, I didn't. At the last second, I decided to make a detour to my fallen friend Eagle Eyes' wigwam to collect some items he would want me to have in his memory. With every step I took in the direction of his wigwam, the chatter of solidified warriors forming their own opinions about how I was able to form such strong medicine echoed inside my eardrum. Strangely, all the talk worked out perfect for me. They were so overwhelmed with trying to figure out my accomplishment that they were distracted from what was really going on in our village.

It's crazy how one small display of courage

can instantly change how people view you. I was official way before that hunting trip, I thought. My behavior is connected to what's inside my beating heart. That's not Kool-Aid. Unbeknownst to these gossiping ass warriors, my grandfather had prepared me to rise to this occasion by being brave. Like most humans, I was a mental slave to foolishness until the Great Spirit extended his hand and pulled me out that grave. Bear witness, as I walk the glory road, my kingdom is being made. My only regret was Eagle Eyes wasn't here to split this glory with me like we had split pouches of k'nick k'neck (tobacco) and buffalo rib dishes.

When I stepped one foot inside his wigwam an eerie feeling consumed my body. Eagle Eyes' spirit was around me, walking with me as my guide. A testament to the good times. Times I wished I could rewind and bring back. I took a seat at his sunken curb of stone Indian style. My thoughts started running races with each other in my mind. I pulled out my tiny stash of rubies and diamonds. In one Holy swoop, the Great Spirit had flipped my misfortune into a fortune. It was his seeds of strength that led to my harvest. My gut feeling was telling me that he was preparing me for something big, but as of right now, I could only guess what that was.

The African-American blood that ran through my veins wanted me to ditch the holier than thou routine and engage in a little buffoonery. I mentally pictured myself walking through this primitive village with various gold trinkets on my wrist and diamonds in my damn chain! I smiled broadly. Even while I relaxed, O-kee- hee-de, the evil spirit was in a tug of war with my soul, but I couldn't just sell out like a Hov and Bey concert. My people needed me. That became even more clear after my grandfather mentioned the great white cloud rising from the east. His comment struck a nerve inside of me. How could I bring myself to look him in his eyes and tell him that in the end, all would be lost? Blood would get spilled, some white, but mostly Native blood. In the meantime, I had to come up with a plan inside my head to slow down this white cloud.

After I put the jewels back into my stash, I pulled out my medicine-bag, which, up to this point, was empty. I looked up through the skylight and asked the Great Spirit for his guidance in helping me fill it up with ornaments that will strengthen me in battle. If something were to happen to me in this dreamworld, I wanted the smooth transition into the Beautiful Hunting Grounds that elders spoke about. The first item that I put into the bag was a long lock of hair from Eagle Eyes: I had taken it off of Red Hawk's body when he perished. The second item was a small piece of pipe from my grandfather. He told me it was from the Pipe Stone Quarry and was given to him by Tso-mec-cos-tee. The last two items were the fur and claws of the body of (O)nyagwai'. These choices should combine to make some strong medicine, I thought. Maybe the strongest medicine in our village besides my grandfather's.

Right after I tied a string around my bag and hung it around my neck, out the corner of my eye, I noticed a shadow staring at me from the wigwam's entrance. It was Mourning Star dressed in a short skirt of mountain goat skins, beautifully garnished with porcupine quills, and decorated with black beads. Her appearance would dazzle any set of eyes, except PETA's. She was even prettier than the last time I saw her. I thought, was that even possible? Smooth skin, long black hair, and pretty brown eyes the color of a copper penny. Mourning Star was easily the best squaw in Two Bear's stable, and it was hard for my eyes to leave her face. I stood up, and she looked me up and down like a project girl would in Syracuse.

"Yes! Mourning Star. How can I help you?" I asked, coming to the conclusion that I had been followed. The eyes do hustle!

"I have come to ask you if you came across the duck quills I requested?" she asked, looking around with her eyes to see if we were all alone.

I flipped on my acting switch and sighed like I cared. "I was hoping to get them for you, but we ran into some Crees, and Eagle Eyes was killed."

Here I was telling her what she already knew. Even the late great Ray Charles could see that when I made my way through the village Eagle Eyes wasn't with me, but here she was still asking me for duck quills. Inside, I felt some type of way about her timing. She moved closer to me with the subtlest of movement, and my nose picked up on a lavender smell that came off her body. The fragrance, combined with her natural scent, began to make my nature slightly rise.

"I am sorry for your loss, Blacksky," she said softly, touching my arm.

Sometimes grief causes people to do the strangest things, I thought.

"I know what you followed me over here for Mourning Star, and it is not for duck quills," I pressed with a bold move.

"Well! Yes, I..." she stuttered, refusing to look at me directly. I placed my hand underneath her chin and lifted her face to mine in the same manner Chocolate did to me. When we were looking into each other's eyes, I whispered to her softly.

"I know Two Bears cannot give you what you desire."

She took a small step toward me. "And what is it do you think I desire?"

Without another word, I let the bearskin fall from my muscular body unto the red Earth. I could feel moisture forming on my chest as she bit her lip in a seductive way that revealed her lust for me. Suddenly, the shit Two Bears talked at the river came to mind. I'd noticed him walk around the village as stiff as a board, which led me to believe that inside the confines of his wigwam, his stroke was mechanical and weak. Why else would his main squaw be stalking me? I thought.

I ripped off my leggings and backed out the weapon of mass destruction, and it damn sure wasn't just to test it like N. Korea Her gaze instantly dropped below my midsection.

"The elder squaws have told the truth," she said. "You have the biggest longpole I have ever seen. Can I touch it?"

"Do what you like with him," I said.

When she grabbed my boner, her small hands could barely fit around my girth. Her touch caused a surge in my loins to start building. I lifted her shirt over her head, and when I got it off, her thick bush pressed up against my skin. Mourning Star dropped to her knees.

"Agádöswé'danih (I'm hungry)," she said. "Dasgöh! (give it to me!)"

"Ihse:g! (you think)" I responded. She started covering my six-pack with tiny little kisses, and the sensation caused my dick to swell to its full potential, poking her in the neck. I could see the shocked look on her face at how big my dick was, and I put it to her lips.

"Ogá'öh (tastes good)," I said, talking nasty in my Native vernacular and getting her ready for a pipe game that's spectacular. This moment would be new gossip for the elder squaws to talk about. Strong "puha" (magic) from the medicine-man who made it rain inside Mourning Star's mouth. When I looked down, I could see her placing tender kisses along the length of my dick and around the ridge under my cockhead. Her hard work caused my longpole to jerk and start twitching.

"It takes so good," she said, placing my dick deep down her throat. Her mouth was wetter than Lake Minnetonka, and I could feel my mushroom-shaped head tickling her tonsils. Suddenly, she began gagging violently, and her drool ran down her chin, splashing my dick, then falling to the wigwam's floor.

I smiled. "There is no need to be greedy."

A porn star look appeared on her face. "Forgive me, Blacksky. I wanted my nose inside your pubic hair." She wanted to tell these squaw thots that she deep-throated my cock. Please! My dick is longer than algebra equations, thicker than two milkshakes in one cup. I reached out and slapped Mourning Star on her butt.

"These things do not happen, but I will help you," I said.

Concerned for her safety now, I restricted her

mouth to only six inches of fun. In no time at all, she started to establish a rhythm. Clear drops of my pre-cum coated her lips, and I could feel a strong surge coming from deep within my body. I didn't want this sex scene to end this way, so I eased out of her mouth and steered her body to the red-earth in the missionary position.

"Are you ready for this longpole?" I asked, looking deep into her eyes and slowly teasing the opening of her twat with my massive dick. She shivered with delight for good reasons. Ladies, this is big cock presoak pussy preposterous talk, and I have the type of stroke that changes walks.

"Stick it in," she begged with passion in her eyes.

When I went deep inside her wetness, she gasped, and her breathing changed; her small chest expanded, contracted. After two small strokes, her breathing continued to accelerate. Clearly, this meant she couldn't take this dick, and I quickly realized that this was a situation that required finesse, not brute force. Not only do I have cock as big as a horse, I know how to use it. Just know that. I started grinding my hips in a circular motion with African rhythm. Gold Ghana. This type of long dick stroke could take your baby momma. Her pussy was hot, creamy, and wet. She was visibly excited. Several thrusts later, her body shook with an orgasm. I could feel her juices run down her legs and splash my thighs.

Suddenly, a loud noise came from her throat. "Stop, Blacksky!"

"'What is wrong, Mourning Star?" I asked.

"Oyĕ'gyö' (lightning has struck) inside of my wetness," she said in a scared tone.

How can lightning strike inside her pussy? I thought. Then the reason she would yell that popped inside my brain. I smiled. I'd hit this bird with the Hitchcock and given her the first orgasm of her life. I let out my War-cry!

"I promise that you will be fine," I said, flipping her over into the doggy-style position and sliding deep inside her.

She cried out. "Two Bears could never go this deep!"

I slid in and out, stretching her pussy with each stroke. My dick glistened with her juices, and her screams bounced off the fabric of Eagle Eyes' wigwam. I pulled her hair, and she loved it. I found my rhythm, owning that pussy. She scooted up and tried to shelter her honeypot from the weapon of mass destruction, but I gripped her hips so she couldn't run and hit deeper inside her bunker. She started to yell things in the Native tongue that was hard for me to decipher.

"Swagwe:goh! (all of you!) Age'wa:ga'has (I like meat), Blacksky."

"What is that you said?" I asked.

"Oyë'gyö' (lightning has struck) again!" she yelled, locking up her pussy around my dick and cumming over and over again.

Sensing that I was on the brink, I pulled out of her wetness and stood up. Mourning Star spun around, placing my dick in her mouth. I let out a loud primal grunt. Hot semen pumped from my body, and I closed my eyes in pleasure.

"It tastes so good," she said as she slurped.

Just as her tiny licks caused me to open my eyes slowly, I saw the flash of metal travel its arc and slash Mourning Star across her face. She opened her mouth and screamed a sound that my memory will never forget. When I stepped toward Fire to disarm her, I never saw the cast iron pot in her other hand, and the force of the blow caused everything to go black. Oh shit! I thought as the red-earth came rushing up to my face.

CHAPTER FOURTEEN:
THE ULTIMATUM

I woke up on a butter soft bedstead with a pounding headache then glanced at a familiar curtain ornamented with porcupine quills and hieroglyphics. My brain quickly let me know that my transgression ended horrifically. I wanted specific details. How did I get back to my wigwam? Who brought me here? I touched my forehead and felt a cartoon size knot. When I rolled to my left, the answers to those questions was most likely looking me directly in the eyes. He was dressed in a stylish buffalo robe with a battle from his life on the front. I looked closely. The hieroglyphics depicted he was on deck for that river war. That's why his headdress of ermine feathers with polished buffalo horns was hard to ignore. In his hand, he held a tin cup with steam rising from it.

"I was worried about you, Blacksky," One Horn admitted, passing me the hot tin cup. "Sit up and drink this, my friend. It will help the pain inside your head go away."

I sat up, then I took the cup out of his hand and sipped it slowly. The hot coffee was strong, and it made me feel mellow. It tasted like shit, though. It definitely wasn't that yellow Cafe' Bustelo.

"How did I get back to my wigwam?" I asked.

"After the smoke, you started cleared," he said. "Ke:awak (my daughter) informed me that you were asleep inside of Eagle Eyes's wigwam." He paused. "I did not think it would be wise to leave you at the mercy of your enemies after Mourning Star ran through the village with her face slashed."

One Horn's answer caused my temporary amnesia to immediately subside. What I did wasn't wise. I thought, how could I get myself jammed up like this? Pussy was my weakness.

I shook my head. "Did anyone see you carry me here?"

"Did anyone see me?" He repeated sarcastically. He shook his head. "I think my daughter struck you over the head a little harder than she thought. Do you remember that the sun was still high in the sky when this happened?"

We both laughed at my ridiculous question.

"Do you think Fire will ever forgive me?" I asked.

"You have decided to make a permanent decision in a temporary situation," he told me. "Because of that, we must talk about about this Two Bears situation." Why did he repeat the same word twice? I thought.

"Let's talk about it," I said.

"You cannot have forgotten that Mourning Star was Two Bears' main squaw? If you have my friend, let me be the first one to remind you that you broke the village rules rules."

"The same rules that all the warriors break in our village. Why do you keep repeating the same word twice?" I asked.

"Sometimes my little speech quirk kicks in. I have tried to control it, but sometimes I cannot, my friend."

There was a pause between us, and I couldn't help but wonder where this little quirk was when he was excepting the gifts my grandfather gave him for his daughter.

One Horn stared at me and said, "The other warriors did not get caught with their hand in the o:nyö'hsowa:nëh (pumpkin) patch like you did."

"This is true," I admitted. "But I did not chase Mourning Star into Eagle Eyes' wigwam, my friend. She chased me."

"Like you, I know that you cannot take from the willing, but that does not change what happened today. Two Bears has said that not only does

Mourning Star have a slash on her face, but you have also violated her special place, and it has no more value to him." He paused. "He has demanded that Mourning Star be replaced with another squaw."

"That is all he wants," I replied. "I will send him ge:ih (four) squaws and this will be over my friend."

"Of course, if it was that simple Blacksky, I would have just given Two Bears one of my many squaws squaws. Two Bears has made it clear to anyone that will listen that he will only accept my daughter in exchange for Mourning Star."

As One Horn's words set into my mind, it became clear that Two Bears was attempting to do the most. Unbeknownst to him, he had the right plan, just the wrong man. I thought, he needed to have several seats around the sunken curb for even trying me like that.

"What has my grandfather said about this situation?" I asked.

"Chief Crowfoot cannot and will not get involved in personal matters when the village rules have been broken."

There was a pause. "No," I said calmly. "My soul will visit the Beautiful Hunting Grounds before I let him take Fire. Tell Two Bears that I do not like his deal, and now he will get nothing."

He smiled. "Your words are honorable,

Blacksky, and that is why I have told Fire that she can do no better than you for ganóöhgwa'shä' (love). There is no doubt that the Great Spirit walks with you, my friend." His facial expression turned serious. "Somehow, the chief knew you would not agree to Two Bear's deal, so he has set up a fight for you in the center of the village. Do you accept?"

"I accept," I said. "My grandfather is not grooming a coward to be chief," I added confidently.

"The glory road is full of valleys and peaks. Is it not?" he asked, staring at me thoughtfully. His question made me think about the Reasonable Doubt album Chocolate gave me for one of my lessons.

"Yes," I agreed wholeheartedly.

"You are still a young warrior, but the youth I used to be has escaped me. As you get older, you will find out that in Blackfoot Nation, no one is who they say they are. Are they?" he asked.

I didn't immediately answer One Horn's question because it seemed like there was an underlying subliminal message behind it. I thought, am I tripping, or does some of his Native lingo seem advanced like mine? My grandfather told that there was no way I was the only dreamwalker. Could One Horn be a dreamwalker? Agwë'nöih (I'm crazy), and my mind is playing tricks on me.

"Why do you say these things, One Horn?" I

asked suspiciously.

"I am one red-man with many thoughts," he said, looking directly into my eyes. "I cannot help but notice that you and my daughter's passion for glory on the battlefield are one and the same." He paused and searched my face for an emotional reaction, but I had my poker face on. "It is my belief that two Ganö'gat's (May's) ago, O-kee-hee-de, the Evil Spirit entered my daughter's soul."

I stayed silent for a few seconds. I thought, why would One Horn say that Fire was the Devil?

"And you say this because Fire wants to do more than just cook and dress skins in our wigwams?"

"No, my friend. I say this for your safety. Do you know what happens when you play with fire?" he asked.

"Of course, you get burned."

"In the future, it will be wise of you to keep that saying close to your heart and both of your sano'e:'s (heads) in the right place," he warned, gesturing towards the weapon of mass destruction.

"You are right, my friend," I admitted." I wish that my flesh was not so weak when it comes to squaws."

He smiled. "Your object in view will get better with age. You must be able to learn from this and move on. There is a lesson in everything, Blacksky. Even an arrow! You must remember that your decisions affect the people that you care about the most most."

One Horn's advice awakened some new feelings and emotions within me. It reminded me of the conversation I had with my grandfather about my deceased father in this world. I didn't want to go down that same path, and I promised myself that after the fight with Two Bears, I would move better so I wouldn't trip.

For the next two hours, I spent nearly every minute with One Horn reinforcing what I already knew. He was way more advanced in every facet of combat than me. Chocolate taught me that repetition is the mother of all skills, and she was right. As sweat poured down my body, I swung a hard front kick in his direction, and he easily dodged it.

"Your timing is slightly off, Blacksky," One Horn said as he squared up with me again. "Two Bears will try to establish his own rhythm, and it will be necessary for you to disturb that." He paused. "Go again," he ordered.

One Horn was elusive, and his feet stayed in motion like Muhammad Ali, so I mirrored his movements and made them my own. This time, he threw several kicks at me with succession, and my new footwork strategy worked. I easily eluded his attempts, and it left him open for my attack. I delivered a right cross with so much power that even though it was partially blocked, it still knocked

One Horn to the red-earth.

He looked up at me in disbelief. "Now you are ready, my friend."

CHAPTER FIFTEEN:
THE SHOWDOWN

By the time the sun reached the agreed-upon level in the sky, word of the fight spread through the village like a California brush fire: I could hear the older warriors in our village gossiping through the skylight about my indiscretion. Some of them thought I needed a lesson. I didn't. My built-in defense mechanism: A subconscious reaction to protect and defend myself from a negative view of myself. Cocky! I have enough mental health to share the wealth, so I predicted smooth sailing in this fight. I'm the Ancient Alien sent here via time travel with composed hypnotic riddles for my fans to unravel. As if my hands were a gavel, I threw hard punches into thin air and pretended they all landed on Two Bears' face. Suddenly, One Horn appeared in the entrance of my wigwam.

"The time has come for you to walk the glory road," he announced.

I smiled. "Let us hold our heads up and walk it high."

One Horn laughed. "Are you sure that you want to toke the dried buffalo shit and k'nick-k'neck before combat?" he asked in a surprised tone.

"Yes, my friend," I responded. "I want to get higher than a shooting star in the sky."

I picked up my pipe, which was already filled with that exotic shit to look at; Zendaya, Naomie Harris, Priyanka Chopra, and that Lucy Liu. I took a few pulls and held the smoke in. Enhanced view, intense euphoria, high energy, and a pleasant body sensation kicked in. I passed it to One Horn.

"Only a prophet or legend would be brave enough to hit this buffalo shit before combat. You are very aloof for such a young warrior. This is strange to me," One Horn said, blowing out some smoke slowly. "My daughter dressed this for you to wear to the fight."

I must have been higher than a ga:da's (ducks that perches in a tree), because those tunic and leggings he held in his hands just magically appeared. That's weird, I thought: the shirt was finely dressed with two white wolf skins and ornamented with porcupine quills. Attached to the seams, from the shoulders to the all-black leggings were scalp-locks that I snatched off the Crees' heads in battle. I took the outfit out of his hands, and the material felt incredibly soft.

"How does she know this will fit me?" I asked.

"All it takes is one time for my daughter to size you up."

When I put it on, I was impressed by her skill set. When it came to her skill set, she was in her bag: It fit just right, and every stitch was where it was supposed to be. The scalp-locks she added made me look savagely fierce. Inside, I knew that's exactly how she wanted me to look.

"Fire told me to tell you that you are a special hosge'egehdoh (warrior), and today the entire village will remember the day when the underdog became the wolf. This is why she dressed your tunic on such short notice. The scalps she danced still have blood on them. I have never seen my daughter forgive so quickly. It is clear for all to see that she has given her awĕnyahsa' (heart) to you, and it will be wise of you not to break it again." How! How!

"Where is Fire now?" I asked in a concerned tone.

"I do not know, Blacksky," he said. "But, I am certain that she will be somewhere only a well-trained ogà:' (eye) can see."

Minutes later, I exited my wigwam with One Horn leading the way. The scalps on my tunic were still damp with the blood of the Crees, and their 'self-esteem' was my evidence of how bravely I fought in that battle. At the first sight of me, the entire village broke into pandemonium. The air quickly became filled with the excitement and chatter of red-men and women. When we reached the halfway point of our walk towards the center of the village, I purposely slowed down to take in the scenery around me. I thought, damn! I'm still high off the buffalo shit.

There I stood, right in the middle of several hundred wigwams covered in dirt. On the tops of these wigwams were separate groups of warriors standing next to buffalo skulls, skin canoes, pots, and pottery. I pivoted like a mountain goat and noticed the suspended poles about twenty feet above the doors of their wigwams. The scalps of deceased warriors flew from them like a flag on a breezy day.

In the distance, blue streams of smoke rose from the coal pits into the afternoon air. When I made it to the middle of the village, the public ground, usually empty, was jam-packed with red-men, women, and children. There were at least five hundred warriors seated shoulder to shoulder on the red-earth around the circular area of the ground.

As I entered the fighting area, a silence fell over the crowd. It was the silence of anticipated violence at my expense. It took a few seconds for their conversations to begin again. Strangely, I could hear a lot of warriors wishing they were in my all-black moccasins. Owenoih (it's crazy). One Horn positioned himself on the right side of me, no question, listening to the same thing I heard.

"Mother-Earth can be a confusing place," he said. "A place where red-men are more than happy to join the village of the dead." He was describing my exact feelings.

"This is true," I agreed.

"And look," he said, pointing out to the crowd with his nod.

When I looked in the direction his finger was pointing at, a group of mothers were decorating their daughters to offer the winner in marriage.

"I see them!" I yelled. It was loud.

"There is no question that whoever wins this fight will have to beat all the squaws off with a stick."

"When I win," I boasted. "I will pass them off as a gift for your loyalty to my family."

"As you know, Blacksky, I do not turn down nothing but a tunic made of duck quills." I laughed. He didn't know duck quills played a role in my conflict.

"What's so funny?" he asked me.

"Nothing. Look who showed up," I said, purposely keeping him in the dark.

"It is about time," One Horn said. "I had begun

to think that he was a so:wäk (duck)."

As two Bears and One Wolf walked the glory road with their entourage, they received the same electric response we got. He was wearing a stylish headdress made of raven quills that would look better if it was on my head. His tunic of buckskin was fringed with scalp-locks and a short chart of his life, which could end today if he tried something stupid. His leggings were mediocre at best. I thought, no wonder why he was trying to muscle me out of my wife. He should've come to her. She could have done it much better, like A-wax said in Menace. When Two Bears entered the fighting area the crowd grew quiet again.

Suddenly, out of nowhere, the whole village erupted in ear-piercing applause, and the expressions on their faces, One Horn in particular, made me look in the same direction that had them so hyped.

"It is your grandfather," One Horn yelled.

"I thought you said he was not coming?"

"I said he will not get involved. That did not mean he would not show up." He smiled. Do not be mistaken, Blacksky. Your grandfather will never miss a chance to make one of his glorious entrances."

My grandfather's appearance caused my heart to swell with pride, and my spirit grew stronger. On his head, he wore the gold crown that I gave him, and he rocked it slightly tilted towards the medicine lodge. His body was draped in white buffalo skin, and it had to be the same one he had on in the painting inside of his wigwam. The costly skin was preserved and looked in mint condition as striking proof of its existence. I could hear the gasps of five hundred red-men at this strange mystery. A white buffalo robe is extremely scarce and of great curiosity in our Nation. Expensive like modern-day couture and will never go on sale, out of all the herds of buffalo that grazed these boundless prairies, there is only a one in two thousand chance that you will see a white one.

The white buffalo skin is considered one of the greatest medicines in our Nation. Usually something like this would be hanging on top of a long pole over the medicine lodge as a sacrifice to the Great Spirit. The second chiefs, doctors, and high-priests all gazed upon my grandfather with intense hatred and envy at his deliberate show of cockiness. My grandfather had the most brilliant smile on his face. He seemed to know that his entrance would cause this type of response, and he embraced it. When he entered the fighting area, the shouts of applause became thunderously louder.

With one wave of his hand, the entire village quieted, and he addressed the onlookers. "I am Chief Crowfoot, the leader of Blackfoot Nation. No one will speak till I have finished talking. If you have a problem with my flesh and blood, feel free to come to me. Do not take any physical action against them without my knowledge, or you shall perish. I am a fair chief, and because Blacksky has broken our village rules, he will be treated no different than any other warrior who has done the same." He paused. "We are here at Two Bears' request to settle this problem between him and Blacksky with a battle of young warrior pride. Swadéhsa'öh? (are you ready?)" he yelled to the crowd.

I smiled. My grandfather was the gówähgo:wa:h (king), and as he did his best Michael Buffer routine, I saw her. She was seated on top of a wigwam, at a safe distance for herself, but in striking distance for the bow and quiver she had slung over her shoulder. Upon careful observation, it seemed like she strategically placed herself in a position where Two Bears and his entourage were oblivious to her presence. It was weird, but also extremely attractive to me. When she nodded to me, I nodded back and thought, her father was right. I had to watch Fire more closely. It wasn't normal for a squaw to demonstrate so much loyalty and courage. She had more heart than most of young warriors in our village.

When One Horn went to meet One Wolf about the rules of our fight, Two Bears and I engaged in a staring match that would've made Mike Tyson look away. Another brief discussion ensued between One

Horn and my grandfather. Seconds later, One Horn walked back over to me.

"What are the rules?" I asked.

"No weapons allowed my friend," he said. "And they have requested one more thing," he added.

"What is that?"

"They have asked that this fight be to the death."

"That is fine with me," I agreed.

My grandfather reapproached the center and called out the rules for both sides to hear. "This is hand-to-hand combat, no weapons, kicking is allowed. Also, Two Bears has asked that this fight be to the death, and Blacksky has accepted."

One Horn got closer to me and said, "Life always means more with the possibility of death."

When I stepped to the center and removed my tunic, sweat dripped of my chest and abs. All the squaws gasped with admiration, and all the warriors looked at me with envy. My medicine-bag dangled from my neck, and I gripped it tightly while simultaneously praying to the Great Spirit for his strength. Two Bears took off his tunic and raised his arms to the crowd like him being pronounced the winner was a foregone conclusion.

"Soon you will join Eagle Eyes," he said, violating.

I was still high, so I smiled. This Two Bears

nigga really was wild, summoning me to the middle of the village like I was on trial. It was ten squaws to every brave, and I was expected to behave? I'm the contrary of afraid. I wanted to beat blood out of Two Bears and toss his body in a grave, but there was no way he could've seen Casino. He was playing crooked Bingo with the kid that calls the numbers out. Victory, no doubt, was of great significance to Blacksky, so I felt sorry for this GUY. Chill. Let's build right quick. I know I talk that shit: about raunchy escapades of my big dick. Who could be smart enough to use this to get rich?

Two Bears didn't know my new powers had turned me into the Native Huey Newton with the pen and the Shotgun. If you don't know What's Happening, start from the top and do 'The ReRun'. I was attempting to be the witty Champ championing the black cause, all while using the talent God gave us all, and Two Bears was mad Mourning Star licked my balls.

"Warriors to the center." was called, and the fight began. We circled each other for about a minute in a slow and boring feeling-out session. I stepped in as a feint and attempted to draw first blood, but Two Bears responded with a light punch that grazed my right ear. Even though I easily eluded its full impact, the punch drove me somewhat backward. Thinking he was doing something now, he threw several slow combinations that showcased my ability to avoid, evade, and duck. Starstruck, the crowd cheers, but I didn't give a fuck. My plan was to stay patient until he made a mistake that I could capitalize on, then hit him with the Cassius Clay and Joe Lewis, put an end to all this foolishness. Two Bears charged past my defense and used his shoulder to ram my body onto the red-earth. As the crowd broke out in another cheer, I could feel some pain in my stomach and shoulder: the same body part that the Crees grazed with their arrows.

Two Bears raised closed fists over his head. "Your future chief is on the ground where he should stay."

One Horn looked at me with confidence. "He has forgotten that it is not how you fall down, but how you get back up. Watch his strut. This isn't about luck. Duck!"

While I appeared to be distracted, Two Bears threw a quick kick at my head, but at the last minute, I eluded it and sprang back to my feet. The crowd cheered at our close encounter, and Two Bears pushed forward swinging with bad intentions. He was trying to end the fight prematurely, he had some high hopes, especially when his attack left him off balance. I landed a hard one-two punch combination that snapped his head back for hating. The blows opened up two small cuts underneath both of his eyes. Shocked, he touched his face with his hand and drew back blood.

I laughed out loud. "Now, all your squaws will call you Two Mouses." Hundreds of red-men erupted into unified laughter. Unable to control his anger, Two Bears attacked on some reckless shit, lost control of his whip. A thudding uppercut put him on the back pockets of his tunic.

"It is never any fun when the rabbit has the gun," I said. M. G. Hardie.

Two Bears scoffed. "What about a knife, Blacksky?"

He backed out a huge two-edged knife that he had concealed, and the entire crowd collectively sighed at his blatant disregard for the agreed-upon rules. Anger swept through me, and it made me want to kill him even more.

He got up off the red-earth and launched himself at me with his knife, but I was prepared and got out of the way with a juke move. When he slashed at me again, I blocked it with my arm. The sharp blade opened up a good size wound on my skin. He lunged again, and a struggle ensued between us for the knife. His grip was solid, and the blade stabbed through my right hand several times. My blood dripped from the blade and stained the red-earth. When he stabbed again, I grabbed him in a bear-hug and wrestled the knife away from his grip. Before he had time to react, I plunged the knife deep into his heart. The impact opened up a gaping wound inside of his chest, and his body jerked and spasmed. I dug my hand into his chest and let out a savage scream, holding up, and claiming in complete silence, the heart and soul of the warrior Two Bears. As the chaotic sound of my own scream echoed throughout the village, almost simultaneously, something strange started to happen within me. Shockingly, my hands and arms begin to fade away, then vanish. I could still see activity in full swing all around me, but it all seemed so far away now.

Suddenly, my vision became cloudy, and everything surrounding me slowly started to go black. There was a lengthy pause inside my body as if the force of the whole universe was pulling me through time and space. Everything stopped moving, and the muffled sounds of the Shaman's voice made me slowly open my eyes and glance at his pockmarked face. His facial expression was one of shock and disbelief.

"In your journey to the spiritual realm, you have managed to amaze me," he declared.

I moved my hand up to my neck, and I was shocked that my medicine-bag was still there. I thought, how could that be possible?

I took a deep breath and asked, "How long have I been seated in this same position?"

"About six hours."

My body felt as if every activity I did in my

dream was real. I stretched my legs and attempted to get all the soreness out of my joints. Sitting Indian style was definitely a dubb for a while.

"It seemed like it was so much longer," I said.

"You should know that six hours in our world can equal many days in the spiritual realm." He paused. "Your journey was a very powerful one."

I didn't immediately answer the shaman, because his statement caused the events that happened on my spirit quest to flood my thoughts like New Orleans after Katrina.

"Does everybody wake up from these dreams with this?"

The Shaman paused and looked at my medicine-bag.

"You are the first," he admitted. "And I have been the Shaman for the Onoda'ge:ga:' (Onondaga, people of the hill) for many moons. The spirits have gifted you with many talents because you were born on a special day in June."

Every word out of the Shaman's mouth had me thinking that forming my medicine was more than just a dream.

"What talents?" I asked.

The Shaman held out a single feather in his hand. "This came from you."

"We:doh (when?)," I asked.

A shocked look appeared on his face. "You know the Native language?"

"I guess so," I said in a surprised tone.

"For you to learn the Native language while you formed your medicine is unheard of. And as it stands, you're the first one on this reservation to shift inside your dreams."

The Shaman's admission quickly took me away from my present situation, like the lovely voice of Yazmine Young on a sunny Buffalo afternoon. I wondered if I could shift in this world too.

"What else did you observe?" I asked. The eyes do hustle!

"I've only heard and seen very little while you were forming your medicine, and that information that I share with you is for your ears only."

"I know how to keep a secret," I promised.

He gave me a long look. "The Great Spirit gave you your powers for a real reason. Reasons that you must figure out while you walk Mother-Earth. Blacksky has replaced the name you were given at birth. In the Onoda'ge:ono' (Onondaga people) culture, we believe that your name should coincide with your spirit animal. You're the exception." He paused and handed me a feather. "That is for you. Put it inside your medicine-bag and don't ever open it again. The value of this bag is more important than any material thing you can buy from the white man. Hold it close to your heart, because it's your guardian spirit in this world. The bag's power will strengthen you. Under no circumstances are you to ever remove this bag from around your neck. I'm impressed by your heart. I predict that your life will get off to a fast start, but it is not how you start. It's how you finish. If you take off your bag, your powers will diminish."

I looked into the eyes of the face in front of me and saw wisdom way beyond my young years.

"I will take your silence as you understand," he said. "The spirits have chosen you to fight all forms of evil while you walk the glory road. There is no question that you will have to spill blood to accomplish this feat. Be unafraid, Blacksky. You walk with Gods so you will not be easy to defeat. Your Native and African blood runs through you like a river of protection. Past spirits surround you with an invisible force." The Shaman waved his hand back and forth to demonstrate the force. His hand movement set off a supernatural effect inside my brain.

The Shaman shifted a little, then he continued. "One of your spirit animals is one of the wisest ji'dë'ö:h (birds) in the sky. It is because of this that you will be capable of imbibing a tremendous amount of information. This gift from the Great Spirit will surface during most any occasion." He paused. "Your strength should increase under the cloak of night, then double when the moon is at its full capacity. If someone wishes to harm you on one of these nights, there will be tragedies. This is also for you."

Nevermind the fact that every time the Shaman gave me something it magically appeared like a trick from David Blaine, the Fanny pack was black and beautiful. Amani Summers. And I couldn't help but wonder was the Shaman handing me 'Soul Glow'? With all this talk about spirits, one will never know. My father used to carry his activator in his fanny pack. I smiled and reached for the bag. When I opened it, there were three tiny vials of some sort of liquid inside.

"What are these?" I asked, holding one of the vials out in front of me and examining it carefully.

"That is liquefied peyote," he responded. "It will make your transition back to the spiritual realm easier for you. Each one of those is to be used three days apart. The vials that you hold can be very dangerous if you do not follow what I said."

"What happens when I run out of this supply? Can I come to you for another batch?" I asked, doubling up my questions.

"We will talk about that when the time is right," he said in a nonchalant tone. "Nothing without value to you comes without a good price."

The Shaman was a crafty old man. For every question I asked, he had a plan. No fool, he knew I would need his services in the future. That's why he slyly stayed away from volunteering all his knowledge of me being a dreamwalker. Just before my mind could form my next educated guess, the Shaman started speaking again.

"It's also important that you don't think you're the only shifter on Mother Earth. To so many others she has given birth. You had better sharpen your shifting skills while you have free time. Don't be blind. The Great Spirit rewards preparation and punishes those who don't use their mind."

I nodded my head. "Who can shift on this reservation besides me?"

"There is some information that is against my code for me to tell you about." He gave me a serious look. "If you pay attention to your surroundings, your question will answer itself. Some shifters use their gift to serve the Evil Spirit. The Blacktop is their hunting ground."

"How do I get better at shifting?"

He smiled and said, "Unlike you, I cannot shift, but I would imagine the faster you get in and out your shift, the better."

"Why come all the shifters don't stick together and fight the real enemy?"

The shaman shook his head with disappointment. "I wish that were true, but it's not. Most Natives are full of jealousy, and most of the time, you cannot get them to come together unless it is for a drink or smoke. Your reception on this reservation will not sit well with everybody, and because your Native blood is mixed with African-American blood, pure blood Natives will try to cast their own judgments on you."

"Why?" I asked.

"That's a good question, Blacksky, especially since Native and black Americans have both suffered unspeakable violence by the hands of the white man. For the Onoda'ge:ono' (Onondaga people), it is a slap in the face for so many black people in Syracuse to celebrate Thanksgiving, a day that the white man has turned into a holiday to commemorate his genocide on the Natives. It is like the Natives having a big feast to celebrate the enslavement of black people."

"I wish I could say something in defense of my African American brothers, but most of them are about as sharp as a bowling ball." We both laughed. "The funny thing about the times is they always change. Not now, but one day I will unite all shifters, and I really don't care who likes it," I declared.

"Well said, my friend. If any Native takes the time to get to know you, they will fall under your spell. You are a wizard with words, and it is hard not to like you, Blacksky. There is so much fire in your young body. For now, your Native name should be kept a secret with the exception of sano'eh (your mother)," he warned.

"You talk as if my name is forbidden."

"Revealing your spiritual name too soon can be used against you, Blacksky. Besides, don't be so quick to volunteer such personal information to your enemies."

"What enemies?" I asked in surprised tone.

"Listen carefully," the Shaman said, staring me directly in the eyes. "The Native supernatural world is full of trickery, and like I have told you before, if you are not careful you will have a Chinese name. Long Gone!"

Twenty minutes later, after soaking up every small detail of our conversation like a sponge, I left out of the medicine lodge feeling stronger, wiser, better than I ever felt before. The mellow afternoon sun was lighting up the small houses and cabins surrounding me like Bruce Leroy in 'The Last Dragon'. As I looked around at the crowd that gathered, a delicious smell floated through the air and made my stomach growl. Someone, somewhere, had prepared a delicacy, and I could easily smell the various dishes.

I assessed that there were about twenty people in front of me. Ten men, five kids, four women, and one Stacy. She was easy for me to spot because nobody had a smile on their face brighter than hers.

As I made my way through the people as politely as possible, the greetings came from each one of them. Each one made me feel excited and accepted. When I finally reached Stacy, she grabbed me around my waist and hugged me as if I just got released from a long stretch Upstate. Her body felt comfortably soft inside my arms. She belonged there. I ran my knuckles down the left side of her cheek, looking into her eyes.

"If I knew you gave out these kinda hugs, I would come see the Shaman every day."

She smiled. "I'm so proud of how you handled yourself that I had to give you back a hundred cool points."

Never a dull moment with this girl, I thought.

"Oh," I said softly." Is this some new shit?"

"Nope," she responded calmly as she folded her arms across her chest. "I've always had it up here." She took two of her fingers and tapped her temple twice. "When I first meet someone that I have regular dealings with, I start them off with five hundred cool points. Depending on how you conduct yourself around me, you can either lose points or earn them. Most people do some cornball shit and make me snatch the whole total."

"What happens then?"

"You ever see all hell break loose?" she asked with her trademark saying.

I sent four Crees to the Great Spirit to decide if he wanted them in the Beautiful Hunting Grounds or not and a fight with Two Bears to the death, I thought,

I smiled. "Have I. So, how many cool points do

I have?"

"Let me see," she said, pausing and looking up at the blue sky like she was making some mathematical calculations. "Five hundred minus one Franklin for ignoring my phone calls. Plus, it would be crazy if I didn't deduct another hundred for smiling in that bitch's face that you helped move in, and last but not least, minus fifty for that stupid Bills hoodie."

I did the math. "Two fifty."

"Don't forget the hundred you just earned," she teased.

What's a point system to someone who knows how to shoot their jump shot? I thought. I put my hand under her chin and lifted her face to mine.

"How many points is this?" I asked as I parted her lips with my tongue. Her kiss tasted like a tropical-flavored fruit. Suddenly, a bell went off from a short distance away, and the mood was broken. Stacy backed up and interlocked her arms with mine.

"Don't worry. I have a way you can earn all your points back later on tonight. That bell means we have to go. The chief is expecting us for dinner," she said like she had been making plans like Wale and Usher.

Like everybody else, we followed the heavenly smelling scent all the way to the pavilion where the dinner was being held. Minutes later, we pulled up like an exercise regimen.

There were several long picnic tables set up. Each one was occupied by Native men, women, and children of all ages. I stood there, taking everything in. Native women had come a long way, I thought. In my dreamwalk the red-women not allowed to sit in the same group as the men. They had to eat with the children and wolf dogs.

The chief, whom I met earlier before I went inside the medicine lodge, was standing up and the first one to greet Stacy and me. He had changed out of his traditional Native garb he wore earlier into a pair of blue Levi's tapered jeans, a black Polo Ralph Lauren shirt, and a black pair of suede Converse with a white star. The outfit was casual, but at the same time, it made him look sophisticated. On his wrist was a Cartier watch that wasn't flashy, but you could tell it cost a few dollars. What does he know about Polo? I thought.

"Congratulations! I'm sure Sage would be very proud of you if she was here," the chief said, sticking out his hand. He gave me an inquisitive stare and asked, "What should I call you now that you have formed your medicine?"

I shook the chief's hand, and his grip was purposely firm.

"Lamar is fine." He released my hand, and I took a step back.

"I see," he said in a tone that made me feel like

he had expected this type of reply from me. "The Shaman doesn't advise everybody to conceal their Native name, but I can see he has given you these directions which you have followed. To do otherwise would be foolish."

I didn't immediately reply to the chief's words, because the fact that he was so persistently obsessed with my Native name right off top, set red flags off inside my head. It was clear that I had to choose my words wisely around him.

"I agree. That would be foolish. The food smells real good," I said, smoothly switching topics.

He laughed at how I cunningly went around the subject he really wanted to know about.

"Sadö'swe'da:nih?" he asked.

"What does that mean?" I asked back, deciding right then and there to keep the fact that I learned the Native language while forming my medicine to myself. He had his games, and I played mine.

"It means are you hungry? No one knows more than me how empty your stomach can be after you have formed your medicine. I had some of our best cooks on the reservation prepare some of their favorite Native dishes for you. Many of the elders who you see would like to speak to you. It would be wise of you to soak up as much wisdom as possible from them. My daughter Layla, whom you have met earlier, is not here yet, but I can assure you that she will make an appearance." He paused. "Follow me," he ordered.

He led Stacy and me over to two empty spots at the picnic table, and we both sat down. Every spread in front of me looked delicious. There was mackerel with chopped onions and cilantro. Fried catfish in bread crumbs, baked salmon, bison tacos, venison sausages with jalapeno cheddar cheese in the middle, and various cakes and pastries. Ogá'öshö'öh (good things to eat), I thought.

CHAPTER SIXTEEN:
LAYLA FIRE

I woke up in a state of puzzlement, and my mind was filled with osha:da' (fog). After two years of dreamwalking, this is the very first time I thought about disregarding the shaman's warning about popping peyote capsules back to back. Drake. Once blinded, my flashlight had entered my life without notification. He put me in a situation, and when I saw the same portrait that was in the Native American Book of Prophecy decorating Chief Crowfoot's wigwam, I couldn't believe it. The portrait could only mean one thing: Blacksky was a shifter. How else could he have accomplished returning to our village wearing a gold crown? Theoretically, these things don't happen: This was the equivalent of Hailee Steinfeld in Balmain at a dice game rolling three straight trip six's. The spiritual fix was in, and Blacksky's glorious success made the hair on my legs stand up. I couldn't help but feeling just a little envious at all the attention he got.

As my eyes moved around my bedroom, a warm breeze blew the dreamcatchers that hung over my bed in different directions, like the emotions of people born in July. Why lie? I couldn't stop thinking about the feelings stored inside my heart for Blacksky. Did he know he occupied a space where others attempted to pay rent? My usually tuff exterior was cracked when I saw Mourning Star's mouth wrapped around my husband's dick. His blatant disrespect triggered murderous feelings inside my body that caused me to react without thinking about consequences.

I sat up on my bed and placed both of my feet on the floor. It is customary on our reservation for the elders to cook a big dinner for any young man who has formed his medicine: I wouldn't miss this particular dinner for all the o:wísda' (money) in the world. I stood up and stretched my arms and legs, then I spread my feet shoulder width apart, manicured toes pointed forward, thick thighs parallel to the floor. I started with a hundred squats in a row, two hundred cherry pickers, and one hundred crunches. This was my routine every time I woke up from my dreamwalk. Most of the Native women on our reservation have pear-shaped bodies that made me decide to make fitness a priority in my life.

After working up a nice sweat, I shed my black Lacoste dress and placed one hand behind my back to unhook my bra. I finally got it off after wrestling with it, then slipped my panties down. I crushed both lingerie items into a ball and attempted a six-foot jump shot in the laundry basket that Hoops would make. It looked good when it left my hand, but it came up short. I have to dunk it like Shaq next time, I thought. When I stepped inside my bathroom, I grabbed my hot pink washcloth off the towel rack and bent down to take the stopper out the drain. After that, I opened the hot water faucet and waited a few seconds for the temperature to rise. Once inside, I stood directly under the downpour of water and slid the Dove White Beauty Bar over my skin. It felt good. All bad bitches love Dove. It's the only brand composed from the heavens above.

After washing my hair with Pantene Pro-V, I began scrubbing my thighs. My own delicate touch caused memories of my first night with Blacksky to dance inside my head like a Ciara video. The lustful thoughts made my nipples harden, and I stuck two of my fingers inside my wetness. The slow massage I started on my clit made me close my eyes and picture his long, thick, and juicy dick. It was still fresh in my mind how he stroked me so deeply that he made one of my kidneys shift. Did he know that when it came to my pussy, his dick was boldly going where no man had gone before. When he touched me, he demonstrated emotion, feeling, and way too much love for a primitive red-man, I thought. His eyes were a dead giveaway, and after repeatedly staring into them intensely, it came to me. Lamar was dreamwalking into Blacksky's body for the first time.

Their mannerisms were too identical to be a coincidence, I thought. Their walk, hand gestures, and stare were both the same. As my body shook with orgasm, I couldn't help but wonder if I was the only one in Blackfoot Nation to notice these small changes in him. Clearly Chief Crowfoot had to notice too. This shit was crazy. Who would've thought Lamar was the one the prophecy spoke of? The elders, I thought. As the hot water ran down my body, I quickly decided to keep this to myself and not even tell my parents. They seemed to be just as interested in Lamar as I was, and it was easy to understand why. When I witnessed what he was capable of on his first dreamwalk, it was clear that he was chosen to alter Native history. I believed in that like rich kids believed in Santa. Of course, I wanted to be right by his side like a Jada Kiss song while he accomplished this. Like Michelle for Barack. Like a gun for a stick-up kid. Like a drink for an alcoholic.

When I decided I was clean enough for my

liking, I turned the faucet off and dried myself off with a big yellow yödä'gö'éwata' (bath towel), and ten minutes later, after brushing my teeth, Q-tipping my ears and moisturizing my skin with Jergen's, I walked naked back to my room. Once inside, I reached inside my lingerie drawer and pulled out my blue Victoria Secret panties. My pussy would be in solid gold panties if they sold them, I thought. I quickly slid gold bracelets from Cartier and John Hardy down both of my wrists, followed by my Blue Nest bracelet that I simply adored. When I put on my 14k Bold Chief ring with the diamonds in his eyes, it complimented the two gold necklaces around my neck. After a quick contemplation, I decided to rock some tight blue Norma Kamali bra and leggings with a pair of white Air JORDAN 4 "Lazers." It took me about a half a minute to go with my Something Blue body spray by Oscar de la Renta. The fragrance had a way of putting a man's head on a swivel. I walked over to the full-length mirror and did a few twirls like Kenya Moore. 34, 26, 40. Body like a model. I'm one bad Leo bitch, I thought.

I grabbed my Gucci bag off the nightstand and walked to the kitchen to get one of my bottles of pink Moet out of the refrigerator. When I picked it up, it was perfectly chilled just the way I intended. I opened it up and drank straight out the bottle. I didn't need any glasses, because I wasn't sharing.

When I stepped outside, I dug into my purse and sparked up half of blunt of exotic weed. As the smoke hit my lungs, I could taste the fruity flavor on my lips. I stood there for a second because there was a decision for me to make: should I walk less than a half of to the pavilion where this dinner was being held? What type of bitch would drive that short ass distance? An ignorant and brash bitch, I thought.

Before I left my house, thoughts of shifting into a gwë':di:s (nighthawk) and flying there definitely crossed my mind, just thinking about the type of looks I would've received caused me to grin. After a short deliberation I thought, I could still fly there. Four minutes later, I pulled up in my 2014 white Mercedes S550 spaceship with custom made black Burberry interior the color of Lupita Nyo-ng'o. I had my window down halfway so Blacksky could hear Keith Sweat's "Nobody" coming out of my speakers. I placed both hands on the wheel and sat still, head turned watching the pavilion. He was looking in my direction. I purposely picked the track to drop a seed in his mind, in hopes that later on when he was alone, that seed would sprout a root and grow. The song expressed exactly how I was feeling about him. Real talk. From a real bitch. I hit the blunt again and held the smoke in for twenty seconds like a professional. Music is so powerful, I thought.

Powerful enough to send a subliminal message right in front of a crowd of Natives.

After Keith was done crooning, I pushed a button and shut the engine off. The combination of Moet and marijuana had me ready to go inside the pavilion, eat the food the elders cooked, slap Stacy in the mouth, tell my father to relax, snatch Blacksky up, and take him home to ride his big dick all night. In that order.

I got out of the car slowly, dressed in all blue like I was banging, but don't be brazy, I've always stood on my own two feet. My walk was so seductive that all the Native men, Blacksky included, dropped what they were doing and stared below my waist. I would imagine their eyes got a good look at the diamond-shaped good pussy gap between my thighs. The closer I got to the picnic tables, the more I could hear flat tire sounds and the breath of Native women getting shorter like they were taking long pipe. It was understandable. I was fly enough to make a star get star struck. My father was the first one to get out of his seat and approach me.

He hugged me tightly and said, "As usual, you are late and dressed naked. Plus, you have driven the white man's expensive toy here."

I had to get away from my father as quickly as possible. Clearly he knew nothing about making a grand entrance, and as far as my Benz goes, I'm too fly to stay low key.

A slight wind blew into my father's hair, and the sun was on his face.

"I see you wore the ahšö'nyashä'(clothes) that I picked out for you. oja:nön (funny)," I said, trying to change the conversation. The collar on his Polo was in disarray, so I fixed it real quick.

"Thank you," he said and smiled. "You know how clumsy your dad can be." He paused. "Obviously, this dinner is very important to our family, and by the way you're dressed, I have the impression that you knew this already. Where were you?" he asked with a serious face and suspicious look.

"I fell asleep," I said swiftly. Then I added. "When I woke up, I knew I was running a little late. That's why I drove my car instead of walking here."

Before he could respond, a few greetings sailed around the pavilion, and I quickly sent my love back. What could I say? I'm that girl on the reservation.

"Has it ever occurred to you that sleep more than anyone on this reservation? I pray to the Great Spirit that you aren't pregna-"

"My beautiful daughter has arrived," Mom announced, interrupting him. My mother's long black hair fell behind her shoulders. Her eyes were the color of brown leaves in gahadago:h (in the woods). In the summer, her skin always turned the color of a Spalding basketball. She was wearing a white tee-shirt that said, "We Are The People Of The Hill" Blue Express Jeans and a pair of NewBalance with a pink N symbol. She stepped closer to me, and gave me a Mafia peck on the cheek. She smelled like food, wine, and rose petals.

"Did I miss anything?" I asked her.

She shook her head. "No, I don't think so. Nothing juicy never gets passed around at the elder table, except for wine and recipes. You know the real party never gets started until you arrive."

"Don't tell your daughter that, Robin. She is Sleeping Beauty, and it is already programmed in her mind that she can show up to these events whenever she feels like it," Dad complained.

Mom made a surprised face. "It's true, Red River. You know just as well as I do that our daughter is a very likable person. Which is why I would assume you always send her to handle all of your important business. Instead of us hassling her for being late and wasting even more time, maybe we should go back to our table and let Layla work the room as only she can."

Dad nodded in compliance and made his way back over to his seat without saying one word. He needed to take several seats, I thought. He was smart enough to know there was no use arguing with Mom. My dad was the chief and the face of our family in public, but behind the scenes, he didn't push any buttons. Mom did. Mom was the shifter, and even though she never talked about it, I know she put a bunch of work in to put our family in position. Even at her age, Mom enjoyed hiking, gardening, rock climbing, and hunting.

"I don't know why Dad is all bent out of shape?" I asked.

"Maybe it's because he isn't any closer to finding out if the elders are right about Lamar."

"Has he announced the Native name the Shaman gave him yet?" I asked.

"The answer to your question is no. It seems the Shaman has advised him to conceal his name."

I shook my head. "Have you ever heard of the Shaman doing such a thing?"

"Not in a very long time. What's even more impressive to me is that he actually listened to the Shaman's advice and didn't fall for your father's trickery."

"Did you meet him yet?" I asked.

"Of course I did."

"What do you think?" I asked, picking her brain on some double agent shit.

"Only the weak speak with tongue in cheek. With that being said, he has a strong presence about him. He is definitely not intimidated by anyone here. It's like his spirit is too big for this reservation to hold." She paused. "When I shook his hand, he looked me directly in the eyes with all the confidence in the world, and he has a green thumb. He can be very useful to our marijuana crops."

I didn't know if his spirit was so big, but his dick damn sure is, I thought.

"I haven't even got to know him yet, and you want me to use him to grow our weed?"

"If you can't be used, then you're useless. Besides, by the way you're dressed I'm sure getting to know him won't be a problem. Look at him," she said looking over in his direction. "He looks like that football player from the Giants. What's his name?"

"Odell Beckham Jr.," I said.

"That's his name. If I had met him before your dad, you would be half African-American too! Why don't you go show Lamar why you're the future of this family?"

"You know that's the plan," I said, kissing her on the cheek.

"Before I forget, Mark has been asking me every fifteen minutes when you would get here." She gave me a serious look. "I want you to handle everything with water and not fire."

"Okay," I agreed.

As soon as I turned around and took a few steps toward my seat, Mark came out of nowhere like family when money is involved. He cut my path off, causing a high level of annoyance to shoot through my body. Mark certainly looked the part, twenty years old, money green eyes, a muscular build with medium height and dark hair. He was wearing an Old Navy shirt with no name shorts that looked like the same design as the cloth on the picnic tables. When I looked down, he had on the ugliest open-toe sandals.

When I looked up again, our eyes locked. He looked away. His softness was comical to me. I like real men.

"Hi, Layla!" he greeted. "I asked sanó'ëh (your mother) what time you would arrive."

I rolled my eyes. "So I've heard."

"You look beautiful tonight," he complimented.

I said thank you and caught his eyes on my pussy print. I guess Mark was trying to be nice to get some nookie. He wasn't getting any of this cookie. I'd been down this road with Mark before. Trust me. It's a real short one. This was a few years ago when I thought big feet equaled big dick. Mark wears a size twelve. I was jacking that shit!

After several dates of him being timid, I took control and asked him to see his cock. It shocked him when I got on some soap opera shit. Bold and Beautiful. Even though his dick was the size of a dó:nya'kdá:ne' (inchworm), I still let him eat my pussy until his tongue got tired. He said I tasted spicy and delightful. I'm Layla Fire. It was my best friend Spells that taught me if a man's middle finger is longer than his ring finger, then he at least has a six-inch dick.

"It's nice to see you, Mark," I lied. "But I just smoked a half of a blunt, and I'm hungry. That means I'm trying real hard to make it to my table. Can we speed this up?"

Mark shifted his weight. "I would like for you to sit with me, Layla. Everybody at my table can't wait for you to recite some of your poetry." I paused like my reply needed some thought.

"Absolutely not!" I said. "My parents have already reserved my seat at that table." I pointed to where Blacksky and Stacy were seated. He had a stupid look. He couldn't believe it.

There was a long pause.

"Really!" he said. "The outsider that you wish to entertain is already causing the Native women to act crazy over him. His oisgwanye'da'e:' (brown) skin doesn't mix with tgwehdae (red)," he added.

Like most female Leos, I hated when people tried to get aggressive with me by saying slick shit out of their mouths. I sat there, thinking for a minute. Out of loyalty to my mom, who I just promised. And my respect for the Elders. I didn't slap the grin off Mark's face.

"Forgive me, Mark. I do have a poem for you," I said. "I choose the path of my fate with each small step I take towards my bright future. The chances of me changing course with you is smaller than your tiny dick. I'm the wrong yehsenowa:neh (female boss) to fuck with." An ugly look decorated his face. "You look sick. Life isn't always sunshine and rainbows. Anyone who's ever experienced pain knows, that sometimes it rains too. And when it rains, it floods...rocks, debris, and mud." I waved my bottle of Moet back and forth in his face. "These hands are dipped in the blood of people who are so quick to judge. I've pulled the plug on so many so-called thugs. In only a second your life could be severed; your soul could be lost. A statistic for my records." I violated his personal space. "Would you like to hear some more?"

"No!" he said. He avoided my direct gaze. I held two fingers up, indicating his size.

"Bye, bye, little Mark," I said, making a right flank towards my table. That's the Mark I knew, I thought. All of a sudden, he had an opinion. He was lucky Blacksky didn't know the Native language yet. I could definitely see him having a problem with Mark's choice of words if he did.

When I sat down at the picnic table, I took a swig of Moet to calm my nerves. I looked around. I wasn't seated next to Blacksky like I planned, but three seats away was good enough for me. The loud I smoked had the 0'ga:s 'a:ka (supper) smelling so damn good. I spent the next five minutes with my fork and plate. The loving hands of the elders on these occasions was magically delicious. Great! The only reason why I didn't demolish each dish was because Blacksky was here. Every time I looked up from my plate, he was clocking me.

This whole scenario of me chasing after a man was different to me. Especially a warrior I'm married to in another world. Men chased me because I'm a smart and beautiful girl. I had to admit, so far, Blacksky had me wrapped around his finger doing twirls. I looked at him and Stacy and shook my head. She was with the man I wed. This was clearly a situation I had to freak. Flirt with him right underneath Stacy's nose, which wouldn't be easy since she was giving me a fighting stare every chance she got. I had to smile. Blacksky's wood made Stacy behave like she was from the hood. I understood why. He laid his lumber on me inside the Dreamworld in the summer. As I picked up on him and Stacy's conversation, my heart beat fast. I could hear gawënoda:je's (it's thundering).

"This is good," Blacksky said as he picked up and examined the glass pitcher filled with wine. "I wonder what kind of wine this is?"

"How would I know?" Stacy responded. "It's not like there's a lab-"

"Patient Cottat Le Grand Caillou Sauvignon Blanc," I interrupted in my best French accent. "The Elders always dump it out of the bottle and put it into pitchers. It's their way of getting all the younger Natives to be themselves."'

"I see. It tastes fruity, and it goes down well with these seafood dishes," Blacksky responded.

If you think that tastes fruity, wait until you taste this gáë'hdä:e' (peach), I thought. I couldn't help it. When he spoke, his lips looked so juicy. Everybody at the table sat in silence for a few seconds until Blacksky broke it. "What do young people do for fun on the reservation?"

"The same thing they do in the city: drink, smoke, and party. And you don't have to worry about guns going off. Are you thinking about spending more time with our people?" I asked.

Blacksky stopped sipping his wine, and his expression turned serious. "I guess that depends on if I'm welcome. Nobody wants to chill where they're not wanted. Right or right, though?"

"You're right, baby," Stacy said. "Nobody has time for that Blacktop Indian vs The Reservation Native." Stacy set her cup down and looked me in the eyes. "How come all the sudden you're trying to be so nice? Usually, you don't want anything to do with Blacktop Indians."

Word to my Native mother, this bitch could work for Ringling Brothers. She had all the qualifications. She could make audiences laugh, she rocked funny looking costumes and makeup, and she behaved in a real silly manner. I hate clowns!

"I'm a boss," I said. "Which means I pick and choose the Natives I wanna fuck with. I don't discriminate when it comes to lames." The Natives at our table shook their head in agreement of the truth. Big facts! I took my eyes off Stacy and put them on my husband. "I've been told to offer you a lucrative job by someone who thinks very highly of you."

"And who is that?" Stacy asked with an attitude. This bitch was in everything but another man's arms, I thought.

"This doesn't concern you," I responded.

"When it comes to my man," she teased. "Everything concerns me. Besides, my baby just got a new job today. Right, baby?"

"Where?" I asked.

"Benz Kitchen," Blacksky said.

"You work for Simon Brown?"

"You know him?" he asked.

My thoughts wandered off like a caged animal finally set free. I was very familiar with Simon and his daughter Spells. About twenty minutes earlier, she popped inside my mind. The universe has a strange way of colliding two worlds when you least expected it. Several years back, when a Federal agent from the Syracuse field office named Greg Davis showed up outta the blue, my father told me to get rid of him quietly. After using some unsuccessful scare tactics, I realized that I had to plan, plot, and strategize. I've become accustomed to knocking all my problems off, but I couldn't just kill Greg. Not unless I wanted the entire reservation swimming with twelve looking for his body.

Because of my profession, I'm so well connected, so respected. All of the above led me straight to Spells. I have to admit, when we first met, my first thought was. "She looks fabulous." She was tall and thick in all the right places with a sex appeal that could stop NYC traffic. Spells had a license to get fly like Bessie Coleman with a touch of Phillis Wheatley. We respected each other after she let it be known she wasn't there to compete with me. Our bond was formed. Shortly after that, she instructed me to retrieve one strand of hair from Greg. I completed the small task, and she said, "Give me one week."

Just like she promised, a week later, I received a manila envelope in the mail. There were ten racy photos inside of Greg eating whipped cream outta Spells' ass and pussy. Those photos made me play in my pussy for hours. They were that nasty.

The next time Greg showed his face on the reservation, I had him follow me to my house. When we got there, I told him he might wanna take a seat and get comfortable on my couch, then I told him that I had something juicy for him to hear, but I really meant eat too. He smiled like I had information that benefitted his pale ass. That was silly thinking. I calmly walked into the kitchen, and I made sure that my ass shook a little more than usual. Seconds later, I was back. This time I was the one with the smile. I was holding some chocolate syrup and a manila envelope that had his future inside it.

"What's that?" he asked me.

I disrespectfully threw the envelope on his lap. "I want two hundred thousand for those, or your sexy wife will get copies." You should've seen the look on his face when he saw the photos! Who gives people new 3-D layouts of their external world? That would be me. He said he never remembered taking the pictures. Spells was an evil bitch, I thought.

"What's the chocolate syrup for?" he asked.

"I want you to toss my salad, too," I responded.

After Greg was done handling his business, I creamed on his tongue, and then he wrote a check for that chicken. Back then, the money was a dope-girl start-up kit that put us in the loop. We never looked back. Spells was just as diabolical as me, so this Blacksky working for her father thing had the potential of going a few different ways; If Spells found out that her new employee had a big ass dick, her next move would be a spell. Afterward, Blacksky would become her personal pleasure, and then she would train him to be ruthless. Maybe Simon would pair him with Poc, a young Eastside general that let his gun go. No doubt, he would teach Blacksky his street smarts.

"Do you hear me talking to you?" Blacksky asked.

"I'm sorry," I said. "Sometimes I zone out. I've been to Benz Kitchen several times; they have great food, and Simon is good people ."

"I thought so too," he said. "On another note, ever since you pulled up in that whip, I've heard whispers about your poetry. I like to play with words too. Spit something for me."

"My pleasure," I said, standing up. I waved my hands, and the entire pavilion quieted down. A light show of power on my soil. Rita Ora in West London, a royal bitch, but classy. "Dear Great Spirit, my creator, father of mankind, forgive me for my sins, forgive me for my crimes. Your life is about to end. That means you're running out of time." I paused to look at Stacy. "She was a killer. I could see it in her eyes, a monster with a stare so bold. It made me shiver with a chill so cold. I froze. In these eyes, I saw a rage so old; an ancient savagery, pure madness. She seemed to embody imminent danger. Her eyes were the epitome of violence and danger. Immobilized by a sudden fear as I stared at this monster's fiery glare. Unable to run, unable to scream, I was shocked by the image of this ghastly fiend. Never in my wildest dreams did I imagine I would one day see, my mirror's reflection replaced by this grizzly monster sneering at me" I did a sexy curtesy, and all my friends exploded in cheer. How could he top that shit? I thought. I'm nice with my shit. That's a whole fact.

Blacksky stood up while simultaneously taking another sip of his wine. Once fully erect, he paused as if he were gathering his thoughts. Behind him, I could see the smiles on mostly all of the elders' faces. Clearly Blacksky was tipsy, and he had to be tired from forming his medicine, which meant the elders would most likely be in for a show they already anticipated when they set the wine on the tables.

"Everybody give Layla another round of applause," he urged. When people did as he requested, he looked over at me and winked. "That was so beautifully dark, don't you agree," he added in a sarcastic tone. "It's a full moon tonight, and thanks to the elders, this French wine is tasting real good. Under these stars, my swagger has doubled like police presence in all-black neighborhoods. I just spent six hours searching for my soul within; it confirmed what I already knew. I was born to win." He paused to look in my direction. "Your eyes commit treason and expose who you really are even through clever disguises, expensive clothes, and your exotic car. The average fool will confuse nothing to lose with something to prove." He directed his gaze toward Mark. "Until I break his bones, leave his body battered and bruised." His words caused me to start thinking, and I missed his next few lines. The only reason he would have to direct a subliminal message towards Mark is if he understood the Native language. Impossible, I thought. "Life is about choices ultimately, the proverbial fork in the road. There is no great secret mystery, no obscure hidden code. First time on the reservation, how can he be so bold? Easily outshining his competition without wearing any gold. My words make your girlfriends wet like reservation swimming holes."

Native men and women broke out in pandemonium as if Blacksky had just given every audience member a car like Oprah.

"That's right, baby! Talk that Blacktop shit," Stacy boasted, squeezing him around his waist.

I finished the rest of the Moet and set the bottle down gently.

"That was real cute," I said.

"I'm not finished yet," he responded.

"Oh yes you are, góíhsagih (monkey)," Mark said, taking small baby steps toward Blacksky.

"Don't forget the rules of the Onoda'ge:ono', Mark," Dad warned.

"It is him that has forgotten his place," Mark said as he pointed at Blacksky.

There was an angry murmur from the elders that stood around my father. They seemed upset that lowly Mark would dare utter a reply after the chief had spoken. Liquid courage is called that for a reason, I thought.

"I can see that the wine has taken over all your emotions, but in case you forgot, I decide who is in or out of place on this reservation. This dinner is now over," Dad announced. "Lamar, the elders have readied one of the guest cabins for you and Stacy to sleep in tonight. The cabin has been stocked with more food and wine at your request, Stacy. Enjoy the rest of your night, Lamar. I have a feeling it will be a long one." Some of the elders chuckled at my Dad's joke, but I didn't.

The darkness of it is a symbol of its violence. Vicious waves swept into the night, shattering the silence. It all started with rain, an ominous omen of the hour, and with a rancorous cacophony it grew to a symphony of power. With a reverberating boom, a crack broke into the dark sky. Angry winds tearing at limbs sweeping debris a mile high. Its howl a testament to its rage. Naked in my bed, unable to close my eyes without this storm building within my body, I stood up and opened my bedroom window.

I shifted into a gwë':di:s (nighthawk), and with one flap of my wings, I flew into the night. The view above the trees was spectacular. There wasn't a cloud in the sky to hate on the full moon and the starlight. As the nighttime air passed through my feathers, I could smell fresh jó:sgwa:ön (cow) manure in the óéhda' (soil). Seconds later, I slowly descended onto a tree branch directly in front of the cabin that Blacksky and Stacy occupied. After a few minutes of staring into their bedroom, they both walked in my line of sight. He had taken off the jeans he had on earlier and was stripped down to his boxers and socks. Stacy had the same dress on. Blacksky seated himself on the bed while she remained standing.

Stacy bit her bottom lip and said, "I've been thinking about the way you kissed me inside my room. That was the best kiss I ever had." She walked over to him in a sexy manner. I could see that her eyes were full of passion and French wine.

"You're lucky your mom came home because just like you say all the time, all hell was about to break loose."

"Nobody's here to stop us now," she responded.

A breeze gusted up from the east and blew Stacy's dress up to mid-thigh, exposing her clean-shaven pussy.

"I imaged you were naked under that dress all night," Blacksky confessed.

Even though I sat there literally riding the pine while Stacy would most likely be riding the dick I wanted, I couldn't deny their desire for each other. they had some Jay-Z and Queen Bey love going on that I wanted.

"Your hunches have always been good," Stacy said, placing her hand on his bare chest.

He kissed her and slowly moved his hand between her thighs, causing Stacy to let out a soft moan. Suddenly, he broke their kiss off.

"What's wrong, baby?"

"I have to tell you something before we do this," he said in an honest tone. "I'm a virgin, and even though it hasn't been easy staying abstinent, I never stuck my dick in anybody. Unless you want to count the imaginary women in my dreams," he joked. "You're special to me, Stacy. Just know that. I would've waited all eternity if I had to. All I ever needed and wanted is right here in front of me. It's time to take it to the next level like you said at your house. Let's make love, fuck, and then make love again. I have to ask you something."

A small tear fell from Stacy's eye. "Ask me?"

Blacksky stood up and let his boxers fall to the floor. Stacy gasped and stood there in frozen admiration.

"Do you think you can take all this dick?"

"Yes! Take your time, because I want it inch by inch," she requested.

When he backed up and took a seat on the bed, my pussy was soaking wet. I could see his big dick from where I sat, standing straight up like the US Armed Forces for the National Anthem.

"Take your dress off slowly," he ordered. In

one quick motion, Stacy did as she was told, and I had to admit, her body was sexy.

"You're so beautiful," he complimented as she stepped forward in a sexy strut.

"What now?" she asked, placing her hands on her hips.

"I want to taste your pussy," he declared.

When Stacy threw her right leg over his shoulder, I glided down to the ground and shifted back into human form. Quickly, I ran behind a pine tree without being noticed. When I focused my eyes ahead, Blacksky was slowly leaving a small trail of kisses on the way up to her pussy. Stacy let out a loud moan and started tugging lightly on her own nipples. His tongue began to separate the folds on her juicy cunt, and he didn't just lick it, he French kissed it with the skill of a seasoned pro. The slurping sounds that his mouth was able to conjure up sounded like a how to eat pussy song.

"Your pussy tastes like a Native delicacy," he said.

With each swipe of his tongue, Stacy arched her back and shivered. I could see her juices running down her leg. Jealousy and envy swept through my body. Why didn't he eat my pussy like this? Without warning, he stuck two long fingers inside of her, and she let out a cry of passion that made me start a slow massage on my clit. She cried out several more times as wave after wave of orgasm shook her body to its core.

"Please stop," she begged.

Blacksky stood up and kissed Stacy, giving her a taste of her own juices. I could see her knees buckle with another orgasm. Before she could protest, he picked her up off her feet, and she wrapped her legs around the small of his back. He didn't just ram his big dick inside of her unprofessionally, I thought. He slowly started teasing her opening with his dick.

"Are you ready for this long dick?"

If she wasn't, I damn sure was, I thought.

Before she could answer his question, he slid what looked like the perfect amount of dick inside of her. The impact seemed to take her breath away. Her fingers dug into his back, and he suddenly began moving as if a slow African drumbeat went off inside of his head. I could see sweat slide down the muscles in his back. Right in front of my eyes, he was ritualistically fucking Stacy like his dick was voodoo. Ironically, it was the same stroke of death that he had me open with, but better. Had my pussy been used as practice for Stacy's? I thought.

For the next five minutes, I watched his dick sliding in and out of her pussy slowly, her wetness coating his pole with a sticky white substance.

"You know much I love you?" Blacksky asked, never breaking his stroke.

"Yes!" she yelled as fresh tears fell down her

face.

"Is this my pussy?" he asked, spinning around and placing her on the bed in the missionary position.

When Stacy didn't answer fast enough, he began to discipline her pussy with long measured strokes. Seven seconds later, her moans told the entire reservation that Blacksky was hitting the right spot. His body in this world was more sculptured and chiseled. It reminded me of a Greek mythology god.

"Ah!" Stacy cried out, pulling violently on the sheets.

Suddenly, he took his body weight off of her and slowly rubbed the head of his dick against her clit. Out of the blue, clear streams of liquid shot into the air like someone else in the room had turned on a water hose. Blacksky gazed at Stacy as if she had grown two heads. Oh, Great Spirit... My own pussy was dripping wet. The mind-blowing scene caused my body to go paraplegic. Stacy's eyebrows moved around frantically, exposing that she was just as surprised as he was.

"What was that?" he asked in a worried tone.

"I don't know," she said in between pants. "That's the first time my pussy has ever done something like that."

"Do you want me to stop?"

"Please don't," she begged. "I can take it."

A sinister smile appeared on Blacksky's face as his massive dick throbbed like it had its own heartbeat. My thighs got hot. I've never been so aroused in my young life.

A moment later, he went back in balls deep, knocking the wind out of Stacy and the air out of her pussy. The impact sounded like the noise a whoopee cushion would make.

"Oh, Great Spirit, Lamar. Yes. Yes. That feels so good," Stacy said.

Unable to hold back my desire any longer, my body started operating on auto-pilot, causing my wet pussy to explode in climax and fertilize the soil beneath my feet with juices. Disoriented, I clumsily stepped backward as if I were drunk off the powerful orgasm passing through my body. A small tree twig cracked beneath my feet. Pop! The loud sound made Blacksky pause mid-stroke.

"Who's out there?" he asked, walking towards the window.

In a split second, I shifted and flew off into the night. The wind from the west was blowing hard, but mild in the east, like a Kendrick Lamar album. As my wings cut through the night air, deep thoughts took over my mind. After fucking Stacy so good, he may never get rid of her. That's where I come in at, I thought. Clearly Stacy had my Mandingo warrior in management like Ann Wolf, and from the look of things, she was bringing out the best in him. I had to wrestle him away from her so I could get all of his hard combinations inside of me, I thought. Are they blind? They cannot see that there are two different worlds inside of me. I cannot believe that what we perceive is all that we receive. I have been open. I have been honest. My mind is focused, but my eyes are jaundiced. Gönóöhgwa' (I love you), Blacksky!

CHAPTER SEVENTEEN:
BLACKSKY GETS TO THE BAG

At 7 a.m. on Friday, I stood at the Centro bus stop on E. Genesse St and Beach, waiting patiently on public transportation. With the exception of the sun, birds, squirrels, and a few vehicles, nobody else in the neighborhood was outside. I looked down at my watch and wished it was Cartier. ETA ten minutes. As I stood there, my thoughts drifted off like a soda bottle thrown into the Erie Canal. The last five days had embedded a kaleidoscope of images and feelings within my soul.

After losing my virginity to Stacy, I couldn't help but feel like I'd taken a small step towards manhood. Unfortunately, the aftermath of the act made me come to the realization of my possibility of being in love with three women. One more than Mr. Cheeks. "And I didn't wanna let none of them go." At the reservation dinner the Elders threw, the wine made me assume that Chin-cha-bee, my wife in the dreamworld, and Layla were the same person. This is what the Shaman warned me about, I thought. Layla was beautiful but so sick. The only thing that could tame her was my Deadwood Dick. She was a fierce little bitch. I'm intrigued. Her style was Clementine Desseaux, Pocahontas, and a splash of Katniss Everdeen. Her freckles were diverse, and her personality was mean, and this wasn't all a dream like the stars in Christopher Wallace's limousine. Chocolate wanted romance for the streets of Syracuse, But I wanted to give the world something they've never seen. Alien negro cock genes concealed inside Balmain jeans. Ancient scrolls for all you trolls that love to read scientific specialties.

I smiled because there are those who will try to copy my perspective recipe, not knowing my revolutionary destiny is to make pussy get wet for me. If it is your time to shine, then may I suggest that you don't stand next to me. Place your head inside the pillory and watch me walk the road to glory. This is a tribute story for all the greats that came before me.

A few minutes later, the big blue bus known as Centro pulled up right next to curb. When the door opened, I walked right up the small flight of stairs and deposited four quarters. The driver of the bus looked like Hal Williams from 227. Somewhere in this world, we all have a twin, I thought. A low beeping noise filled the air, an indication to Hal that I inserted the correct change into the machine.

"Good morning, young man! Do you need a transfer?" the driver asked with an inquisitive look.

"Yes, thank you," I said.

The bus was uncrowded, and because of my new shifting gift, I was able to systematically scrutinize every passenger not named Blacksky. One middle-aged white man wearing 'Beats By Dre' over his ears, a blue v-neck tee shirt, black Levi's jeans, and blue Santoni sneakers. My hatred of the Patriots made me quickly realize how much he looked like Danny Amendola. From his gestures while he recited a song, you could see he had some African-American swagger. I secretly wondered what he was listening to? Probably the best of Justin Timberlake, I thought.

These are the kind of wholesome American white men who occasionally chose to dip their sticks in the chocolate pudding and miraculously ended up with an actress or sports star. How bizarre is that? These things do happen, I thought. Seated two seats down from him are two young black men. They were wearing red bandannas, white tees, blue jeans, Gucci Belts, Jordans, and matching Hermes watches. In my assuming eyes, they both looked like the beneficiaries of the Syracuse dope game.

Nowadays, in every hood in America, a few Simone Biles of the opiate could turn average nickel and dime hustlers into bonafide thousandaires, but if they only knew what was in their pot of gold at the end of the get money rainbow, they would be scared.

As I walked, an invisible magnet started pulling me to the back of the bus. It wasn't like I didn't have any knowledge of the sacrifice Rosa Parks and countless others made so I can sit anywhere. Two steps later, my eyes set on a beautiful white woman in her late twenties. "Becky with the good hair," I whispered to myself. Please believe me when I say, it wasn't her fresh to death salon styled hair with blonde highlights, each strand meticulously brushed down the small of her back, or the fact that her perky breasts, light-green eyes, olive-colored skin, and pretty feet would send a telegram to any man's dick. Nope, it wasn't her beauty that had me mesmerized. It was her round booty. Have you ever seen an ass so juicy that you could see it poking out from the sitting position? She has more óä'hgwawänöe' (cake) than Little Debbie, I thought. She was rocking a Utility Shift dress worn open over a lingerie slip dress with L.K Bennet suede sandals that would make Elvis take a second look. In a materialistic way, her Fendi studded leather satchel officially made me the brokest individual on the bus.

As I got closer to the seat that I picked inside my head, her scent gave me a tingly sensation. It was as if she ordered a special arousal oil from the back pages of a magazine just for moments such as these. A white woman with a pretty face and round posterior of a black woman. I immediately imagined many negros tucking their race cards deep inside their billfolds at first glance at this Ashley Graham look alike. This is the type of Caucasian persuasion that Beyonce alluded to on 'Lemonade'. She slowly examined my hair, face, neck, chest, arms, dick print, and shoes. Suddenly, our eyes locked in on one another, and we engaged in an early morning stare down. High noon style. Satisfied with what is in front of her, she smiled broadly like a Kardashian at the Million Man March. So many different flavors of niggas with good hearts. Sensing my imperturbable confidence, one of her eyes dropped real low like the sexy Tracee Ellis Ross.

Bingo, I thought. We have action. I'm rocking Axe body wash black, a black Polo Ralph Lauren shirt, vest, pants, and black Bruno Magli dress shoes. Notable sources of inspiration while I picked out my clothes this morning; Hova and The Snowman. "Go Crazy". I looked good enough to have my own fragrance, I thought. My slogan will be unforgettable to your ears, ladies. "Cologne that entices sexy women who love men with substantial pipe game."

It definitely had a catchiness to it that could make women get in "Formation'. I smiled at the belief I had in myself and took a seat directly across from my mystery woman. I sat there in momentary contemplation for a few seconds trying to figure out what opening I should go with, but before I could make my mind up, she stole the ball and shot her own jump shot.

"First day on the job?"

"Are you a psychic?"

She smiled. "Truthfully, there's nothing supernatural about my guess at all. One if I told you that I've taken this same bus to work for a year and some change to save mileage on my car, would you believe me? You're actually the first black teenager to get on this bus, at this specific time, wearing a nice suit. So I figured that you must be headed somewhere important."

Her response immediately indicated that she had brains to go along with her nice body. She was a challenge. Which meant this was the perfect opportunity to put Chocolate's teachings to good use. I paused before I spoke and switched my demeanor into an actor like Trump does in public.

"Who wouldn't believe a face as beautiful as yours. It has honesty written all over it. Thank you for complimenting me on my suit, but it's the person inside the suit that needs your attention." I paused. "To answer your question, though, it is my first day of work."

"Congratulations!" she said. "I remember how I felt when I got hired for my first job. Where are you working?"

"Benz Kitchen," I responded proudly.

Weirdly, her eyes sprung open all of a sudden. My answer seemed to cause a change in her facial expression.

"I've never been there before, but the word around town is they have delicious food. Did the owner give you a job title yet?" she inquired.

"Actually no, they haven't. That's nothing for me to worry about, though. I've always been great at adapting to different situations. I'm hoping they plug me in anywhere someone's needed."

"I know what you mean," she agreed. "Doing the same task over and over again at work can get mundane, but everybody has to start somewhere. Heck! Even Obama worked at Baskin-Robbins. It's called your humble beginnings," she added, throwing her hair back over her shoulder.

Her comment caused me to glance out the window behind her. The morning sky was free of clouds. Tall buildings suddenly started to appear in the background with heavy traffic. We were almost downtown. Time is winding down; the clock is ticking, I thought. I had to make my move. Unexpectedly, the phone inside her Fendi bag rang in a waterfall ringtone. She scrambled through her bag and fished out an iPhone 6, then she paused, looked at the screen, frowned, and held up one finger for me to give her a minute. According to Yo Gotti, the iPhone 6 had been used for tracking African Americans, so he was about to buy a beeper and fall back from technology. How could he accomplish this if it was always going down in the DM, I thought.

"Hello, Harry," she greeted in an aggravated tone. Fuck, I thought. This Harry fella was about to take up whatever time I had left to make an exhilarating connection.

"Are you trying to tell me that the narcotics file just up and disappeared from your office?" she asked in disbelief. "Your incompetence really bothers me, and you're a royal pain in my ass, Harry. Do you realize how important that file is to both of our careers?"

There must have been some highly classified shit in that file, I thought. After all, my mind is a palace of 'imagiNative' scenarios. What did Prince Harry do with that cream-colored file? Was the substance white or tan? If it was that tan, was it that Meghan Markle? When you opened the Ziplock bag up, did it sparkle? What would be the Royal Observers' reaction if Harry married a nigga as dark as charcoal? I could picture the clock at Windsor Castle stopping. This was no big deal for most proud African-Americans watching, little did

Britain know, we've been popping. Once you go black, you never go back. There are no more options. Suddenly, the bus came to a stop right in front of Dunkin Donuts.

"Did you question everybody?" she asked Harry. "I see. When?"

She glanced up towards the front of the bus at the digital clock, and then she ran her fingers through her hair. "No!" she said. "My bus just got downtown. Tell Jhon to meet me inside my office in five minutes."

She hung up the phone and placed it inside her Fendi bag.

"I'm so sorry for being rude."

"An apology is never needed when you're taking care of business," I said. "These things do happen."

She smiled at Chocolate's slogan.

"In my case, you're so right," she agreed, following me as I exited the Centro bus. "I really have to get going, but before I get going, I would like to wish you good luck today."

"Thank you."

"Since we catch the same bus in the morning, I'll see you Monday."

"Okay. I hope your day sounds better than it did on the phone," I said.

"Thank you so much."

When she turned around and walked away, I

stood there looking at her ass, and what direction she was headed in. After she took several steps down N. Salina St, I quickly concluded that she worked around the corner for the DA.

When I got off the bus in front of Benz Kitchen, there was one truck in the parking lot: A money green Ford F-150 Raptor. It looked like a monster truck to me, and you could tell that whoever drove it had a personality just as big as the truck. Simon and Sharon's luxury vehicles were nowhere in sight. I assumed they had the kinda money to come in when they felt like it. I glanced down at my watch. It was 7:40 a.m. My father told me that the Greasy Spoon usually opened its doors at 8, so I was twenty minutes early. It was quiet, so when my Bruno Magli's hit the pavement, it caused an echo like I was the 'Sandman'. I stopped to bend over and pick up a stack of Post-Standard Newspapers.

There were lights on inside the establishment, and when I pulled on the front door, it was open. Upon entrance, the small bell over the threshold made a noise and alerted whoever was driving the Ford F-150. "Autumn Leaves" by Leslie Odom JR was coming from the jukebox in the corner and the smell of sautéed onions with home fries, eggs, bacon, sausage, and corn beef hash, filled my nose with its delicious smells. As I made my way to the back to finally meet who was responsible for making my stomach growl, those same watchful eyes of African-American leaders from before stared at me in full awareness of my capricious plight to join them in suspended air. Their gazes were warranted because it was a "big day in a small town" for me. Brandy Clark.

If Obama's path to glory had gone through Baskin-Robbins, then I couldn't have a quarrel about mine going through Benz Kitchen. According to Chocolate, these were the kind of ominous events that would influence my writing career. At the very least, I could stack o:wísda' (manage money)for my school clothes and do some networking on the south side. Suddenly, I heard my name being called over the rhythm and blues tunes.

"Lamar! I'm back here, young blood!" I looked in the direction of the voice and walked towards it. When I bent the corner, a dark-skinned man with a wide smile on his face and gleam in his eyes was standing by the grill. He had an afro tucked neatly inside a black hairnet with all-white chef scrubs on and a pair of Chippewa Service Boots. Dangling from his neck was a gold ji:yäh (dog) chain. He turned and faced me.

"Gator," he said, looking me in the eyes and extending his os'óhda' (hand). I pushed my hand forward, and we did a traditional Syracuse handshake. When I looked deep into his face, I guessed that Gator had to be about fifty. David

Robinson's NBA number. From the eye-contact to the handshake, his demeanor was old-school authentic and militant. Real recognize real.

He looked me up and down. "Simon told me to be on the lookout for a sharp young man, but damn! You're cleaner than the inside of a Clorox bottle in that suit."

"Thank you," I responded. "Do I look like the type of young man you would tip nicely for a job well done?" I asked, brushing some imaginary dirt off my shoulders.

He smiled, exposing three permanent gold teeth on the top row of his mouth. "Shit! You look like one of them light-skinned niggas on the Golden State Warriors without the jumper."

"Yeah, right!" I said. "Ask those musty Cougars about number 10 on the Bulldogs. They know my shot is water."

"Never heard of you," Gator challenged. "As a matter fact, you look like The Weeknd on a budget, so can I call you the Weekday?"

I laughed because when dark-skinned brothers cracked jokes on brothers with lighter skin, they would always say the same group of celebrities. Drake, The Weeknd, Chris Brown. I didn't mind, though. I like being put in a category of people with money.

"Only if I can call you SnoopSnipes?"

"SnoopSnipes," he repeated.

"You have a face like Wesley Snipes with the body of Snoopdog."

Our eyes locked, then we broke out in laughter. My African American bloodline and Native side were more different than the scripture that's right in front of your face. I'm so ahead of the field. This is Carl Lewis in a foot race. You should feel significant to be a participant on an epic journey where wordplay brilliance, swagger, and imagination come together. If you're pursuing pleasure, ladies, I'm honored to be your heavenly host. Enjoy this stronghold of your mind, from the aspiring author who does the most. Every man has a story, but this is straight from the horse cock's mouth. Italian stallion dick for black, white, and Latina mothers who love to fuck in three different positions on expensive covers. If your time is a precious gift, then hurry up and be my new lover. I'll crack those legs open and gently stick my longpipe deep inside your pussy until you beg me for more. Chocolate's teachings forbid pillow talking, so you can be my secret whore. Suddenly, I heard two things simultaneously: A car pulling up inside the parking lot, and Gator calling my name.

"Lamar! As long as you have a sense of humor and an open mind, you're going to do fine at The Greasy Spoon," Gator said, fully snapping me out of my imagination.

"Are you sure about that?" I asked. "I hear

Sharon is tuff on new employees. I hope she doesn't try to run me off because I need this job."

My understanding of altering my style and conversation to fit each person I'm dealing with had soared to new levels after my shift, so my question was wrapped in hidden motive. I needed more information on this 'bama conceived deep down south.

"The real question is, are you going to let her run you off? At the end of the day, Sharon is a strong young black woman. Do you know what type of men freeze up around her?"

"Tell me," I said.

"Weak ass men! Are you a weak man?" Gator asked, looking me up and down.

I gave him my yeah right face. "Absolutely not."

"Good. There are two types of men in this world, and since your in the presence of the Syracuse general, I'm going to break those two down for you, but before I do, tell me who the original Cuse Town general is?"

My mother's dislike of Keith Smart came to mind. Gator probably would've stomped me if I wasn't a Syracuse sports historian.

"The authentic General," I said. "Great passing ability, ball handle, defense, and an automatic scoop shot. Sherman Douglas."

Gator smiled. "You're the first young man to

get that question right. I'm impressed. There's players like Sherman, and men who sit the bench. I'm the type of man who likes to come off the court fully drenched. Players don't chase women, women chase them. Always make a woman deal with your terms, or they'll make you squirm."

Gator's advice made me associate wisdom with the gray hairs on top of his head. I thought about the mystery white woman on Centro.

"Preach!" I said, egging him on for more of his knowledge.

"Not this morning, young blood, but I will give you a small sermon to wrap your mind around. Listen carefully. You're talking to T.D. Jakes of the ghetto. I don't care if a woman is hotter than two niggas selling drugs in Auburn N.Y., don't pay her no mind when you see the rest of those thirsty dudes sweating her. Eventually, that's gonna get underneath her skin, and she's going to wonder why you're so calm around her. In her mind, this makes you different from her other stalkers. You feel me?" he asked.

"Yes!"

"A true player has a plethora of beautiful women that he can fuck whenever he chooses. This keeps him cool when a new beautiful woman approaches him."

"Are you saying that would work on Sharon?" I asked.

His facial expression turned to a suspicious one.

"You're bold. I don't think nobody Simon hired has ever thought about fucking the bosses daughter on the first day."

"Whoa!" I said. "Easy. You didn't hear me say nothing about fucking. I just wanted to know something about the people I'm working around," I lied. Truth be told. He made the right call, like Nick Buonicotni. I am bold. Bolder than a Kayne West microphone snatch from the president. You would be too if you suddenly found out you were a walking enigma full of ambition. Sharon probably was a strong black woman, but even tuff women need a source of pleasure. How would she react when I showed her the weapon of mass destruction? Just because she was a strong black woman, she immediately qualified for a honey tone piece of steel wrapped ever so neatly in a Crown Royal bag. A long and thick delicacy for women.

"Chill out! I respect audacity. Sharon is a tuff nut to crack, though, because she was raised with game from both parents. I've seen her turn some of the wildest niggas in Syracuse into marshmallows. My advice is don't go down that road until your paper is right, and when she sends you on a job, impress her and complete the task with style." He paused. "Sharon will be in here today, but until then, it's just me and you like Tony! Toni! Tone my brother. So let's get to work." He picked the spatula back up and turned over .the home fries.

"What do you need me to do, Gator?"

"Go grab that 'House Special' sign that's in the window and the marker that comes with it."

Fifteen seconds later, I was back in the kitchen, erasing yesterday's house special with a dry washcloth.

"What's going on here?" I asked.

Gator turned to face me. "As long as old Gator here is the chef at Benz Kitchen, Fridays will always be fish Fridays. That's the ritual around here. Today I'm cooking fried haddock with salmon pasta and a tasty beverage on the side for ten dollars."

"Is that it?"

"Nope!" he said. "Let them know we got slices of blueberry cheesecake for the low low."

"And what's that?"

"Five dollars," he said.

Five dollars, I thought, while I walked over to the window to place the sign back, must be some good ass cheesecake.

"Put one of those aprons on over that nice suit of yours!" Gator yelled. I went over to the row of coat hooks and removed an apron with pockets on each side, then I took my last ten dollars and placed five dollars in each pocket. Money brings money. If they wanted me to be a hagä:gwas (collect fares), then I'll be the best waiter Benz Kitchen has ever seen, I thought.

Once the apron was on properly, I walked over to the jukebox and pressed a button to review my choices. Simon had some SWV, Mary J, R. Kelly, Next, and many more. I stopped at Chicago '85. For those who missed it, it's a classic album. Mood music! When the CD began, I smiled. Talk to them, Dave, I thought.

One song later, my first two customers came strolling in. Both were women. One was light-skinned like yours truly with a cute face and blonde hair styled in half curls. 36, 26, 39. Nice! She was wearing a lace cardigan, a high-waisted skirt, and heels.

The other woman was Spanish with a face like Kirby, the Fashion Fair model. She had the same sexy mouth, I thought. 32, 24, 39. Body like a Coke bottle. She was rocking the shit out of this pink blouse with matching heels and cropped blue jeans.

While the two women took their seats, I sat in the cut like peroxide. As they talked, I gave myself the once-over and readied myself to rise above Syracuse mediocrity. Pen and pad in hand, I approached their table with swagger and spotted the blue Ford Focus RS they arrived in. Their eyes took me in slowly like I was the one on the menu, and traces of smiles slowly decorated their lips. With looks that could stop traffic, It didn't surprise me that whatever they were talking about wasn't important when I pulled up.

"Good morning, ladies," I greeted. "My name is Lamar. Would you like something to drink while you look at your menus, or are you ready to place your orders?"

"Es ud Espanol?" the Latina woman asked.

I shook my head. "No!"

"Has anyone ever told you that you look like that fine ass receiver from the Giants?" the light-skinned one added.

I looked into her eyes for a moment and shrugged. "Maybe once or twice. I'm sorry, ladies. Can you please let me take your orders before more people show up, and I fall behind?" I asked, keeping it business.

"How rude of us," the black girl said. "Bring us two orange juices, but tell Gator that it's for Tee-Tee and Rosey. Plus two breakfast specials with sausage."

"Will that be all?" I asked pump faking like I wrote all that shit down.

Tee-Tee dropped her eyes down to my crotch. "Tell Gator we would like those thick, long, sausages. Not those round ones."

Her aggression was veiled and indirect. Just the way I like it. "That's a lot of meat, ladies," I said with a smile. "Are you sure you can handle all of that?"

"Yes!" they both said in unison.

I laughed. "Excuse me. I'll be right back with your drinks in a second."

As soon as I turned my back, their conversation started again. My special powers had increased my hearing tenfold, so as I headed to see Gator, I could hear them word for word.

"He is not lying, girl," Tee-Tee said.

"Lying about what?" Rosey asked.

"About having enough meat for both of us."

"Bitch, you're delusional. He didn't say anything like that. Let me guess, though. You think he has the big one you've been looking for?"

"I'm telling you Rosey when he was just standing here, his hands and feet both were long. Look at his walk. It caused my big dick alarm to go off."

"This is the same alarm that predicted Calvin had a big dick?"

"That was a false alarm, bitch," Tee-Tee admitted.

They both laughed.

"Even if he does have a big dick, he looks like a high school student, and I bet he doesn't know how to use it," Rosey assumed.

"No wonder all these teachers are fucking the kids. If he was my student, I'd put that ass in detention by his self. Once the other kids left for the day, I would bend over the desk and let him bust it open."

They both laughed again. Coincidently, the jukebox was playing 'One woman Man' while they talked recklessly behind my back.

"Are you just gonna stand there or give me the order?" Gator asked.

"Two women named Tee-Tee and Rosey asked for you by name. They want two breakfast specials with long sausage links and two orange juices."

Gator gave me a long look. "How them hoes looking today?"

"Fine as hell," I admitted.

"Be careful," Gator cautioned. "It's Friday. You ain't seen fine yet. Wait until all the rest of those ghetto fabulous women come in here." He paused. "I bet Rosey thought you were Spanish, didn't she?"

"How did you know?"

He looked at my hair that I had in a ponytail.

"You could pass for one of them Spanish niggas. Shit! If you were upstate and pulled up on a dorm, you would have a bowl of rice, beans, and plantains."

"Get the fuck outta here!" I said.

"That's a fact, Jack! And most of the black men would be sizing you up." He shook his head in displeasure. "Black people oppressing black people. Anyways, If you like big tips, you better be whoever the customer envisions you as. Black, white, Spanish, and Jamaican. The only color that matters this summer for you is green." Gator gave me a quizzical look. "Before it slips my mind, I want to know what you know about that Chicago '85 album?"

Does he know who I think I am? I thought. The collector of knowledge.

"Blackstreet." I said one word.

He laughed a hearty laugh. "You got some shit with you, boy!"

"Maybe a little," I confirmed.

As Gator filled my order, his skill level as a chef was on full display. He gracefully made two plates, two orange juices with vodka, and kept an eye on the fried fish and pasta.

"Isn't it a little too early to be drinking?" I asked, looking at my watch.

"If you say so, Dr. Phil! We don't concern ourselves with why people do what they do. We fill the order. Besides, alcohol equals bigger tips for you." He placed everything on a huge serving tray. "Okay, son," he said. "Get out there and get your money. "

I quickly scooped up the serving tray in my right hand like I'd seen countless others doing on TV. Unbeknownst to them, they provided me with the experience I lacked. When I got close to my destination, I set the entire tray down at an empty table and distributed each item one by one. I observed both women observing me with an easy smile on my face. "Can I get you two beautiful ladies anything else?"

"Did Gator add the vodka to our orange juice?" Tee-Tee asked with a slight smile.

"Taste and see," I advised like SWV.

They both took small sips from their glasses.

"Perfect," Tee-Tee said. Rosey smiled but didn't speak. It was as if the right words to say to me had momentarily escaped her.

"Is this your first day of work?" Tee-Tee asked, while seductively biting into one of the sausage links.

"Yes."

"You're a natural, Papi," Rosey said in her Hispanic accent. "Simon did well by hiring you."

"Did he!" Tee-Tee agreed.

I hit them with the smile my parents gifted me. "Thank you. Hopefully, by working hard, I can make his decision justified."

They looked at each other like my words had opened a secret safe inside their hearts. Must be two Virgos, I thought.

"You're so well-spoken," Tee-Tee said, complimenting me. "How old are you, Lamar?"

I weighed her words carefully. The wise weigh everything. Clearly I knew they were attempting to look into me. Obviously, their flattery was disguised in ulterior motives. What they didn't know is, I was a savage like Rihanna in a Polo suit with the ability to dangle the dick they craved on their foreheads like an okdëä' (carrot) for rabbits.

"A high school student," I said, confirming what they already knew while cleverly ducking the age question.

"What school do you go to?" Rosey asked.

"Nottingham!" I said proudly.

They both looked at each other again like I said something distasteful. The alcohol had begun to drop their front even more, I thought.

"Did I say something wrong?" I asked Rosey, whose name rhymed with nosey.

"That school is a joke, and I heard it's still a fashion show," Tee-Tee said.

I looked into her. "Do you believe everything you hear, Tee- Tee?"

She laughed a girl laugh. "Not everything, but some things never change. Can you say my name again, though? It sounds so dope coming out of your mouth."

I smiled. "What school did you graduate from?" I asked, while purposely dubbing her request.

"We both graduated from Fowler," Rosey jumped in, answering the question for her friend.

Thinking it, but not saying it. I frowned! As a proud Bulldog, other schools in the city got no love from me like a Faith and Diddy song. Traditionally, the only thing fly about Fowler girls were the Falcons on their jackets. Which should be replaced with a pigeon, I thought.

Out the blue, the restaurant door opened. The tiny bell made its noise. Four black grandmothers came in.

"Excuse me, ladies," I said. "Enjoy the rest of your breakfast."

Before I could walk off, Tee-Tee took a long gulp and finished her drink. "After you're done taking the gangster grandmothers' orders over there, can you refill this for me?" she extended her hand and passed me the empty glass.

"Of course I can," I said. "I'll be right back with that for you.

I quickly turned my attention back to my new party of four. Gangster grandmothers, I thought. What would make Tee-Tee say something like that? Then again, the only person that wasn't a regular so far was me. Blacksky. After they were comfortably seated, I made my way over to their table. Black imagery. Each one was dressed and looked like the Syracuse version of the Pointer Sisters. They smelled like hair dress, cocoa butter, and marijuana.

"Good morning! Can I bring you something to drink while you look at your menus?" I asked.

"Why yes, you can, you fine young man. Looking all exotic and shit. Let me find out Simon done started importing niggas to work in this raggedy bitch! Bring us two waters and two apple juices." She paused. "And while you're fetching that, you tell Gator's ugly ass that GPD and the gang is here."

Her language caught me by surprise. This wasn't the 'Big Momma' I was used to. The other three ladies at the table broke out in laughter.

"You gonna scare this young man half to death, Renee, talking like that. This is probably his first day working here," her friend across from her announced.

"Please, Joyce!" Renee said. "This ain't no sitcom and we damn sure ain't Diahann Carroll, Mabel King, Marla Gibbs, and Phylicia Rashad. This establishment is in the heart of the hood, Joyce, so if he's scared of a little shit-talking, this ain't the place for him."

When I made it to the kitchen Gator had his back turned to me and was straining the pasta. Steam from the noodles rose up and shrunk the naps in his hairnet.

"Some old lady named GPD said the gang is here," I said.

Gator shook his head and smiled. "Good pussy Donna." The faucet was on, and he was running the spaghetti noodles underneath cold water. "Put some plastic gloves on, then spread four plates on that tray." I quickly did like he asked. "Put sausage, eggs, home fries, and grits on every plate," he ordered.

While I was doing my job, I could see Gator out the corner of my eye, making two waters, two apple juices, and an orange juice with vodka. Gega:'s (eyes) do hustle! So I had to ask. How did you know Tee-Tee wanted a refill?"

Gator looked upside my head like I grew an extra one.

"So far, everyone that's made that bell go off on the door comes here on the regular. Most people wanna go to a place where everybody knows their name like "Cheers". While you're working here at Benz Kitchen...." Gator's voice and words had that old 70s Marvin Gaye rhythm. It was what my pops sounded like when gigantic jewels were about to be strewn around like Castle Hill, New Zealand. "The name of the game is pay attention. I'm gonna give you a chance to be different than the rest of these young knuckleheads running around here. Cooking a delicacy for your woman with your bare hands will turn her on. Believe that! Gator ain't the best looking nigga in the streets, but because of these trophies." He held up both of his hands for me to see." Gator keep a bitch. Why you think all these young girls got older niggas on their arm? These new school niggas can't boil hotdog water. A real woman values a man's man over his material possessions. A real woman wants a man who can teach their son how to be a man. At your age, knowledge should be your best friend. So soak up what I'm saying like a sponge because old Gator ain't never gonna tell you no bullshit, boy!" He paused. "Look at what I'm cooking. This ain't no fancy shit that you couldn't make by yourself...." While Gator quickly broke down how to make the house special, I looked at all the ingredients he had on the table. The haddock was sitting in seasoned egg wash before it got fried. I needed pesto, cherry tomatoes, salmon, and grated parmesan cheese for the pasta. I locked the entire recipe in my memory.

"Them niggas Sharon ran out of here didn't pay attention, but when I look into your eyes, I can tell you wanna learn. You wanna know why I've been the chef here for so long?" Gator asked.

"Why?"

"Over the years, I've learned how to do everything around here. I can play every position on the court like Magic did when he was a rookie. Simon depends on me. Which makes me irreplaceable." His eyes slid to the breakfast tray. "Now run that food out there before them old trout mouth bats get restless."

Seconds later, after dropping off Tee-Tee's refill, I made my way back over to GPD's table.

"Look, girls!" Renee exclaimed, pointing to the hot food. "I'm hungry like two kids with crackhead parents." I laughed along with everybody else and placed their plates and beverages on the table.

When I was done, Renee reached across the table and picked up some jelly for her toast.

"We didn't get your name light-skin." she asked.

"Lamar," I said.

"What's your daddy's name?" She sipped on her apple juice. "As cute as you are, I must've heard of him," she added.

"I doubt that you'd know my father because he's from Georgia."

Renee smiled. "This is Syracuse, not New York City. You'd be surprised who GPD knows, baby."

"Cosby," I said.

She glanced down at my crotch and shifted in her seat.

"Cosby Jones," she said in disbelief. "I knew your face looked familiar." Two more customers walked in.

"Can I get you ladies anything else?" I asked politely.

"No, baby, we're good," Renee said. "This is plenty."

Her demeanor seemed to suddenly change, and my subconscious wanted to know why. As I walked away, I could hear their whispers over my shoulder.

"You do know who Cosby Jones is, don't you?" Renee asked.

"The bootlegger in the bricks?" Joyce

responded.

Renee sucked her teeth. "Bitch, you're dumber than a milk crate on the side of the road. Only an alcoholic would come up with an answer like that."

"Well, who is he then?" Joyce asked.

"Girl, that's 'Big Meat''.

"I thought that 'Big Meat' nigga was just folklore. How do you know if this man is for real, Renee?" another one of her friends asked.

Renee responded, "A long time ago, that country nigga took me home from the bar on State St. He was a smooth cat, and he didn't even press me for the pussy. That shocked me because everybody knows GPD got that fire. I start thinking he had a little dick or something. When Big Meat got me home and backed out, his dick was longer than the rescue mission free lunch line! Now I've seen some big dicks in my lifetime, but this was the one. I'm telling you, Joyce, I felt him way up in my stomach. No man has ever made my pussy cum so much. Then not long after that, I heard he jumped up and got married to some Native bitch."

Renee violated, I thought. I looked out towards her table from the kitchen.

"And that's Big Meat's son?" Joyce asked. She stood up. "I'm about to get that young dick."

Renee laughed. "Bitch, if you don't sit your old ass down! I mean, have several seats."

I laughed so hard, my stomach hurt.

"What's so funny?" Gator asked.

"Hold up, Gator," I said, still spying. At Tee-Tee's and Rosey's table, I could hear their conversation get started again.

"Bitch, I knew it!" Tee-Tee bragged. "That's Big Meat's son!"

Rosey laughed a cute laugh. "Bitch! You do not know Big Meat. With your nosey ass."

"Oh, I will!" Tee-Tee promised. "You watch."

Twenty minutes later, the ebb and flow of customers at Benz kitchen picked up considerably.

"You all right out there?" Gator questioned.

"Yeah, I got this OG," I said, picking up yet another tray for delivery.

Then I stepped inside the dining area and looked around at the surrounding people, most of whom were in heavy conversation or enjoying their food. I sat the hot plates down on my clientele's table, and that's when I saw Sharon. When did she get here? I thought. The song on the jukebox changed to "Everything is Gonna Be Alright" by Naughty by Nature.

Word to the block I live on, this woman was so sexy. She had on Carolina blue jeans with .a black beater slightly cut to show her belly button. A tad bit under that was the Gucci mascot telling people their belt cost a stack or better. Her ass in those jeans looked like the February 14th symbol for lovers. A heart. I looked at her Whole body again just one more time. 34-D, 24, 38. She had a Gucci Backpack with Donald Duck's hands raised triumphantly. Her custom made jewelry from Avianne & Co. Jewelers made Donald's bragging justified. She ran her fingers through her hair and looked at me with those grey eyes. Young, beautiful, spoiled. I was mesmerized. When I got down to her feet, all the great things I said went out the window. All black Gucci Loafers with red and black snakes on the front. Simon's story came to mind. This bitch really did know some voodoo shit, I thought.

How else could you explain a black girl in her twenties wearing snake loafers? Regular black women don't wear shit like that. Clearly this chick had some issues. The Italian wizards over at Gucci were on some bold shit. It was as if they had secretly gotten Frances Gumm's enemies to design Sharon's shoes. Witches.

She quickly worked the room over like an aspiring comedian then made her way directly in front of me. She smelled like warm vanilla & jasmine blossom. "I'm sorry I threw you to the wolves on your first day, but I had to go handle some business, then stop at Page West and get you this." Sharon went inside her Gucci Backpack and came out with a brand new Galaxy Note. "This is for you, Lamar." I smiled.

"For me?" I asked in a surprised tone, taking

the box from her soft hands. "Thank you."

"Open it."

When I opened the small package up the screen on the Galaxy looked like a mini TV.

"I programmed it for you with my phone number in the contacts as well as Benz Kitchen's. When you see those two numbers, call us back A.S.A.P. I've also added you to the 'Greasy Spoon' Facebook Page. You just have to upload your own picture." She paused. "Is this your first phone?"

"Yes."

She smiled. "I remember when I used to use my phone for silly shit. Now every time it rings, there's money on the other end. If you handle your business, your phone is the money magnet. I want you to take a break for thirty minutes before it gets anymore busier in here."

"Are you sure, Sharon?"

"Very," she said, then turned her back and walked away.

Her plump ass in those jeans could make a synthetic Muslim switch his religion. Change his vision. Abort his mission. The pure sight of something so damn juicy made my nature rise. I quickly looked across the room and spotted Tee-Tee. Nice. She would suffice. From where I stood, I evaluated that her mouth was sloppy and slippery from the drinks she consumed. Premeditation set in. What I was about to do was unprofessional on my first day of work, some people would use the word berserk, but I wanted dessert. When I approached Tee-Tee from behind, she was in deep conversation with Rosey. I crouched down to whisper in my victim's ear. Rosey looked at me like I had chosen the Honda over the BMW.

"D keeps telling me to speak to you in private," I said in my deep Barry White voice that made pussy get moist.

She turned her head slightly so she could see my face. "Who the fuck is 'D'?" she asked in a ghetto tone.

"Deez nuts," I whispered so only she could hear me. This was a bold ass pick-up line. Just know that. And it only could be used by grown men with the baby leg in name brand briefs. Big Beef.

"You play too much," she replied. She ain't never lied!

I grabbed a hold of her hand. "I'm so sincere. Come and talk to me privately right quick." Sorry, Simon, this was that Jodeci shit-talking at a high level.

"Okay, but only for a minute," Tee-Tee said as she got up. My power to influence mortals was growing rapidly. Coldness. No Apathy. I winked at Rosey and led Tee-Tee to a secluded closet in the back. While we G strolled, I looked around for Sharon and quickly spotted her. She was busy in traffic.

"Where are we going?"

"To my office," I said, opening the door to the tiny room and leaving it cracked so I could be on point.

Before I could give this whore her first instruction, she sprang forward and started undoing my buttons. In seconds, she had my trousers pooled around my ankles. Suddenly, she dropped on her knees. Wifey material? Bitch, please! Be skeptical when they do it with ease. My dick stood straight out like a black man in a small town, and he didn't care if he got unequal treatment. Nope! He wanted to be confined inside her throat. Tee-Tee reached out and freed the package like it was dope.

"Damn! You got a big ass dick," she said, licking her lips.

"Do you wanna suck it?"

She nodded her head in a trance. Dick-matized.

"Yes!" I palmed her head and rubbed my dick slowly over her forehead, eyes, nose, lips, and chin. I baptized her on a Friday with the mighty staff. She let out a cute laugh, and fresh drool ran from her mouth like a crazed dog. Her wet tongue slid up and down my shaft as her hands balanced my family jewels.

"Open your mouth," I ordered. When she complied, I violated by sticking more than half my dick down her throat. Strangely, she didn't gag. Instead, her cheeks hollowed out and coated my dick with cool spit. Holy shit! My toes curled in shock. She looked up at me and smiled.

"You didn't know you was fucking with a head monster?"

The muscles in her neck began to tighten as if she had a pussy inside her throat. Head this good could keep a nigga broke. Clearly, I stumbled upon a talented hood professional. Gulping sounds mixed with her moans filled the tiny closet with lust.

She took my dick out of her throat and gave me a naughty look. A kinky blow job. I could see the pulsing veins on my cock going up and down as if my dick had a heartbeat. Impressed, she paused to admire my massive erection and focused on just the head of my shaft. This was long neck mastery. A giraffe. Her rhythm was relentless enough to make my toes curl once more. Pleasure slowly came out my pores.

"Don't hold it," she said. "Cum down my throat." On another note, Tee-Tee was passionately proving to me that project girls gave the best head. Word to the dead. A surge of pleasure passed through my body that made me wanna tell somebody.

"I'm a cum sucking slut," she declared as my dick tickled her lymphoid tissues. She is official, I thought.

I closed my eyes and enjoyed the moment as she increased the pace on her sucking. Spasm after spasm made a thick coat of my pre-cum glaze her lips. I opened my eyes and veered them to the right, I could see Sharon peeking at us from behind some boxes.

I quickly asked myself how long was she standing there? She had a shocked look on her face that indicated she wanted to 'touch me tease me'. Case. I decided to give her a show, and I grabbed the back Tee-Tee's head. What kinda weirdo would I be if I didn't grant my manager's fetish? My balls were ready break the plane. Jerome Bettis.

After sticking several more inches of the BBC down her throat, plenty of her drool hit the closet floor. I moved my hips back and forth in an R&B rhythm that made Sharon look at me in amazement. Suddenly, my dick exploded in climax, and my warm load shot out in spurts. As she swallowed every last drop, she made a guzzling and gulping sound. A wicked smile appeared on Tee-Tee's face.

"Damn big daddy! Your dick is still rock hard! I want to feel you inside my pussy."

"I don't have a condom," I said. When you're dealing with a thot, no glove, no love. Just know that!

"Are you going to call me if I give you my number?"

"My phone is off," I lied. "That's why I'm working. I'm broke."

She sucked her teeth at my game, but I wasn't

a lame. The Great Spirit constructed my frame for fame. "I'll see what I can do."

"You better call me, though."

"Why wouldn't I?" I asked.

She smirked. "I just sucked your dick in a closet, but I have absolutely no limits when it comes to my desire."

"Talk that freaky shit," I said.

"I'm not a liar. I knew within the first five minutes that I was going to swallow your babies. This ain't the 80s. I'm gonna get your phone turned on, but don't be corny and don't call me back. My pussy is good too. Nothing about me is wack."

At least this bitch knew what she wanted, I thought. But just because she slobbed my knob doesn't mean she would get married to the mob. I had to get back to my job. I stepped forward and wiped the dried cum off her chin.

"I promise I'll call you."

"Bye, Lamar," she said, turning around and shaking her round ass for me to see. Tee-Tee would show up here every day if I hit her with this dick that could made her kidneys shift, I thought.

After pulling up my Polo dress pants, I smoothly headed back to Gator's sanctum. Simon wasn't here today, but if he was, I would kindly thank him. Tee-Tee's dedication to my mental well-being was insane. That's good brain silly and another spectacular touchdown for Big Willie. I smiled, and I told you before, I got a sexy ass smile. Uzo Aduba. But don't let my facial expressions fool ya. This is a celebration of the medulla. I was scared of heights, got pushed off a cliff, then became a daredevil. When I start talking dirty dick dialogue, stop and get you a shovel. Watch me glorify my sac while simultaneously getting to the sac. You're a hater if you don't jack that. To my loyal sex fiends: I'm oil-based crack. This is only fake news for Trump, but for highly intelligent women, this is that long dick in a round rump. A scrumptious breakfast and a light lunch, an anaconda pelvic thrust inside a tight cunt. Make no mistake about this; it's contagious jungle fever for your eyes when Blacksky writes. Black ink imposed on white paper. Peace to Wesley Snipes. I'm about to make America great again. I don't give a fuck about the gripes. This is a pipe dream from the pussy pleaser. Sharon's ass snapping me out of my thoughts is the only reason I'm giving you a breather.

She had just watched me empty my seed into a thirsty throat but moved around graciously as if she didn't. When Sharon stopped at the head monster's table, I wondered if she was the type to knock the hustle, and I quickly used my special powers to eavesdrop on their conversation.

"Damn, Tee! I've heard you have some skills in the oral department, but take a bow, bitch!" Sharon advised. "It took some talent to engulf all that dick. Women like you can suck their way right to the top of the food chain. Men are weak for good brain."

Rosey sat up in her seat. "You sucked his dick? That's crazy! We sucking dick in tiny closets now?"

"'Oui' is 'French, bitch, and you're Spanish. And how the hell did you know that the closet is tiny? I guess we is sucking dicks in closets."

Everybody at the table laughed, and I did too. These girls were on some other shit, just something I had to admit. Tee-Tee starting talking again.

"I have two hundred for him. He said his phone is off. I need his dick on my team."

Sharon smiled. Game was discovering game. My parents didn't raise lames. How else could you explain someone paying just to 'Lick The Lollipop? I'm Lil Wayne. Stop playing."

"Give it to me then," Sharon said, sticking out her hand. "Big tips on the first day means he was thinking of a master plan. He fits in at Benz kitchen then. The whole crew is in high demand."

Suddenly, Sharon looked at Rosey in a sexy manner. "I was wondering if you wanted to chill with me tonight while I prepare 'Tripple S'? Drinks, music, and good food."

Rosey smiled. "You're finally letting me chill with you? Even after ducking all my calls?"

Sharon made a sad face. "Perdónane, mi amor. Let me make it up to you?"

"I'll be there," Rosey promised.

Gator ain't never lied, I thought. Sharon was a bad bitch. Her wordplay was just as impressive as mine, and I liked it that way. I had to come up with a way to enjoy the show tonight. I needed a peek at the queen's sugar. Ava Duvernay. After a hard day of work, I needed some time to play.

After making sure Sharon watched me get on the bus, I got off on the very next stop and cut through a few backyards, avoided a dog, and jumped a fence. My efforts landed me right behind the Benz Kitchen Waste Management dumpster. Stratagem. In no time at all, I stripped down butt ass naked and folded my clothes up in a neat pile. I stood up straight and began my chant.

"Dear Great Spirit, you could have made me who you wanted, but you made me who I am. I now walk the glory road with blessings from your hand." I opened my eyes to make sure I was all alone still and closed them again. "Jinohdaiyo'go:wa:h (rat), jinohdaiyo'go: wa:h (rat)," I said.

Before I opened my eyes, a hundred different smells hit my nose all at once. The night air blew through my black fur and white whiskers. When I opened my tiny eyes, everything around me seemed colossal sized. Cookie and candy wrappers, empty weed bags, half-smoked cigarettes, my clothes, and shoes.

Sometimes you have to do things you don't

want to, and this was one of those times. To my extreme disapproval, I had to turn into the mascot for cowardly people who voluntarily cooperated with the police for reasons that benefit them. I felt small and insignificant. Is this how rats felt when they helped divide a family? Get themselves out of trouble, returned to the hood, rented party buses, went to the club, got women's numbers. Or, were they proud rats? Clearly the rats in my generation had grown extremely bold. They threw parties, drove a Benz, carried a gun, shot a gun, had a bad bitch, and wore a wire. James Bond, I thought.

After doing several laps around the building, I finally managed to find a small opening. I took a deep breath of air and commenced to twisting and turning my body in a way that made people sick on sight. Exorcism shit! Ironically, these same twists and turns symbolized my path down the glory road so far. Topsy-turvy. I won some and lost some, but thanks to the Great Spirit, and constant honing of my powers, I could now ambush each situation with caution. Now firmly inside the hole, I stood there and looked at the darkness with very little signs of light. It made me think about amassing enough money to get my family out of the city.

Sautéed onions, garlic, and olives worked as a GPS for the direction I needed to head towards. Seven rights, a climb, six narrow lefts, and a two feet drop later, I slid behind some big pots in the kitchen. The fried hamburger and sweet sausage smell over the eye over the stove made my tiny legs weak with hunger. Suddenly, Sharon walked directly in my line of sight. Just that fast, she had changed her clothes into pink Yoga pants over a blue swimsuit by Bikinis That Create Curves, but with all that ass on display, I knew soul food was partly responsible. She was stirring the sauce and lightly bouncing her ass at the same damn time. The groundbreaking Album "Lemonade" by Beyoncé played on the jukebox. "Hold Up" was playing, and Sharon knew every word by heart. Her Resume: One/Bad/Bitch. The savage inside me almost forced me to return to human form, pull her Yoga pants down as well as swimsuit, then slide the BBC inside of her.

Out the blue, a tiny claw tapped me on my shoulder. It shocked me, and I turned around slowly. Another rat was looking me dead in my face; a fat old gray rat with black whiskers. He squeaked a couple times before I realized I had to use my Beastmaster powers to translate his lingo.

"Who the fuck are you?" I asked him.

"Hold up now." He held up a claw. "You sound a little aggressive. I don't want no smoke."

"What's your handle?"

"Sammy," he responded.

I smiled. "The Bull?"

He sucked his teeth and frowned at my guess.

"I'm Sammy Smooth. Real rats never go behind the wall for that long. Don't insult me, kid. My name rings bells with the law. Some of my boys are..." Sammy had the kinda face you wanted to punch. I'm talking about straight Thomas Hearns his old ass. "Alpo, Mel G, Lewis, Rob, AG, and The King..." I held my claw up to stop him.

"What the hell did you just say?"

"You heard me, nigga," he said. "And I'm not talking about Elvis."

I yanked Sammy up by his fur coat. "You're a liar. Cliff would never chill with you. That's the Rubberband Man, self-appointed King of the south. I can't jack that, Sammy."

"Believe what you want to, but stop making all that noise before Sharon puts you in that pot. Besides, I keep a paper trail on me for moments just like this.." Sammy produced several pieces of paper from behind his back like a cheap magic trick. I snatched it from him and started reading it. For Negros with high intelligence, Cliff was the modern-day Cliff Huxtable with more swagg.

It was as if Cliff had shotguns off and sold coke while he was raising Rudy and Theo, and Cliff didn't have to slip the women at Spellman anything. They flocked to him naturally. Maybe it was because they could get whatever they liked, or his face in butt technique, I thought.

Like the rest of black America, when I saw

Cliff, an ex-felon, get jammed up in a federal gun case, I thought, not even Ehrich Weiss could have got out of that shit. He did, strangely. Had Cliff and Clair been Junebug and Bonequita, they still wouldn't be around next year. Craig Mac.

Hmmm, I thought. Cliff was so militant, though. Could he actually be a rodent? He did leave his loyal sidekick on national TV for a bad side bitch, but that didn't mean he was a snitch. All niggas upgrade when they get a few dollars. Would 'Dough Boy' give him his own personal throne on Hollywood Squares if he sent people up the river? Cliff didn't eat the fried chicken on the one episode I did see. A nigga from the south who passes on fried chicken. Suspicious indeed.

"I just rented this party bus and all the bad bitches coming. They don't care about telling like they used to."

I punched Sammy like Diddy did Drake. "Fuck your party bus. If you tell on any of my friends, I'll hunt you down."

"You're one of those tuff gangster rats, aren't you?"

"From now on, every time I see you, I wanna know who you've been chilling with? What block is hot? And that new paperwork." I kicked him in his ass. "Now, get the fuck out my sight!"

TO BE CONTINUED

References

Catlin, G., & Matthiessen, P. (2004). North American Indians. New York: Penguin Books.

English - Seneca Dictionary. (n.d.). [ebook] Available at: https://www.akronschools.org/site/handlers/filedownload.ashx?moduleinstanceid=6603&dataid=9898&filename=english-seneca%201-18-12.pdf [accessed 8 nov. 2019].

ABOUT THE AUTHOR

AE Butterscotch is the author of the series, *The Legend of Blacksky*. His passion is writing fantasy novels which incorporate multicultural themes, time travel, and especially displaying his own musical writing talents. He is currently working on other books in this series, so stay tuned! He is a proud father and resides in Syracuse, NY.